# DUKE OF DEBAUCHERY

## SINS AND SCOUNDRELS BOOK 6

SCARLETT SCOTT

**Duke of Debauchery**

Sins and Scoundrels Book 6

All rights reserved.

Second Edition

Copyright © 2020, 2021 by Scarlett Scott

Published by Happily Ever After Books, LLC

Cover Design by EDH Professionals

This book or any portion thereof may not be reproduced or used in any manner whatsoever without the express written permission of the publisher except for the use of brief quotations in a book review.

The unauthorized reproduction or distribution of this copyrighted work is illegal. No part of this book may be scanned, uploaded, or distributed via the Internet or any other means, electronic or print, without the publisher's permission. Criminal copyright infringement, including infringement without monetary gain, is punishable by law.

This book is a work of fiction and any resemblance to persons, living or dead, or places, events, or locales, is purely coincidental. The characters are productions of the author's imagination and used fictitiously.

For more information, contact author Scarlett Scott.

www.scarlettscottauthor.com

## CHAPTER 1

Monty had expected a host of reactions to his proposal of marriage.

Laughter, however, had not been one of them.

He stared at The Honorable Miss Hattie Lethbridge, whose wild peals of mirth were echoing through the salon where they sat on opposite settees, attended by an abigail.

Whilst he had never proposed to make a lady his duchess, he had certainly made a number of offers to females. Demimondaines, it was true. But each one of them had been only too pleased to accept his offer of *carte blanche*. Not a single, bloody one of them had *laughed*.

"Forgive me, Montrose." Miss Lethbridge at last caught her breath and used a handkerchief to blot the tears from her eyes. "I must have misheard you. I thought you asked me to marry you just now."

His ears went hot.

*God's fichu*, this was not proceeding well.

Not at all.

"You did not mishear me," he said. "I proposed to make you my duchess."

"Marriage." The levity fled from her countenance now.

"Marriage." He tried to keep the consternation from his voice.

He had known Miss Lethbridge for years. As the younger sister of his best friend, Viscount Torrington, and the bosom bow of his sister, she had been a fixture in Monty's life since her comeout. But if he were honest, he had scarcely taken much note of her before, aside from the waspish verbal jabs she insisted upon sending his way. She had always been a vexing creature, which no doubt had tarnished her luster on the marriage mart.

But he noticed her now. Her black curls were gathered into a becoming hairstyle that framed her heart-shaped face. She was lovely, though not a traditional beauty. Taller than he preferred, it was certain. Still, he found himself suddenly curious about just how long her legs were and how they might feel wrapped around his waist.

Supposing he could convince her to wed him, that was.

Which was becoming increasingly unlikely by the moment.

"You want to marry me," Miss Lethbridge repeated.

"As I said." He flicked an irritated glance toward the abigail, who was seated in the corner of the salon, head bent over some sewing.

He truly did not prefer an audience for his humiliation, but he supposed there was no help for it. He could not very well sit here unchaperoned with Miss Lethbridge given his reputation.

One second alone with the Duke of Debauchery was enough to ruin a lady.

Though, in all fairness, he could not accomplish seduction in a mere second. Three, certainly. Two, perhaps. One? Nay.

"You must realize that you are the last gentleman I would ever wish to take as my husband," she said then.

His ankle was paining him, and he longed for the welcome oblivion only laudanum could bring. Indeed, he felt itchy everywhere. For a moment, he wondered why he had even bothered to present himself here today, and then he recalled the sight of his friend, Torrie, lying insensate following his phaeton crash.

*Ah, yes.*

The need to pay for his many sins.

"You find fault with me, Miss Lethbridge?" he asked calmly.

Of course, he already knew what her objections would be.

"I find fault with drunken reprobates who recklessly race my brother when he is in his cups, leading to injuries so severe, he almost did not recover." She paused, twin patches of color darkening her cheeks as she rallied to her cause. "So severe he still, in fact, has yet to recover entirely."

What Miss Lethbridge did not say was there remained a possibility Torrie would not *ever* recover. The extent of his friend's injuries, along with the part Monty had played in them, would not leave him. Like the pain of the broken bone he had suffered in the same crash, the guilt would not go.

"I was wrong to race Torrie that night, and I know it," he admitted, for he may be a scoundrel, but he could acknowledge his mistakes. "Marrying you is a means of attempting to atone for my actions."

"I am no sacrificial lamb, Montrose." Her chin tipped up, and her voice was steeped in haughtiness. "Marry someone else if you feel it will unburden you. Marry *anyone* else for all I care. All I know is, it shan't be me."

She was wrong about that, and he would prove it.

He shook his head slowly. "It cannot be anyone else, Miss

Lethbridge. You are the only woman I will have as my duchess."

She dared to laugh again. "How much gin did you drink before you came here, Your Grace?"

"None at all," he lied.

She wrinkled her nose. "You stink of it."

*Beelzebub's earbobs.* She was not going to make this courting business easy, was she?

"A small tipple, only to make the pain in my ankle bearable," he amended.

This, too, was a blatant falsehood. But he was accustomed to lying to everyone around him. He was Monty, drunken scoundrel, who went through life bedding more women than he could count and being the life of every ballroom, drawing room, or gaming hell he inhabited.

At least, that was the Monty he showed the world.

"Your ankle has been healing for weeks," she told him, unimpressed by his injury.

The trouble with a broken bone, was that it never set quite properly. True, his demons had sent him down the steps in search of liquor, upsetting the work of the sawbones. True, he had also punched a footman in the eye and pissed on the Aubusson following that unfortunate series of events.

Opium was his friend now. Well, opium and gin. Along with the occasional smuggled whisky. And brandy. And port. Anything to keep his mind enrobed in bliss. Anything to silence the ghosts of the past.

But never mind all that.

"My ankle is still paining me a great deal," he protested.

"If you expect my sympathy, Your Grace, you are more foolishly deluded than I supposed." Her expression was pained. Pinched.

Her cat chose that moment to make an appearance. It strolled, the plump, beastly thing, right up to his settee as if it had not a care in the world. As if it owned the bloody chamber and all its inhabitants.

"Why is the feline here?" he muttered.

For it was a long-standing argument between them that he could not abide by her creature. That pompous spawn of Satan with the most ludicrous appellation he had ever heard.

"Sir Toby Belch is his name," Miss Lethbridge said, a wintry note of reproach entering her dulcet voice. "I will thank you to refrain from disparaging my companion."

Sir Toby Belch. Her *companion*.

"Is it not a feline?" he asked, skewering the white ball of fur with a glare as it padded ever nearer. "How is the truth a disparagement?"

Her lips tightened. If there was an expression she wore when she was gazing upon a pile of dung, he would venture a guess he was bearing witness to it now. And it was directed solely upon him.

"Sir Toby is much more than a mere feline," she snapped. "I do think you should go, Montrose. You have done enough damage already. A moment more in your presence, and I shall be addlepated myself from the fumes on your breath alone."

That cut rather deep.

If she wanted to see him in his cups, she would have to cross paths with him at half past three in the morning when he was on his second bottle of gin. He was on his best behavior today, on account of the proposal.

"Forgive me, Miss Lethbridge," he said, still watching the cat, which had sidled to his mistress first and was now receiving an adoring caress from her that made a sharp spear of jealousy cut through him.

Imagine that.

The Duke of Montrose envious of a goddamn cat.

"Apologize to Sir Toby as well," she had the audacity to demand.

"To a cat?" His cravat, styled in some bloody new knot with a name more ridiculous than her feline's, seemed to be strangling him. And the itchiness was returning tenfold. Reminding him he needed more laudanum soon.

Thank God there was a bottle in his carriage.

"Yes." She scooped the feline up from the floor and settled him into her lap, not even sparing Monty a glance. "To Sir Toby."

"Sir Toby Belch," he could not help but to point out. "Do not forget the beast's full name, lest you dishonor him."

He was making light of her. Prodding her when he was supposed to be wooing her, and he knew it. But he was growing irritable. Nothing about this interview had proceeded as he had hoped it would, and now she was upbraiding him about the damned cat. All whilst he was beginning to crave more oblivion.

His ankle throbbed. All the more reason to settle upon his panacea as soon as possible.

"He is named after you," she told him then, her tone most unkind.

To the beast in her lap, she cooed something nonsensical before delivering a kiss to the top of his head.

The next time he called upon Miss Lethbridge, Monty was going to pay a footman to lock the damned thing in a closet until he departed. He vowed it to himself.

"I have no wish to have a cat named in my honor." He gave her one of his most cutting frowns, an expression he resorted to infrequently, because ordinarily he was too sotted to care. "As I am not a baronet, and my given name is not Toby, I fail to see how I can be his namesake."

Her lips compressed for a beat as she finally gave him her

full attention, her green eyes assessing. "You do not recall, do you?"

His frown deepened. "Recall what, Miss Lethbridge?"

This conversation was growing deuced old.

"Sir Toby Belch is one of Shakespeare's characters," she said.

The information proved uninformative. He had not attended the theater in years, and even when he had, he had been too deep in his cups to pay attention to the stage, aside from picking out the next actress he would make his mistress.

Now he was going to have to find out what the devil Sir Toby Belch had done. Monty was reasonably certain he did not wish to know.

"Of course I recall," he lied instead. The itchiness was growing worse. And the solution was awaiting him. "Thank you for the honor, Miss Lethbridge. Hattie. I may call you Hattie, after all our years of acquaintance, and on account of our future nuptials, may I not?"

Her eyes narrowed. And he swore the feline's did as well. "You are prevaricating, Montrose, and you may call me Miss Lethbridge, or you may call me nothing at all."

"Of course, Miss Lethbridge. When we are wed, however, you will be my duchess," he could not help but to point out. Nor could he keep the smugness from his tone.

For she was no chit fresh from the schoolroom. And despite his many faults, he was still a duke. No matchmaking mama would refuse his proposal, not even hers.

"We will not wed," she snapped. "And you are lying about everything. About how much gin you have drunk today, about recalling who Sir Toby Belch is, about wanting to marry me. Every day, you lie to yourself, to your sister. You think I do not see your hands trembling or your bloodshot eyes, or the wrinkles in your coat, but I see it all. I see *you*, Montrose. And I do not want you."

She rose to her feet following her astounding speech.

The silent abigail looked up from her sewing, casting him an expression of pity.

*Damnation.*

As he watched, Miss Lethbridge dipped into a remarkably elegant curtsey, given that she held a fat cat, and abruptly quit the room. He was left sitting there, alone with the abigail. He glanced down at his lap, and he realized she was right. His hands were shaking.

It was time to go.

He needed his medicine.

\* \* \*

HATTIE FLED from the drawing room and from the Duke of Montrose so swiftly, she almost collided with her brother in the hall upstairs. Sir Toby, who objected to traveling in such haste, hissed.

In the wake of the phaeton accident he had suffered while drunkenly racing the Duke of Montrose, Torrie was fortunate to be alive. He was a pale, gaunt figure, quite unlike himself. But that was not the sole manner in which he was unlike himself.

For he had no memory beyond when he had finally woken. He had suffered a severe head wound in the crash. His physician could not be certain if Torrie would ever regain his full memories.

"I am sorry, Torrie," she said, reading the confusion in his expression. "I did not mean to trample you in my haste."

"Think nothing of it, Harriet." He gave her a pained smile. "I was lost in my thoughts and not taking care."

She suppressed a rush of sadness at his use of her full

given name. Sometimes, it was difficult to comprehend that her beloved brother considered her a stranger. But he was wary and hesitant, uncertain of everyone and everything these days. He did not often stray from his rooms. Not even since he had recovered enough to resume walking once again.

Indeed, that he had deigned to leave at all was a surprise.

"Are you well, Torrie?" she asked, clutching the cat to her, searching her brother's face. "Is there something I can fetch you?"

"I am as well as I can be." He paused, his stranger's gaze searching hers. "Nothing you can fetch me will bring back my memory. Vast portions of my life are gaping holes. Almost all of it. Do you know, Harriet, it is like walking about wearing a blindfold?"

"I am so sorry," she said, hating the distance that existed between them now. "Will you not call me Hattie?"

His expression remained tight. Rigid. Odd how this new version of him even looked like a stranger. He held his jaw differently. "I do not remember you."

There it was, one of the many reasons why she could not marry the Duke of Montrose. He had taken her brother from her. Oh, Torrie was still alive. His heart still beat and breath still flowed through him. But he was not the same Torrie.

"I remember you, however," she managed calmly. "And your memories will return to you, in time."

"I have no promise they will," he said coolly. "You must remember this, Harriet. The brother you once knew may be forever gone. We are beginning anew."

For a brief, desperate moment, she wished *she* could begin anew, that her memories were as locked away as her brother's. Because she had secretly loved the Duke of Montrose for as long as she could remember.

Loving him did not mean she was going to allow herself

to become his next victim, however. The duke collected hearts. He was reckless and wild, broken and jaded and cruel. He was driven by demons only he could see. And she had no wish to fall headlong into his darkness.

One thing was certain. She could never marry him.

## CHAPTER 2

"*His* Grace, the Duke of Montrose."

As Monty was announced that evening at a ball being hosted by his friend and cousin, the Marquess of Searle and his marchioness, the chandeliers suddenly seemed hotter than the fires of Hades. The milling guests, whirling and chattering in their finery, gold winking from their throats and hair, blended into a garish blur. He was itchy already.

*The good Lord's chemise.*

He had not fortified himself with laudanum or gin this evening, knowing he would need to be sharp. But now, he felt the opposite of sharp. He felt…lost. Adrift in a sea of people who did not know him, trying desperately to keep from drowning. Desperate for spirits of any sort. Something to appease the endless need crawling through him, eating him from the inside out.

"Monty." Searle stood before him, thank God.

"Searle, I need a goddamn drink," he announced.

Quietly enough, or so he thought, that no one else would

overhear, even in this crush. Perhaps there was a gasp from the fringes. If there was, he did not care.

"You look like the devil," his cousin said, raking him with an assessing gaze.

A judgmental gaze.

Rather the way all his acquaintances seemed to look upon him these days. Especially Miss Lethbridge.

*Hattie.*

Also, his own sister, Cat, who was off in the country with her husband. And his mother. Her nattering grew particularly wearisome.

"I am the devil, according to some," he told Searle, aiming for a levity he did not feel. "Have you any gin? Whisky? Brandy?"

Better yet, laudanum.

But he dared not make such a request. For if he did, Searle would assess him with more than a gaze. And he had no wish for his cousin to begin shining a light upon his darkness.

"You need it?" Searle asked, his jaw tightening.

"To get me through the night? Hell, yes." He was being utterly honest. *God's fichu*, he needed it to get him through the next bloody hour, let alone the whole night. He despised polite society.

He had been a fool to think he could go all these hours—at a damned ball—without finding at least a few sips of what he needed most.

"Come," his cousin said.

Blindly, Monty followed. The blurs of color and faces and voices continued. Until they made their way through the vast show of revelers to the relative peace of Searle's study. They may have crossed a hall. They may have even climbed a set of stairs.

But as Monty gulped down some whisky offered by his

cousin, he could not be bothered to recall how the hell they had gotten to where they were. Only that there was liquor there. He drained the glass and held it out to Searle.

"Excellent. More, if you please."

Searle raised a brow. "I thought you intended to court Miss Lethbridge this evening."

"I do." In his mind rose an image of Hattie with her luscious dark hair, her expression of disapproval, clutching that fucking cat. "I will. But I am not feeling the thing at the moment, Searle. I need some fortification."

To say he was not feeling the thing was an understatement.

Searle splashed a bit more whisky into his glass before returning the decanter to a sideboard. "You would better serve yourself to avoid the whisky, do you not think?"

Monty was feeling a bit more like himself now. He had not slept the previous night. Balls were deadly boring. He had scarcely bothered with such mundane festivities before. That he had stooped so low now nettled. But Hattie would be in attendance.

Just because she had told him she had no intention of marrying him did not mean he was giving up. Quite the opposite. He was more determined than ever.

"The whisky is a requirement for courting," he said, finishing his next glass with ease. Returning to the swirl and crush of the ballroom did not seem as overwhelming now.

"I cannot think Miss Lethbridge would be impressed by a drunken suitor," Searle observed.

If his cousin thought he was in his cups, Searle did not know him at all.

Monty almost laughed. But there was nothing humorous about the state in which he now found himself. So, he raised his glass once more, only to find it empty. He held it out again. "I am hardly drunken."

"Monty." His cousin's tone was laced with disapproval. "You have arrived at a ball and demanded three glasses of whisky."

Unperturbed by the assessment, Monty shook his glass. "I demanded three, and yet I have only been given two."

"Do you *require* a third glass?"

"Beelzebub's earbobs." He pinned Searle with a glare. "Is this what marriage does to a man? You sound like my bloody mother."

"Aunt is concerned about you," Searle said, hovering near to the whisky decanter, as if he were guarding it. "As am I. How is your ankle?"

"It pains me." Though the accident had taken place some time ago now, he did not think his ankle would ever be the same. Much like the rest of him.

"You were drinking enough to drown an infantry brigade before the accident," Searle pointed out, not making a move to replenish the spirits in his glass.

Very well. If his cousin would not pour him another, he would simply get it for himself. He stalked across the study with his walking stick, then reached for the decanter.

"I am suffering, Searle. I cannot even walk without my stick. The bloody bone is healed, but it throbs like the devil. If I do not have a drink, I will not be able to attempt a waltz with Miss Lethbridge this evening."

Most of what he had just said was tripe. He was sure his cousin knew it. But Searle did not attempt to correct him. He watched. Monty tossed back the third glass, relishing the burn of the whisky down his gullet.

"Monty."

Monty did not want questions, seriousness, or sympathy. He wanted to comfort himself in whatever fashion he deemed necessary and for everyone else to go to the devil.

"Do you think I should compromise Miss Lethbridge as

you did with Lady Searle?" he asked, seeking to distract his cousin from the inevitable sermon he had been about to deliver.

He contemplated a fourth glass of whisky, but decided against it.

"No, I do not recommend compromising her." Searle stalked forward and thieved the glass. "Court her properly, if you truly intend to marry her."

"Of course I intend to marry her." He had first seized upon the notion during his convalescence. "It is the only means of making amends for my sins."

Well, some of his sins.

He would never forgive himself for what had happened to Torrie.

"Marriage to atone for your actions is not a good reason." Searle settled the glass out of Monty's reach, his tone grim.

"I need an heir," Monty argued. "Miss Lethbridge needs a husband. I need to do something to make up for what happened to my friend. See? Everyone shall be happy."

Except Monty. Happiness was an ever-elusive chimera for him.

But he did not say that.

Instead, he followed his cousin back into the throng of revelers, searching for the one woman who could save him.

\* \* \*

HATTIE COULD NOT ABIDE by balls.

She spent most of her time on the periphery, trying not to be noticed.

Which was how she happened to overhear a conversation between two of the Season's reigning diamonds of the first water, Lady Ella Linnane and Lady Lucy Ross. Sometimes, lurking in the potted palms had its advantages.

Sometimes, not.

"Did you see her dress?" Lady Ella asked, *sotto voce*.

"What a dreadful shade of Pomona green," Lady Lucy agreed. "With her complexion and the jonquil robe, it is a dreadful *faux pas*."

Hattie frowned and looked down at herself. *She* was wearing an evening gown of Pomona green satin and blonde lace with a yellow robe.

"I confess, I am surprised to see her in attendance," Lady Ella was saying now. "I thought her firmly on the shelf. She is quite old now, is she not?"

"An ape leader," Lady Lucy agreed, her tone unkind as she fanned herself. "It is being said the Duke of Montrose intends to wed her, but I cannot fathom such a mésalliance."

"That is because you have set your cap at him," Lady Ella said. "I would not fret. Everyone is saying he only wants to marry her because he feels guilty about what happened with Lord Torrington."

"No one would ever want to marry her for any other reason," Lady Lucy said. "She is quite plain and far too tall."

Hattie's stomach clenched at the confirmation they were indeed speaking about her. She told herself it did not matter what two empty-headed society chits said about her. Nor did it matter if they thought her tall and plain. She *was* taller than most ladies, after all, and no one had ever declared her a remarkable beauty. She was not fair-haired and blue-eyed in the fashion of Lady Ella and Lady Lucy.

"Do not forget her hair," Lady Ella added. "It is the color of—"

"Ebony," interrupted a low, masculine voice Hattie recognized all too well.

"Your Grace!" Lady Ella and Lady Lucy said in unison, dipping into curtsies.

What more could her humiliation need? There stood

Montrose, towering over the simpering ladies who had just been insulting her gown and appearance. Hattie closed her eyes for a moment before casting a glance around to determine her route of escape.

Surely if she slipped through the space between the potted palms and the corner, no one would take note. Lady Lucy's and Lady Ella's backs were to her.

"Perhaps no one has ever told you, Lady Ella, that there is nothing uglier than idle gossip motivated by envy," Montrose said then, his voice cutting. "But fear not. You have no need to worry over competing with Miss Lethbridge."

Hattie froze in the act of retreating, wondering what Montrose was saying. Had he changed his mind about marrying her, just as she had known he would? Montrose's interest never remained settled upon one thing for long.

She ought to feel relief at the notion.

So, why did a small pang of regret pierce her?

"Of course, Miss Lethbridge could not compete with Lady Ella," Lady Lucy said. "Lady Ella is one of this Season's most celebrated beauties, whilst Miss Lethbridge is…"

"My future duchess," Montrose said, his tone harsh and quite unlike the lazy drawl she had become accustomed to expecting from him. This Montrose sounded serious. Somber. As if he meant what he said. "You could not possibly compete with her because she is your better in every way and far lovelier. Even so, do not forget that beauty fades, my ladies. A shrewish nature never does."

Hattie bit her lip to keep from smiling. How unlikely. Montrose had defended her. Ne'er-do-well, scapegrace, scandalous Montrose. Without waiting to overhear more, she made good on her escape, heading for the French doors that led to the balcony.

Her cheeks were flushed, and there was another warmth she could not shake burning brightly within her. A warmth she did not want and dared not trust. Some mind-clearing evening air was what she needed. Because there was no other reason why Montrose championing her to the horrid Lady Ella and Lady Lucy should make her feel like this. Indeed, there was no reason for warmth and the Duke of Montrose to coexist within her.

No other reason save her heart, that was.

She tried not to think of the awful things those two wretches had said about her as she made her way into the night. Cool air kissed her cheeks as she stepped against the stone balustrade, resting her arms over it.

She had heard all the whispers about her before. Since Montrose's pronounced interest in her had become common knowledge, the whispers had grown stronger. Although Montrose was known as the Duke of Debauchery, he was also a wealthy peer. A handsome duke. The tales of his licentiousness did nothing to deter debutantes from swooning over him. Nor did it do anything to stop matchmaking mamas from throwing their daughters in his path like matrimonial sacrificial lambs.

She was the Honorable Miss Lethbridge, a plain long Meg who would rather be at home with her cat and a good book than whirling around a ballroom. Who had no intention of marrying anyone. But that did not stop the vitriol being directed toward her.

She sighed, wishing he would leave her alone. Despite her eternal pragmatism, she could not deny that his pursuit of her filled part of her with a longing she had no wish to feel.

As enjoyable as it had been to overhear him giving the twittering ladies within such a crushing setdown, it would likely only increase her misery. The ladies would be outraged, and they would talk about her all the more.

"I am sorry you had to listen to the evil nattering of those two harpies," said a voice, interrupting her solitude.

She jumped and spun about, a hand pressed to her heart. The glow of the moon illuminated him, and even in the lack of light, he was disturbingly handsome. That was the thing about the Duke of Montrose. He never failed to take her breath and make her heart pound, no matter how much of a drunken reprobate he was and no matter how many occasions upon which their paths crossed.

No matter how much damage she knew he could do to her if she but let him.

Belatedly, it occurred to her that he had known she was hiding behind the potted palms all along.

"How did you know I was there?" she asked, for she was certain she had been unobtrusive enough behind the thick gathering of vegetation.

"I watched you dance with the Earl of Rearden." He moved another step nearer, bringing with him his scent.

It was shaving soap and delicious man and, as was always the case with Montrose, a hint of spirits. How she wished he did not often smell of his vice. One of many, she was sure.

"I danced with Lord Rearden quite some time ago." Though his nearness affected her, she was determined to stand her ground. To avoid retreating. Any movement whatsoever on her part would be surrender.

"He is a scoundrel, Miss Lethbridge." Montrose flicked at the sleeve of his coat, as if he were bored by their conversation. "You ought not to give him your time."

"*You* are a scoundrel, Montrose," she pointed out, and if there was bitterness in her voice, it could not be helped. For part of her—the most foolish part, surely—still wished he were not.

If Montrose was not a drunkard and a scandalous rakehell, the feelings she had always entertained for him would not be wrong. Those feelings could be controlled, she reminded herself firmly now. They could remain buried.

Tamped so deep inside her heart, they would never see the sun and have a chance to grow.

"My intentions toward you are honorable," Montrose insisted. "Rearden's are not."

The earl had only ever been kind to her. He was a widower, and she had once been friends with his sister, who had died in childbirth two years ago. He often sought her out at balls, but there was an unmistakable sadness in his eyes, such loss. He had never been untoward, and as far as she knew, his reputation was quite impeccable.

"The earl is a friend," she defended, though it was not any of Montrose's business what the earl was to her. She was not marrying either of them.

"Do not trust him." He took another step. "Do not trust any gentlemen."

"Least of all you." Her tone was pointed, as it must be, even as his proximity did strange things to her senses. A moonlit balcony was not the time to lower her defenses, however, or give in to weakness. "I should go back inside, Your Grace. If you will excuse me?"

"Not yet." He reached out, grasping her wrist.

A spark skittered up her arm, despite his hands being gloved.

She held still, suddenly breathless. "Unhand me, Montrose."

To her surprise, he did.

"Hattie." His voice was low. It sent a ridiculous trill down her spine.

Though he no longer stayed her, she found herself reluctant to flee. "What do you want, Duke?"

He flashed her a wicked grin, and she felt the force of it tugging low in her belly. "You know what I want."

The warmth churning through her went molten. Montrose was *flirting* with her. Wielding his rakish charm with expert precision. And she longed to hear his unspoken words. Perhaps it was the darkness. Perhaps it was his kindness earlier in telling Lady Lucy and Lady Ella to go to the devil. She could not be certain.

But he was a rakehell, she reminded herself. He had made conquests of half of London's ladies. He also was accustomed to getting what he wished. He must never know her true feelings, for he would only use them against her.

"I will not marry you, if that is what you are implying," she told him crisply. "Not even if you champion me to all the harpies in the world."

"How many harpies are there in the world, do you think?" he asked idly, stroking his jaw.

She resented the way the subtle action drew her attention to his mouth. The Duke of Montrose had lips that made a lady think about kissing. Hattie was not impervious to them, although she knew precisely what he was.

She forced herself to recall that, once again. To remember his question. "It is an unfortunate fact of life that although there are far more good people than bad, the rotten apples ruin the rest of the fruit."

He tapped the fullness of his lower lip with his forefinger, as if he were deeply contemplating her words. "Or the rotten fruit makes wine, depending upon how one views it."

He was teasing her. Montrose had never done that before. Nor had he looked at her in such intense fashion. Mayhap it was the darkness, but he seemed to be sweeping over her form, as if he could envision the curves hidden beneath her gown.

He was looking at her very much like a rake looked upon a woman.

She knew that look, had seen it many times from other men. But it had scarcely ever been directed at *her*. And never before by Montrose.

Even his proposal had been bland by his standards. He had not even attempted to touch her.

But she was not about to be wooed by him. If this was a new tactic, he could throw it over the balcony as far as she was concerned. "Why did you follow me out here, Montrose?"

"Because those horrid creatures were talking about you, and you looked pale when you scurried away."

Dreadful man.

"I did not scurry. Mice scurry, and I am no mouse." She gave his arm a stern tap with her fan.

He was still touching his lip, and she could not help but to allow her gaze to dip there once more. To think about that mouth in a way she should not. Heat raced through her.

"You are certainly not a mouse, Hattie." He smiled then, and the full effect of Monty smiling was not lost on her. "You are far too beautiful to be a mouse."

First, he had called her lovely and now beautiful.

It was enough to cut through some of the heat and unwanted longing. To restore her senses. "Flattery will not change my decision, Montrose. And I have not given you leave to refer to me in such a familiar fashion."

Even if she did like the way her name sounded in his deep, delicious voice.

Even if it felt right.

*No, it does not,* she scolded herself firmly. *The Duke of Montrose is a scapegrace, drunken rogue who has never taken anything seriously in his life.*

*But you love him in spite of all that,* taunted a different voice. One she promptly banished.

"I would never flatter you," he said solemnly. "You are far too intelligent. You outshine those two insipid chits and every other lady in the ballroom."

"And that is why I am inundated with dance partners," she scoffed before she could think better of it.

But Montrose seized upon her revealing words. "I will dance with you, Hattie."

"That is not what I meant." She delivered another rap with her fan. "I have no desire to dance with you. And do cease calling me Hattie at once."

"When we are wed, I shall call you Hattie," he drawled as if pondering the thought. "Unless you prefer Harriet? That is your true given name, is it not?"

Where to begin? His persistence was growing more pronounced. He had been incredibly attentive at every social event she had attended in the last few weeks. But now he was calling her Hattie and making her think about his lips and cornering her on a dark balcony.

He must be checked.

"We are never going to be married." Her tone was not as firm as she wanted it to be. Indeed, there was a breathless undertone she could not like. "Therefore, you must carry on with referring to me as Miss Lethbridge. Or if you wish to be perfectly proper, The Honorable Miss Lethbridge."

His grin deepened.

All those very bad, very unwanted, altogether dangerous feelings returned.

"Oh, darling. You know I never wish to be proper." He moved nearer, reaching out to press the same forefinger that had been on his lips to hers. "And you are wrong. We are going to be married. You may as well accept your fate."

She wished his hand were ungloved.

That was her first thought.

Because if it were, she would be able to feel the texture of his bare skin on her lips. The pad of his finger. To flick her tongue over it, taste him... No, she must not think such thoughts.

She stepped away from him, severing that decadent contact. "You only want to marry me to appease your conscience."

"No, that is not why." His expression was somber. "I want to marry you because I want *you*, Hattie."

But she did not believe that. Could not believe it. Because despite his many faults, the Duke of Montrose remained one of the most handsome, sought-after men in London. She could not believe he truly wanted to marry a wallflower scarcely anyone had ever noticed.

His lie hurt more than she had expected. It was akin to a knife in her heart. A reminder of the awkward girl she had been, the lady she had become, who haunted the periphery of every gathering.

"Do not lie to me, Montrose." Her voice was shaking, which she regretted. But it could not be helped. Her emotions would not be reined in. "Lie to everyone else all you like. But do not lie to me."

With that parting shot, she dipped into a mocking curtsey and left the balcony.

## CHAPTER 3

*Lie to everyone else all you like. But do not lie to me.*

Hattie's words echoed in Monty's mind the next night as he prepared himself for an evening of debauchery. She was alarmingly close to the mark there.

He had spent a good portion of his life deceiving everyone around him.

He had to lie to them, just as he had to lie to her. Because if anyone—if one single soul—knew the truth, it would be the end of him. He could not bear it. He would jam the barrel of a pistol into his mouth and...

Wincing, he halted that particular thought.

Marrying Hattie was the answer

He simply had to convince her. Or compromise her.

*Yes! Compromise her. To the devil with Searle's advice.*

He could bloody well seduce her, put an end to this nonsense with the balls and the musicales. He would not have to court her or send her flowers or chase after her. He would not have to find her on moonlit balconies and attempt to steal a kiss, only to be thoroughly rebuked and abandoned.

He had enjoyed a drop of laudanum in his tea earlier. It

filled him with a familiar warmth. His ankle did not even ache. He felt invincible and light as a feather all at once.

Instead of leaving his laudanum behind, he tucked it into his coat. There was no telling how long he would be gone and whether or not he would need it before he returned. His body was positively buzzing as he left his chamber and descended the stairs.

Halfway down, he realized his damned mother was standing at the base, gazing up at him with a pinched look of reproach.

*Fuck.*

He carried on, making an extra show of using his walking stick. "Mother," he greeted her when he reached the last step, bowing deeply.

"Montrose, I was wondering if I might speak with you." She eyed him in that suspicious maternal manner of hers, the one he could not abide. "Have you been indulging?"

"Of course not," he snapped, tired of her endless castigation.

This was her fault, after all. Her brother was the cause…

But he would not think of that despicable bastard now. Arthur Parkross would burn in the fiery depths of hell for his sins one day.

"You seem detached," his mother accused. "As if you have been drinking spirits. Did you recently wake from a nap?"

"Madam," he reminded her sternly, "I am the duke. It is not your place to question or otherwise make demands of me."

She jerked as if he had struck her.

"Montrose…"

"Your Grace," he interrupted, emphasizing formality. "You have overstepped your bounds."

Servants were lingering, not far. He did not want them to overhear this particular quarrel. For even as scandalous as he was, some subjects—namely himself—he guarded with a zealous need for privacy. This part of his life was not to be discussed. Not even if he pissed on every rug in the damned house.

But enough of that. He had decided what he was going to do with this evening. His mother was keeping him from what he wanted. Which was a visit to The Duke's Bastard, followed by a trip to Hattie's bedchamber.

He knew which chamber was hers. And there was an accommodating tree conveniently located near it, he was reasonably sure. If not, there was always the servant's entrance. Bribery was a possibility…

"Yes, of course," his mother interrupted his thoughts, frowning at him, hurt evident in her expression and tone. "I merely wished for a few minutes of your time."

"I cannot spare it," he dismissed. Because he had no wish to listen to yet another one of his mother's lectures. If he wanted to hear a sermon, he would attend church. And he did not want to hear a damned sermon, which was why he had not warmed a pew in years.

Instead, he had been warming beds.

Legions of beds.

He was not proud of that, as he thought upon it. But worshiping women had seemed a remedy. The first of many he had sought to ease the pain within. None of them ever fully healed the bitter wounds. No matter how hard he tried.

"You cannot spare a few minutes?" his mother pressed. "I am worried about you, Montrose."

He laughed at her pronouncement. A bitter and deep laugh, no levity in it at all. "You are about twenty years too late in worrying about me, Mother."

With that, he brushed past her, stalking from the townhouse he reluctantly shared with her. In truth, he should have sent her to the dower house. But since he had yet to take a wife, he had not done so. He had sent her to Scotland not long ago with his sister Catriona, but their absence had been cut short when Catriona had returned to marry the Earl of Rayne.

Long story, that. One which began with the earl shooting Monty in a duel.

Walking stick in hand, he settled in his carriage. The last year of his life had been devilishly trying. But he was convinced it was time for fortune's fickle wheel to give him a good turn.

* * *

Sir Toby was playing with her hair again.

That was the first thought in Hattie's mind as a gentle stroking over her unbound locks pulled her from slumber. Eyes still closed, she stretched.

"Do go away, you little scoundrel," she murmured.

His fluffy, warm body was a comfort she adored. But occasionally, the cat decided to bat at her hair in the midst of the night.

"Hattie."

*Dear heavens.*

Sir Toby could not speak.

Her eyes flew open, a scream rising in her throat. A hand clamped over her mouth.

"Do not scream, love." She knew that voice. That deep, decadent rumble.

"Montrose," she said against his bare palm.

She had the fleeting, foolish thought that she was having her wish from the other night on the balcony at Lord and Lady Searle's ball. His skin was against her lips. It was warm. Surprisingly smooth. Some wild impulse inside her wanted to kiss that palm.

But then she recalled it was the midst of the night, and he had somehow stolen into her chamber, and that he was a roué of the worst order.

So, she bit him instead.

He emitted a strangled howl of pain, removing his hand. "Damnation, Hattie. That bloody well hurt."

She felt not a moment of guilt. "Good. Perhaps next time you will think twice about the wisdom of sneaking into a lady's chamber."

"Your teeth are sharp as your wits," he grumbled.

Hattie remained unmoved. She would bite him again in a trice if she had to. Anything to keep herself from falling into his dangerous flame. "What are you doing in my chamber, Montrose?"

"Getting bitten by a vicious she-cat."

Speaking of cats, where was Sir Toby? She patted the counterpane and found him curled up alongside her, apparently unmoved by her altercation with the duke. Lazy ball of fluff. Did he not know he was meant to guard her from scoundrels?

"I would not have bitten you had you not trespassed in my chamber." She reached alongside her, investigating the counterpane. Her hand met with muscular thigh.

*Oh.*

She snatched her hand away. Montrose was sitting on her bed. And she had just touched him. None of these things were good.

"I wanted to see you without other eyes and ears," he grumbled. "How is a man supposed to convince a lady to marry him if he is forever having to observe the bloody proprieties?"

It occurred to her that Montrose had likely never before courted a lady.

All his conquests were demimondaines.

"I can assure you that you do not go about it by sneaking into bedchambers." She frowned at him through the darkness. Her window dressings were askew, lending just a hint of moon's silver light to the room. "Did you climb into my window, Montrose?"

There was a tree in the small gardens below, with large, sturdy old branches.

The rogue must have somehow scaled them and made his way to her chamber.

"Had I known a bite was awaiting me, I may have reconsidered putting my life at risk." His tone was still wounded.

"Montrose, you should not be here." And not just because his presence in her chamber was highly improper. But because there was something about being alone with him in such intimate quarters that made her feel quivery inside.

Longing unfurled deep within her.

"Of course I should not, but as long as we are quiet, no one will ever be the wiser." He stood then, and she felt his weight lifting from the bed. "Where is the bloody tinderbox? I can scarcely see anything."

"Alongside my bed, on the table," she said, grateful her bedroom was at the far end of the hall where neither her mother nor her brother was likely to overhear.

The familiar sound of the tinderbox opening reached her, followed by the striking of flint. A spark flared to life as he lit a spill, then the brace of candles, bathing the room in a warm glow.

She could see him quite clearly now, and she wished he had not lit the candles at all. Because seeing him made it so much more difficult to resist him. His gaze seared her, traveling over her as she sat up, the counterpane falling to her waist.

Sir Toby at last stirred, waking and stretching before

nimbly climbing over her legs and approaching the edge of the bed. He sat, staring at their unexpected guest.

Montrose's stare flicked to the cat. "You sleep with the feline?"

"He is my companion." She gave the animal a soft head scratch. "He belongs here. Unlike you. What was it you wished to convey to me that necessitated breaking into my chamber like a common thief out to filch the silver?"

He passed a hand over his jaw, his expression turning rueful. "To the devil with your teeth being sharp. Your tongue is the sharpest weapon in your arsenal. A thief, am I? If I am to be compared to one, perhaps I ought to steal something for my troubles. At least, then your words would possess a hint of truth."

The notion of the Duke of Montrose stealing something from her made the quivery sensation turn into molten heat. Instantly, she was thinking of what he might steal. A kiss. Or…

Her cheeks burned. "I have nothing worth stealing."

He gave her a slow, wicked grin. "Oh, how wrong you are, darling."

Did it count if he stole her breath?

Montrose seemed different this evening. She had not even detected the faintest trace of spirits.

"You must not call me that," she said weakly.

He reached out to Sir Toby, and much to her dismay, the cat arched his back into Montrose's slow caress. She watched his large hand traveling over Sir Toby's snow-white fur, and thought she could not blame her cat one whit. To have that hand traveling over her exactly thus…

*No*, she ordered herself. *Stop this madness at once.*

"What must I not call you?" he asked slowly, his drawl sending another frisson of desire through her. "Darling? Or Hattie? Would you mind making a list for me? When we are husband and wife, I shall refer to it regularly to keep from displeasing you. Though I must admit, nothing makes me want to kiss you more than when you frown at me as if you are a governess, and I am your recalcitrant charge."

He wanted to kiss her?

*Yes.*

It was the voice she had been silencing for years now, as she had watched from afar while her brother's handsome, rakish friend had run rampant all over London. Stealing hearts, stirring up scandals, and otherwise earning his status as one of the most scandalous—and sought after—gentlemen in Town.

She forced herself to recall what he had just said. "You must not call me anything other than Miss Lethbridge, Montrose. For that is what my name is and what it shall remain. There is no need of a list of any sort as I have told you, ad nauseam, that I will not marry you under any circumstances."

"You're still frowning," he said, his voice low. His head dipped.

He continued petting Sir Toby, who was now purring loudly. Of course, only the Duke of Montrose could win over a cat who did not like anyone but Hattie. Even when he did not like Sir Toby himself.

Sir Toby was too foolish to realize it, apparently.

She knew the feeling all too well.

"I am frowning at you because you are a reckless cad without a thought for my reputation." She gave him a forced smile just to irk him. "There. Does that suit you?"

"I am afraid not." His gaze was on her lips. "Your smiles also make me want to kiss you. Indeed, as I stand here now, I cannot think of one reason why I have yet to do so."

Indecent longing flooded her. Settled between her thighs in an ache.

What to do with such words? The Duke of Montrose was not for her, and she knew it. He would only break her heart. The only reason he was flirting with her and trailing after her now was because he wanted to marry her and lessen the burden of his own guilt. He did not truly think her beautiful. He did not truly want to kiss her.

She furiously repeated all those reminders to herself.

But the intensity of his expression and the heaviness of the moment seemed to bely all that. There was an awareness hovering in the very air, sparking and shimmering.

She swallowed. "Because you know that if you attempt to kiss me, I shall punch you in the nose."

Her words were unsteady. Revealing far more than she would have preferred, to herself as well as to Montrose, if he but listened.

"Will you?" he asked softly. He leaned closer. He stopped petting the cat. His hand was instead flattened on the bed, bracing himself as he raised a knee to partially join her there once more. His other hand cupped her jaw. "Do it now, Hattie, if you must."

His face was close enough to hers to touch. His mouth near enough to kiss. He stroked her cheek with the pad of his thumb. It was the only point of contact between them, and yet it felt like the most intimate of caresses. She could feel that tender caress in her core.

It made her weak.

Her fingers curled into a fist at her side.

"Go ahead, darling." He gave her a slight smile, a taunting one. His breath was warm and faintly wine scented.

It was an improvement over gin.

She wondered where he had been before he had arrived at her chamber. Who he had been keeping company with? Why he had come here? Surely not just to steal a kiss? Surely not just to speak?

"What do you want from me, Montrose?"

She would not strike him, and they both knew it. Her heart was not in it, for she would far rather prefer to kiss him instead.

"You, Hattie." He dragged his nose against hers. "You in my bed. You beneath me. You bearing my children. Is that so difficult to believe?"

It was. And it was also starkly, shockingly attractive. His words set off a reactive pang inside her that said she would not be averse to such a future. Indeed, part of her would like it far too much.

"You only think you want that," she protested. But her hand, the one she had tried to make into a fist, was open now. And it had traveled of its own accord to his face.

She was touching his cheek. Feeling the prickle of his dark whiskers on her skin. He was so alarmingly masculine. So tempting. The rational part of her knew who he was, what he was. The rest of her did not give a damn.

"I know what I want, Hattie." He pressed his lips to hers then.

The contact was brief. Fleeting.

Unexpectedly soft.

Disappointingly bereft of passion. She had expected him to brand her with his mouth. To consume her. Instead, he had given her the barest of kisses.

He retreated a few inches.

Here was where she should tell him to leave. Demand that he go. Insist she did not want anything to do with him at all.

Her lips opened. Her tongue moved.

"Is that the best you can do?" she asked.

The question was a mistake, because in the next breath, his mouth was on hers. Consuming. Ravishing. Not exactly punishing, but this was the kiss of a practiced seducer. It was knowing. His lips moved over hers, demanding she open. And she did, allowing his tongue to sweep inside.

She tasted him, Monty and red wine and sin and everything she should not want.

It would be far better to be a wallflower, to die a spinster, than to burn herself in this man's flames. That was what her mind tried to warn her, anyway. None of the rest of her listened.

Because kissing Montrose was incendiary.

It was revolutionary.

She wondered if this was the feeling inventors felt—this deep sense of discovery, this heady excitement—when they realized their creation would work. When they understood they had made something that had never previously existed, something rare and unique.

That was how she felt kissing the Duke of Montrose in the middle of the night, alone in her chamber where he decidedly had no business being, whilst Sir Toby Belch witnessed their madness. She felt as if she had just found something incredible. She wanted to capture this feeling, this moment, him, and keep it forever. To relive it again and again.

To always feel this way.

But that was a sheer impossibility.

He jerked his lips from hers suddenly, ending the kiss as abruptly as it had begun.

He stared at her as if he were seeing her for the first time. "Hattie. You felt it, too, did you not? The rightness between us cannot be denied."

*The rightness between us.*

She did not want those words to hover in her mind. To dazzle her with a promise which would go unfulfilled. But it happened anyway.

"There is no *us*," she denied.

Also a useless action, wasted words. Because she could hear the lie of it, taunting her.

He took her hand and brought it to his chest. His capricious heart beat within, a reassuring thump. "I am here." He released her wrist and pressed his hand over her heart. "And you are here. Our hearts are beating fast. You enjoyed that kiss every bit as much as I did, Hattie. Do not dare to deny it."

His chest was solid and warm, as warm as his lips had been, as warm as his palm, seeming to brand her through the cotton of her night rail. "You are well-versed in the art of kissing, Montrose. If I did not like your kiss, it would be a surprise."

Her words made him frown, and she realized this, too, was the wrong thing to say. For she had just taunted him.

"Are you suggesting you would enjoy any man's kiss as much as mine?" he asked, his tone silky with menace.

She clung to her bravado. "Yes. I am saying precisely that. As long as he were a skilled kisser, of course. Any gentleman would do."

He made a sound deep in his throat. A growl or a curse, she could not determine. And then his mouth was fused with hers once more.

## CHAPTER 4

He should have kissed Hattie Lethbridge a long, damned time ago.

He should have married her as well.

He should have bedded her a hundred times over by now. A thousand times. It still would not be enough. Need for her was a rising tide within him. A raging river threatening to overflow its banks. He had not felt this alive in as long as he could recall.

These were Monty's turbulent thoughts as he moved his lips over hers. Kissing her was a revelation. *She* was a revelation. Her lips were soft and full, giving and lush. Her tongue moved against his, exploring, filling him with desire.

He was glad he had added a drop of laudanum to his wine at The Duke's Bastard. Because it heightened his senses. And he wanted to soak up every second of this embrace. He wanted to commit her taste to memory. He wanted to remember her sweet response forever.

He was supposed to be a hardened rake. Cynical and jaded. Aloof and unaffected. But he could not deny the way she moved him. *Damnation*, how she moved him.

And she knew how to kiss.

Hers was not the highly skilled kiss of a courtesan, but neither was it the kiss of a tyro. Possessiveness surged inside him. Who had taught her to kiss? He would find out. Later. Challenge the bastard to a duel.

He smothered the thought and deepened the kiss. For now, her lips were beneath his, and that was all that mattered. His body hummed with the longing to feel hers beneath it. To have her softness cradling his hardness. To pull her virginal night rail over her head.

It was white, of course. High-necked, too. Those pearl buttons at her throat had been a beacon calling to him with the need to be undone. He wanted to rumple her, muss her, unbutton her. To make his mark upon her with his mouth, with his teeth. Her chastity tempted him. Taunted him.

He could not deny there was something irresistibly alluring about the prospect of being her first lover. Of teaching her pleasure. Of instructing her in the finer art of how to be wicked. Burying himself inside her tight heat. He had never had a virgin before. Hattie would be his first, and he was heartily glad none had come before her. Indeed, he wished, in this moment, he had never had another lover. That she was his only.

Why had he never noticed her before now? Why had he never suspected the fire lurking beneath her prim exterior? Had it been because she was his friend's sister, or had he simply been too damned stupid to see the glory awaiting him?

Whatever the reason, he was making amends in the only manner he knew how—worshiping her with his mouth. With his hands, too. He cupped her breast, found her pebbled nipple through her night rail with unerring ease. He worked his thumb over the sensitive tip. She made a breathy sound of need low in her throat, and his cock twitched.

*Yes*, said the voice inside his head. *More. Everything.*

He wanted her the way he wanted a drink. The way he wanted more opium. He craved her. He wanted her complete surrender. To possess her. To claim. To fill. Above all, to please her.

She was intoxicating. He left her kiss to trail his mouth down her throat. She smelled of violets and herself. He licked her skin. Salty and delicious. Next, he found her ear. Kissed her there. Pressed his lips to the delicate hollow behind it. Felt her shudder.

"Tell me again, Hattie," he whispered in her ear, careful to make certain his lips grazed the whorl.

Her breaths were ragged. She was not as unaffected as her perennially disapproving mien suggested. She wanted this, wanted him. And she was silent. He hoped it was because he had so addled her wits, she had forgotten what they had been speaking of before he had kissed her senseless.

Monty caught her nipple between his thumb and forefinger, rolling it, plucking at it. "Tell me any other gentleman would do. Tell me you would respond to another man as you have responded to me. That you would want another the same way. Go on. Lie to me."

"You are sure of yourself," she whispered.

He could have told her this was the *sole* arena in which he was sure of himself. But what would be the point? He was who he was. She already knew him as the selfish rogue, the scandalous rakehell.

He kissed her ear instead, then kissed down her throat. Leaving her breast, his fingers found her buttons, sliding them, one by one, from their moorings. With each fresh expanse of creamy flesh exposed, he kissed. Hattie made no move to stop him.

"I did not hear the words yet, darling," he taunted against her bare skin.

He found her frantic pulse at the base of her throat. Found the satin flesh of her décolletage. Explored the curve of her full, round breast. He had never taken his time to admire another lover more. Everything about the night, about this, about Hattie, was different. He knew it to his marrow, even if he did not have the slightest inkling of what he ought to do with the information.

Continuing to tempt and tease and kiss her seemed the obvious answer.

Sinking his cock inside her seemed an even better one.

"Any other gentleman would do," she said.

He froze. Surely, she had not just said what he thought she had said. His ears were deceiving him, he knew it. For there was no way she could be as far gone as she was, as flushed and desperate for him, and then tell him she would react thus to another man.

Monty used his teeth on her, gently biting the full swell of her breast. Not hard enough to cause pain or even a mark. But enough for warning. He gave up on the civility of buttons. Instead, he grabbed a handful of her night rail and tugged. The fine material rent, splitting in two. Her breasts burst forth as her gasp sliced through the room.

His eyes were intent upon his prey. This part of her, too, was beautiful. Her nipples matched the color of her lips. And they were hard, jutting out. Puckered little buds. Begging for his mouth. For his teeth.

"Would you let another man do this?" he asked her.

And then he lowered his head and took one of her nipples into his mouth and sucked. He was not certain which of them he was intending to teach a lesson more. She arched her back, thrusting her nipple deeper into his mouth.

She was so responsive, his Hattie. He could not get enough of her raw, unbridled enthusiasm.

"Yes," she gasped. "No. Yes."

He used his teeth on her, for she brought out the mercilessness within him. The need to pleasure within an inch of pain. "Which is it, Hattie darling? Yes, you would allow another man to suck your pretty, pink nipples until you moan? Or no. No, these sweet nipples are mine and mine alone?"

Her breath left her in one hot exhalation. Her verdant gaze was fixed upon him, her lips parted. Her pupils gave proof of her desire. "No."

He flicked his tongue over her, back and forth, before withdrawing and blowing upon the wet peak. "Say it, Hattie. All of it."

"What do you want from me, Montrose?"

*Oh, no.* She was not going to avoid it. He would have the victory of the forbidden words he wanted on her lips.

"I just told you what I want." He blew on the taut bud of her breast. "Answer the question, sweet."

"No." Of course, she was stubborn to the last.

Had he expected anything less from her? Even pliable and filled with desire, she was still Hattie. And Hattie's stern sense of self was one of the characteristics he admired about her most. That and her brilliant wit. Her beauty, rare and unique, was additional.

"No?" he repeated. He licked her nipple and then raised his head, locking gazes with her.

She swallowed. "No, I would not allow another to touch me thus. Only…only you."

Her words made his desire surge.

The need to be inside her almost consumed him. Ruled him.

He forced it back, tamped it down.

"There, now. Was that so difficult?" He rewarded her by sucking the peak of her breast into his mouth, hard. And then he lowered his lips to the other and lavished all his attention upon it in similar fashion.

A most unwanted noise interrupted the heated moment between them.

He released her breast and turned his head in the direction of the sound, which was one-part growl, one-part hiss. The damned cat, which he had quite forgotten in all his raging need for Hattie, was perched nearby, growling low in its throat.

Perhaps the creature thought Monty was hurting his mistress.

Perhaps the thing was jealous.

Mayhap Hattie had trained the feline to perform just such a distraction on the odd chance a scoundrel would find his way into her bedchamber and attempt to seduce her.

"Oh, my sweet lad," Hattie cooed.

And it took him a full minute to realize she was addressing the goddamn cat instead of him.

*Preposterous.*

The devil of the thing was, she looked so bloody tender and adorable, calling to the creature, he could not even be angry. He did, however, reach a realization. He could not bed her while the infernal feline looked on. No matter how badly longing for her was raging through his blood and hardening his cock.

One thing was certain: he had never before been interrupted in the act of seduction by a feline. A practiced rakehell like him should have done better. Instead, he was sitting here, his prick harder than stone, jealous of a cat.

Why had Hattie never gazed upon him with such tenderness?

*Foolish.*

He was a sapskull. Did he want tenderness from her? He had never before longed for anything more than slaking his lust with a woman. Was Hattie somehow different from all the others who had come before?

Monty had no wish to consider such a damning notion. Instead, he turned his mind to the matter of getting what he wanted in most expedient fashion.

He kissed her breast. "I have compromised you, Hattie."

The wrong words to say, it would seem.

For they had the opposite of their intended effect. Her hands settled on his shoulders, shoving him with surprising force. "You have seduced me, is what you have done. Fortunately, no one knows. My reputation is not yet in tatters. You will have to leave the way you came, however."

He had not come at all, and that was the problem. But she was not speaking of carnal matters. She was speaking of his departure, as though it were imminent. The devil of it was, now that he had clambered up the tree, he found the prospect of his descent rather daunting. Perhaps breaking his foolish neck would be just the solution he sought, however. He had not wanted a woman as badly as he wanted Hattie in…ever. Now that he had kissed her, touched her silken skin, felt her body respond to his, his hunger had only grown. His need for her had intensified.

She was frantic, shaking hands attempting to cover herself with the tattered remnants of her night rail. Robbing him of the sight of her beautiful breasts. The cat strolled over, planting his bottom on the bed next to Hattie as if staking his claim.

*Not a chance*, he told the cat with his eyes. *She is mine.*

"I am not ready to leave just yet, darling." He gently brushed her hands aside and repaired the night rail for her as best he could, given the damage he had done. It was enough to preserve her modesty, but there would be no repairing the tears. "We need to speak."

"You have already said a great deal." She eyed him mulishly. "Far too much, in fact. You must go, Montrose."

He could not resist trailing his finger up her throat, all the way to her lips. The shape of them fascinated him. Everything about her did.

"I cannot go just yet until we speak about our nuptials."

Her frown returned. "There will be no nuptials."

He wanted to kiss the furrow from her brow. He settled instead for following the sweet bow of her upper lip. "Do not be foolish, Hattie. You must wed me now, of course."

She grasped his wrist, staying his explorations without pushing him away. "No."

Stubborn woman. He admired her spirit and boldness. But not quite as much when it was keeping him from what he desired most. Her hand on his wrist was the sweetest brand, burning into him. Touching her lips had been a mistake, because it only served to heighten his lust.

It was blazing through him. Heat and need were a fire within him which could not be tamed. But he could indulge in none of this.

Time to resort to more desperate measures. Prevarication was in order.

"You could be with child," he lied.

Her pretty lips compressed. "That is impossible."

*The good Lord's chemise.* Her knowledge clearly surpassed that of virginal miss. He ought to have suspected as much. This was Hattie, after all.

Still, he was not pleased about the notion she understood something more would have been required in order for her to grow his child in her womb. Strangely, the thought of Hattie bearing his child filled his chest with something...an unfamiliar sensation. It did nothing to dampen his ardor.

He forced himself to breathe. To stop touching her mouth.

He seated himself on the bed at her side, switching positions. "And how would you know whether or not it is impossible after what just passed between us?"

Her cheeks went rosy. "More would have to have happened. You did not…enter me."

Two words, and she almost ended him.

*Enter me.*

*Beelzebub's earbobs.* How was he to concentrate?

He inhaled slowly. She was still holding his wrist, as if she were reluctant to sever the contact. With his other hand, he covered hers. "How do you know this, Hattie?"

She bit her lip, as if considering her response. Just when he thought she would not speak, she rocked him with another two words, but in a different way entirely. "Your sister."

His gut clenched. It was true that he had arranged for Catriona to marry the Earl of Rayne. It was also true the two had found happiness together. But the notion of his sister's marital bed made him want to retch.

He shuddered. "You have said enough. I suppose I should not be surprised my minx of a sister was the source of your knowledge."

"The fault is mine," she said, surprising him. "When she told me she was *enceinte*—nay, I suppose, it was actually Olivia who told me. Never mind who did the telling, however. I asked her…I was curious about the marriage bed, knowing I would never enjoy it myself."

He did not know which fact she had just imparted he ought to dwell upon first, that he was going to be an uncle, that she had been curious about lovemaking, or that she had supposed she would never marry.

In the end, his love for his sister won out over his rampaging lust. "Cat is having a bairn?"

"Yes." Her frown deepened. "Did you not know?"

This evening was going from bad to worse. All his carefully laid plans had been blasted to hell. He was not currently deep inside Hattie's welcoming cunny. Nor was he any closer to convincing her to marry him. And now, he was learning his sister was with child.

"Of course, I did not know," he said, shock still roiling through him, warring with the desire for her. "When the devil was she going to tell me?"

"She wanted to tell you when she was here in London, but then Rayne came for her, and they ran away to the country together once more. She was so desperately happy with her husband that it never occurred to her until it was too late. She said she had sent you a letter. Several, in fact, but that you had not answered them."

*God's fichu.* He thought of the stack of unopened letters strewn haphazardly over his study desk. He did have a great deal of neglected correspondence.

Hattie guessed the truth before he could craft a clever excuse.

"You have not been reading her letters, have you?"

He did not particularly care for the judgmental tone in her voice. "I have not been reading anyone's letters."

"Montrose."

"I have been ill." He rubbed the top of her hand idly. Even her skin was luxurious. Intoxicating. He could not wait to strip her bare and explore her everywhere.

"You do not seem ill now." She was watching him, that green gaze seeing too much.

"I have an injured ankle." He flashed her his rake's grin, the one that never failed to make the ladies melt.

Hattie did not melt. She yanked her hand away from him. "You just climbed a tree, Montrose."

Yes, so he had.

"A grand gesture to win you." He pressed his hand over his heart. "I will happily suffer for my lady."

"I am not yours."

Salt in the wound. If he could not have her tonight, he was going to go home and drown himself in gin.

He gritted his teeth. "You will be."

"I will not be." She cocked her head, considering him. "You do not even have your walking stick."

Laudanum had a way of making a man feel invincible. Capable of anything. Including climbing two stories high in a tree. In the midst of the night. He did not say any of that, however.

"I do not always require it," he hedged. "Only when my ankle is particularly paining me."

She was the Hattie he knew once more, her armor firmly in place. Looking distinctly unimpressed with him. He missed the flushed, acquiescence of his passionate lover. He would have kissed her again, but he did not trust himself.

"You should read your letters, Montrose," she said pointedly.

Yes, he should. Procrastination was as excellent a vice as any, however. If he did not read of trouble, how could it exist and shatter his illusion of opium-laced tranquility?

"My correspondence is none of your concern."

Her expression shifted. Closed. He regretted his stiff response, the coolness in his tone. She was drifting away from him. It was as if all the distance he had erased between them with their earlier kisses had returned.

She was still caressing the cat, cuddling the misbegotten little creature to her side as if to offer him protection. For its part, the damned feline looked remarkably pleased.

*She may have won this battle*, he told the cat silently, *but I shall win the war.*

"Go now, Montrose. Before you are seen and I am ruined in truth."

Her voice had softened, imploring, almost.

"I will go, but do not think this is over between us." He rose from the bed and offered her a mocking bow.

"Just as I told you earlier, there is no *us*," she denied. "There is only Miss Lethbridge and the Duke of Montrose. We do not belong together."

Stubborn Hattie.

Delicious, beautiful, passionate, stubborn Hattie. Bedding her would be exquisite. He now had to climb down a tree in the dark of the night with a raging erection.

Without falling to his imminent doom.

He gave her a smile. "How wrong you are, darling. In time, you shall see."

CHAPTER 5

"There is another arrival for Miss Lethbridge."

Their stony-faced butler made the announcement whilst Hattie was having tea with her mother. Just as well, for the tea was tasteless. The distractions not nearly distracting enough.

"*Another* arrival," cooed Mama, giving Hattie a pointed look. "What can it be now, Oswald?"

The Torrington House butler had a look of perpetual long-suffering. Hattie had no doubt the antics of Torrie and Montrose, over the years, had helped to facilitate his pinched expression.

"A crate of books, I believe," Oswald declared, stoic as ever. "Where will you have me put them, Lady Torrington?"

Montrose had already sent flowers, and in true Montrose fashion, he had seen to it that not one bouquet had arrived, but a dozen. That had been the day after his unexpected and thoroughly improper appearance in her bedchamber.

She had supposed he was offering penance.

Now books? How did Montrose even know what she preferred to read?

"Is there a note?" Mama asked.

"No, my lady," the butler said.

Of course there was no note. The first bouquet of flowers had contained one. The subsequent eleven had not born a single letter. Sending such a tremendous waterfall of gifts to an unattached lady was scandalous, even by Montrose's standards. He knew the rules of society. He simply eschewed them. All whilst laughing and drinking himself to oblivion.

Except, his laughter never reached his eyes. Strange how she had failed to note that before. There were ghosts in his gaze. And those ghosts haunted him.

"See them brought here, if you please, Oswald," Mama directed.

"Of course, my lady." Oswald bowed, then took his leave of the room.

Hattie was alone with her mother once more. And her mother's assessing gaze saw far too much. "These books, too, are from the Duke of Montrose."

"I do not know," Hattie prevaricated, lowering her gaze to the tea swimming in her delicate china cup. A safer place to direct her attention, it was certain. For if she met her mother's gaze, she had no doubt Mama would see through her.

"Nonsense." Her mother's voice possessed an unusually sharp edge. "The books, like the dozen bouquets you have already received, are from the duke. He has paid a marked amount of attention to you."

Yes, he had.

And he had also sneaked into her chamber and kissed her to oblivion. He had asked her to marry him repeatedly, though she dared not tell her mother.

He had made her weak.

And foolish.

And weak.

Her weakness for him was not to be borne.

"There is no note, Mama," she argued. "The flowers and books could be from anyone."

"Yes," said Mama drily. "Your suitors are legion."

Her words were most unwelcome reminders. She was a failure as far as her mother was concerned. A wallflower. A spinster. Nearly too old to be unwed. Only a handful of suitors she was not keen on pursued her, and in time, they, too, would fall away like leaves from an autumn tree. None of them made her feel even the slightest hint of what she felt for Montrose.

She compressed her lips, inhaling slowly, counting to ten inwardly before responding. "What are you suggesting, Mama?"

"I am suggesting that the Duke of Montrose has decided to marry you, and though he is a despicable scoundrel and tawdry rakehell, you must accept him," her mother snapped. "You will be a duchess in your own right, Hattie. Only think of it."

Her mother's icy blonde beauty had not been passed on to Hattie. Nor had her fine-boned, elegant figure. Hattie was tall. Well-curved. Her hair was dark. Whilst her mother had been the toast of London in her season before Father had married her, Hattie had never been considered a diamond of the first water. She was a perennial disappointment to her mother.

But as irritated as Hattie was with her mother's perpetual judgment, she could not like the manner in which she had described Montrose. *Despicable scoundrel. Tawdry rakehell.*

She took a calming sip of her tea before proceeding. "Mama, I must not *accept* anyone. And Montrose is neither despicable nor tawdry."

Her mother emitted an inelegant sound of disapproval deep in her throat. "Of course you must accept a husband. At your age, you must accept any husband who will have you.

What else is there for you, Hattie, hmm? Perhaps you would like to become a companion or a governess?"

Hattie flinched. This was an old argument between them. Though she possessed a small annual income in her own right, it would not be enough to sustain her. The Torrington line was simply not that flush with cash. She had no wish to take on either of those roles, as her mother well knew. Nor was she convinced, however, that she wanted to become a wife.

And most assuredly not the next Duchess of Montrose.

No matter how delicious the duke's kisses were. And no matter how much her heart and her body ached for him, in ridiculous, unwise, reckless, altogether wrong tandem.

He would break her heart. Disappoint her. Hurt her. He was as glorious to behold as an angel and as tempting as the devil.

"Surely I have several seasons remaining before I must become either companion or governess," she argued primly.

"You must decide."

A footman appeared then, bearing a crate of books.

Hattie's heart leapt at the sight of so many leather-bound volumes. All for her. She adored reading. But how had Montrose known? She was sure she had never shared her love of the written word with him.

The footman deposited the crate at Hattie's feet. With a bow, he was gone again. Hattie abandoned her tea in favor of the new arrival. It was better than flowers. Better than flattery.

*Not better than kisses*, whispered a voice inside her.

She promptly stifled the voice and wished it to Hades. She plucked the first book from the top of the opened crate and found it to be a book written by Mrs. Radcliffe. Beneath it was a volume of poetry by William Wordsworth.

She adored poetry. She flipped open the volume, unable to keep from perusing the pages, eager to begin reading.

"Have you listened to a word I have spoken, Hattie?" Her mother's voice interrupted her pleased examination.

She snapped the book closed and reluctantly returned her attention to Mama, who wore an expression of intense displeasure, her lips pursed, jaw clenched.

"Forgive me. I was distracted by the books."

And by the thoughtfulness of just such a gesture. Sneaking into windows, stealing kisses, arrogantly proclaiming his suit as if she would have no choice but to accept his offer of marriage—these were all actions she expected of him.

Sending her one dozen bouquets?

Choosing a crate laden with books, and not just any books but books she would enjoy reading? She was almost dizzied.

He was doing it again, the devilish man. Just as surely as he had scaled that tree and made his way into her chamber, he was skirting all her defenses. Marching straight to her heart the same way an invading army would storm a castle in days gone by.

Just when she thought nothing the Duke of Montrose would do could possibly surprise her, he did. The realization was troubling. Worrisome. He was becoming increasingly impossible to resist.

"You and your books," Mama said with a dismissive sniff. "I never could understand your penchant for burying yourself in pages and pages of words."

"I love them," she said, holding the Wordsworth book of poems to her heart as if she expected her mother to wrest it from her grasp. "I never understood your dislike of words."

"Words are silly," her mother snapped. "You ought not to waste your time with fictions. If you had been more interested in conversing, Hattie, in attending balls and routs and musicales, instead of forever feigning a headache so you could stay at home..."

"I do not care for society in the way you do," she defended herself, stroking the cover of the book. "And I have not always feigned the headaches. Some of them were real."

Most of them, however, had been ruses so she could stay home with Sir Toby and cuddle up beneath her counterpane with a good book. As far as Hattie was concerned, reality often paled in comparison to the vibrant intensity of the imagination.

*Unless the Duke of Montrose is involved.*

*Drat it all*, she thought she had banished that voice.

She would simply have to try harder.

Her mother sighed. "I was far too lenient with you, it is clear. I have failed as a mother. All these seasons, and you have not managed to find a husband. Now a duke wishes to marry you, and you still do not show interest. What is the matter with you, girl?"

She may not show interest, but that was because within, she hid a great, burning interest. And *that* was what was wrong with her, far more than anything else.

"You would have me marry a tawdry scoundrel?" she asked weakly.

The book seemed to burn her fingers.

For all his badness, there was some good in the Duke of Montrose. It was that which frightened her most. Because the goodness was what could make her love him even more.

"A *duke*, Hattie," Mama said, frowning mightily. "You could ignore his wild ways. Forgive him his foibles. In return, you would be a duchess. You could command society. Do not forget that you cannot forever cast yourself upon the mercy of your brother. Already, your relationship with Torrington is strained."

"Of course it is strained." Reminded of why, Hattie returned the book of poems to the crate at last. "Have you forgotten the reason for his loss of memory? We are fortunate he is even alive after the phaeton crash. Who was there at his side, racing him?"

"The Duke of Montrose is not alone responsible for what occurred that awful night," her mother told her. "Torrington chose to race. Torrington chose to drown himself in drink that night, just like so many others. He is in his father's mold, much to my shame. Have you wondered what would happen to us if Torrington had died that night?"

Hattie's blood went cold. She loved her brother. The thought of a life without him…it was unthinkable. She could not forget the fear when she had discovered he was lying insensate after nearly perishing.

"Of course I have not thought of it," she said. "Why would I entertain such a horrid thought?"

"Because it is the way of our world." Mama's countenance was even grimmer than it had been before. "Your brother has no heirs. If one of your father's country cousins would inherit the viscountcy, our circumstances would be significantly reduced. Is that what you wish? Are you truly that selfish?"

Hattie stared at her mother in consternated silence.

She had never thought marrying the Duke of Montrose could secure her future.

All she had ever thought was how marrying him could ruin it.

And her.

She did not like this reminder of the fragility of life or the precariousness of their places within it. Nor did she like the growing realization that Montrose may have been right after all.

\* \* \*

AFTER TWO DAYS OF WAITING, Monty had Hattie alone again.

Unfortunately for him, they were in his curricle, which meant they were parading before half the fashionable world. Which also meant he could not kiss her senseless. Or unbutton her bodice. Or suck her nipples until she begged for more. Or even hold her damned hand.

No, he was courting her. In proper fashion. At the fashionable hour. Like a true swain. A lovesick suitor. A milksop who cared about rules and getting out of bed before noon.

He almost shuddered at what he had been reduced to, all in the name of winning this woman's hand. At some point, his attempted conquest had become a great deal less about the amelioration of his guilt over Torrie and a great deal more about his desire to get Hattie Lethbridge into his bed.

He had even stopped drinking gin until the evening, instead having a morning drop or two of laudanum to carry him through to night. All because she had scented gin on his breath for one of his proposals. He had been particularly plagued by nightmares the night prior, and it had not been one of his finer moments.

Sometimes, he was weak. Mindlessness proved an excellent distraction in such times. He could inure himself to the demons nipping Cerberus-like at his heels best by getting tap-hackled. But Hattie, too, and his attraction to her, which only grew stronger by the moment, served much the same purpose.

And he had intended this ride as a means of furthering his cause, not suffering through her silence.

"It is a lovely day, is it not?" he asked, casting a sidelong glance in her direction.

Her dark hair was largely obscured by her bonnet today, but even as she sat stiffer than an ancestral bust at his side, she held undeniable allure. Was it his imagination, or had he just caught the scent of violets on the wind?

"The sun is not shining," Hattie returned, her voice bearing the same edge of disapproval it always possessed.

Unless he was kissing the breath out of her, that was.

"But neither is the sky raining," he could not help but to point out.

London had suffered a spate of dreary weather of late that—even for London—proved dreadfully morose. He had despaired over finding an hour during which the mists and rains would cease to fall. At last, fickle fortune's wheel had given him a good turn.

"Hmm." She made a noncommittal sound, then said nothing else.

Clearly, Hattie had no inclination to make this easier upon him. Had he expected anything less?

He kept his attention firmly upon the road ahead of them as they proceeded to Rotten Row, where they might be seen.

"Did you enjoy the gifts I sent you?" he could not resist asking.

It was his pride, he supposed. He had never before made such an effort to woo a lady. With Hattie, it was different.

*She* was different.

"The flowers were quite pretty, Montrose. Thank you." Her voice was soft. Tempered with an unknown emotion. She was less disapproving now, yet still guarded.

"It was my pleasure to send them." He sent her another glance. "What of the books?"

"The books were from you?" she asked innocently. "There was no note accompanying them. I confess, I had assumed they had come from Lord Rearden."

The devil she had. His fingers tightened on the reins. "They were from me, and you know it." Misgiving swamped him, along with a possessive surge. "He is not still courting you, is he?"

"Of course he is." Her tone was bright. Blithe.

He had warned the blighter to leave off. Perhaps Monty would need to pay him another call.

"The books were from me," he gritted, nettled although he suspected she was intentionally misleading him. "I know how much you love to read."

"You do?" she asked, a note of surprise entering her tone now.

"Of course." He flicked her another look. "Your nose is forever betwixt the pages of something, Hattie."

It was true. Though he had not often heeded her, he had seen her enough over the years of his friendship with Torrie to know she was a voracious reader. He did not recall ever having seen her without a book nearby, unless she was at a social event. Even in her chamber, there had been a neat stack of volumes on the table alongside her bed.

"I did not realize you had noticed me," she said quietly.

Almost so quietly he did not hear.

But he had heard, and he did not miss the implications of what she had said. He needed to reassure her, he knew, that his motives were pure. Hattie was a proud woman, and she would not marry anyone—not even him—for the sake of settling a conscience.

He had to convey to her that his proposal was about more than that for him now. Indeed, mayhap it had always been.

"I noticed you, Hattie." He glanced back at her. "How could a man *fail* to notice you?"

Her cheeks flushed, and she turned toward him, her gaze burning into his. "Many have failed. Legions, in fact. I shall not be duped by your flattery, Montrose. If you expect me to believe I am suddenly the most glorious woman you have ever beheld, or that you are this eager to marry me for any reason other than the guilt eating you alive, you shall have to do more than offer hollow encomiums."

*By the good Lord's chemise*, how could he convince her every word he uttered was true?

He clenched his jaw, returning his stare straight ahead. "You are a beautiful woman in your own right. Believe me when I tell you, no amount of guilt could coerce me into the parson's mousetrap. I seek to be caught willingly."

"Was that meant to reassure me, Montrose?" Her tone was tart. "If so, you failed quite miserably."

The saucy wench.

He was making a muck of this, as usual. But curse it, did she not realize he had never courted a proper lady before? Had never considered the prospect of taking a lady to wife until his accident?

As he had lain there in the mangled wreckage of his phaeton in the wake of the crash, his ankle hurting like the devil, he had realized something, he had no heir. If something more serious than a broken bone had befallen him, and if he had died, his mother and sister would have been left with precious little aside from his mother's dower and some property in Scotland.

Lying in bed, delirious with agony, laudanum, and whatever liquor he could find, he had settled upon a solution—marriage. And then, when he had considered the idea further, he had settled upon an even better one, marriage to Hattie. Thus, he would secure the future of his line and his family, repay the debt he owed Torrie for his recklessness, and also gain a beautiful, intelligent woman as his wife.

Of course, his sister Cat had since married the Earl of Rayne, making the necessity to consider the future on her behalf less of a concern. But all the rest of his motivations remained true, though they had been eclipsed by his carnal need to make Hattie his.

"I want to marry you, Hattie," he said, his voice low. They would soon be near the fashionable crush of carriages, and he did not want to be overheard. "Because I want you in my bed. Is that so difficult to believe? Did you not feel how much I wanted you in your bedchamber the other night?"

"Montrose," she hissed. "Do not dare speak of it."

Ah, perhaps here, at last, was the means of persuading her. Certainly, it was a way to give voice to all the pent-up desire coiled within him, like a snake ready to strike.

"Do not speak of what?" he pressed. "The way you kissed me back as if you enjoyed every moment of the passion sizzling between us? Shall I not speak of the way you responded to my lips upon your breasts? Tell me, Hattie, how did you explain your rent night rail?"

She said nothing for a lengthy pause, and he wondered if he had finally shocked her into silence.

"I burned it in the fire grate."

Again, she spoke so softly, he had to strain to hear her over the din of the horse's tack and the familiar clop of hoof beats. "Excellent thinking, my dear. I ought to have done so myself, to spare you the trouble."

He had been reckless with her, he realized now. Reckless with her reputation.

A strange realization settled over him then, as they passed down Rotten Row along with the half of society. Hattie was important. Precious, even. The instinct to protect her rose within him, strong and undeniable. Along with shame that he had allowed himself to proceed as far with her as he had.

If he had been caught in her chamber, or if anyone had called into question the evidence he had left behind, he shuddered to think what the results would have been. Or, worse, if he had fallen from that blasted tree, she would have been blighted forever. He would have caused an irreparable stain upon her reputation.

And as he had an irreparable stain upon his soul, he had no wish to inflict a similar torture upon anyone else. Especially not Hattie.

"The fault was mine every bit as much as yours," she startled him by saying then. "I...welcomed your liberties, much to my shame."

"Why shame?" he countered smoothly, maneuvering them through the crush with ease. "Are you embarrassed of me?"

He held himself stiffly as he awaited her answer. Here was yet another shock; he cared. Her opinion mattered to him. No one's opinion—not even his mother's or his sister's—had mattered to him in as long as he could recall. He knew he drank far too much, that he had become reliant upon opium to carry him through the day. He knew he was damaged and bitter and jaded. He knew he would never be whole.

But somehow, some foolish part of him hoped Hattie did not see him in the same light. Oh, he knew she disapproved of him and his ways. That much was undeniable. But he could not help but feel she found some redeemable qualities in him.

"I am embarrassed of the way in which I so easily abandoned my morals," she said. "You are a practiced and highly skilled seducer. But even so, I should have been able to resist you."

And yet, she had not.

This, more than anything else, made his heart surge. Buoyed his spirits. Filled him with optimism, that most foolish bedfellow of all.

"There is far more to you, hiding beneath your prim exterior," he observed. And *God's fichu*, but he could not wait to discover it, if she but allowed him to. If she made her sultry lips say *yes* instead of *no*.

"There is nothing hiding beneath my exterior," she countered. "A lack of common sense. A lapse in resistance. That is all. But with a man of your reputation, my weakness was only to have been expected."

*A man of your reputation.*

What the devil was happening to him? Not long ago, he had taken great pride in his reputation as a dastardly rakehell, as the fastest of all London's libertines. And now, Hattie's mere allusion to his reputation nettled. Worse than nettled. It pricked him straight to his marrow.

He was not about to allow her to dismiss what had passed between them as his rakish prowess. There had been something else, something far deeper. Undeniable. The hunger they shared, the attraction, it was hotter than flame. He had never before wanted a woman in the way he wanted her. And that plain truth had nothing to do with his guilt over Torrie or his desire to secure the line or any other blasted sense of duty. It was purely Hattie.

Hattie and the way their bodies seemed to be in concert with each other.

He sent her a long, searching look. "You felt it, too."

Her flush returned, deeper this time than before, just as telling, and she jerked her gaze from his to stare into the opposite direction. "No."

She was persistent, his Hattie. But he was more persistent. His determination burned hotter than a thousand suns. He wanted her. In his mind, she was already his.

His desperate longing goaded him on. "Look me in the eyes and tell me you felt nothing when I touched you, Hattie, when I kissed you, when I sucked your sweet nipples."

She gasped. "How dare you?"

"How dare I speak of your nipples?" he asked, taunting her now. "Or how dare I suck your nipples? How dare I notice the way you enjoyed it when I sucked them? I confess, darling, I am a bit confused what has distressed you."

"Do hush! *You* have distressed me," she said. "You with

your wrongheaded insistence you wish to marry me. You sneaking into my chamber. Your kisses, your touch, your wicked words. Those books. How did you know I enjoy reading Mr. Wordsworth's verse?"

"I did not know for certain," he admitted, "but you had another of his volumes alongside your bed. I took note during the call I paid you."

Hattie was distraught. Her voice shook. Her hands trembled in her lap, her gloved fingers twisting together. *Damn it*, upsetting her had never been his intention. He was meant to be wooing her with this curricle ride. He was meant to be reminding her of all the pleasure he could give her, all the reasons why she should agree to marry him in spite of all the common sense she possessed, which undoubtedly urged her to tell him *no* and to run like hell in the opposite direction.

"I had not realized you were so observant, Montrose," she said.

That was all she could manage after the trouble he had taken to obtain reading material he thought would suit her? A whole bloody crate worth, at that.

"I can observe as well as the next man." He was being curt with her now, and he knew it. But it was his sole defense.

A tense silence hung between them, permeated only by the steady plod of his horses. They reached the end of Rotten Row, and he turned them back in the direction of Hattie's home.

"Forgive me," she said suddenly, sounding torn.

He flicked her a surprised glance. She was looking at him, her lovely features framed by her bonnet. Her face was a study in pink and cream, innocent beauty, everything he coveted.

"I beg your pardon?" His voice sounded rusty, even to his own ears. Husky with suppressed emotion.

No one had ever apologized to him before. At least, not

anyone who was not a servant already in his employ, required to adhere to a strict code of politeness. No one had ever cared enough, though there was any number of apologies he was owed, Christ knew.

"I hurt you," she said, her gaze searching his. "That was not my intention, Montrose. As Torrie's friend, you are almost another brother to me."

He made an inarticulate sound of objection. Her revelation she cared about him had been overshadowed by her suggestion she considered him another brother. He could easily prove otherwise. But the suggestion still irked.

"You cannot hurt me, Miss Lethbridge," he assured her, keeping his tone remarkably cool. Thoughts of the past inevitably filled him with misplaced rage. With a feeling of helplessness. With dread and shame. He had no wish to inhabit any of those emotions now, seated so very near to the woman he wanted to make his duchess.

He wanted Hattie to be his benediction.

His salvation.

The means by which he finally buried the past.

"The books pleased me, Montrose."

Her words dragged him from the mire of his thoughts. He kept his stare trained on the road ahead, however. Because he was afraid of what he would do if he looked upon her countenance and read the need he swore he heard in her voice now. Holding himself back would prove impossible, he had no doubt.

And he could not very well ravish her in his curricle, in the out of doors. Before half of the peerage.

"They are all of interest to you?" he asked carefully, realizing her response mattered.

Realizing *she* mattered.

Far more than he could have ever supposed.

"They are," she affirmed.

"Excellent." He nodded as if they were discussing something of no greater import than the skies overhead. "I am glad I was not mistaken in my choices."

A companionable silence fell between them as they neared Torrington House once more. Monty's spirits were lifted yet again. He could not help but to feel, in spite of their clashing of wills and wits on this drive, they had reached a tentative understanding, of sorts.

It was only as they neared the front façade of her home when Hattie broke the silence. "Montrose?"

"Yes?"

"I still cannot marry you," she said, stubborn to the last.

"You *can*," he returned smoothly, equally stubborn, and more certain of her now than ever before. More certain of the both of them. "And you *will*."

## CHAPTER 6

Hattie was returning to the Whitley ball after a trip to the lady's withdrawing room when there was suddenly an obstacle in her path.

A tall, handsome, sinful, all-too-familiar obstacle.

"Montrose," she hissed at him, casting a frantic glance about the hall to ascertain they were alone.

Thankfully, they were. But for how long? That was the imperative question.

"Just the lady I was looking for." He grinned his scoundrel's grin at her, the one that inevitably made heat wash over her.

The one that made her weak for him.

Oh, so weak.

But she must be strong. She gathered her fortitude. All her disapproval. "You cannot accost me outside the lady's withdrawing room at one of the biggest balls in London."

He quirked a brow. "First, I am not accosting you. I just happened to cross paths with you. Secondly, if you do not want to risk being seen speaking to the scandalous Duke of Montrose, you can accompany me."

DUKE OF DEBAUCHERY

And then, he held out his hand.

His big, beautiful hand. For yes, even his hand was somehow attractive—masculine, long-fingered, seductive. She stared at it and recalled how deliciously he had brought her body to life when he had touched her.

She swallowed. *Stay strong, Hattie. Do not fall prey to the pretty duke with the bedchamber eyes.*

"Anything you have to say to me, you can tell me now, here," she told him, attempting her sternest voice.

But her sternest voice was terribly unimpressive, because ever since he had kissed her, he had been robbing her resistance one gesture, one look, one word at a time. In truth, the ballroom was a hot crush. She had no wish to resume her position on the periphery or to pretend enjoyment whilst she danced a country reel with the odd gentleman.

All she wanted stood before her.

More fool, she.

"Come with me," he said, his hand still outstretched toward her.

*Do not take his hand*, warned her inner sense of practicality.

For surely, going anywhere with this man at a ball would be tantamount to the end of her reputation. She would be ruined. Hopelessly compromised and forced to marry him after all if they were caught. She should step around him. Bid him good evening. Forget they had crossed paths. Forget all about the maddeningly handsome, devilishly tempting Duke of Montrose.

She took his hand. And she went with him willingly, allowing him to pull her into a nearby chamber. The door clicked closed behind them, and by the illumination of a lamp on a desk at the opposite end of the room, she could see they were in a salon of sorts. Perhaps even a study. But too much of the chamber remained in shadows for her to tell.

She forgot to care when he turned toward her, his strong masculine arms banding around her waist, hauling her into an equally hard, muscled chest. His embrace felt right and wrong all at once. She was eager and yet desperately uncertain. Longing and terrified. She did not dare trust him, though being in his arms felt like returning home.

"What are you about, Montrose?" she forced herself to demand. "This is—"

The rest of what she had been about to say was swallowed by his mouth. He fitted his lips to hers in a sudden, voracious kiss. It began with raw carnal intent, open-mouthed. Starving.

She forgot all about speaking.

Forgot this was wrong and dangerous to her reputation and against every admonition she had peppered herself with on the way to the ball, knowing he would also be in attendance.

Forgot everything but the Duke of Montrose's mouth upon hers, coaxing her to open. She slid her arms around his neck, pressing herself against his tall, lean body as if she were no better than a common strumpet. His warmth and strength burned into her, along with his delicious scent of musky man and clean, sharp soap.

She opened for him. His tongue slipped past the seam of her lips, tangling with hers. The kiss became erotic. Shockingly wicked. It was wet, ravaging, demanding. He tasted of wine and the sweet, sensual intoxication of possibility.

Hattie had lived her entire life according to the rules. She had never once engaged in an impropriety with a gentleman until Montrose had descended, hell-bent upon marrying her. She had scarcely even been kissed until that night in her chamber, when he had climbed the tree just to reach her.

She kissed him back now with all the furious longing she had tried so hard to bury and ignore. Her emotions—all her wants and needs—were suddenly unleashed. All she could think about was kissing him. Getting closer to him.

It did not matter that they were in danger of being caught at any moment. If anything, that only served to heighten Hattie's excitement and awareness. *Dear Lord*, what had gotten into her? This was all the fault of the Duke of Montrose.

And she would be properly angry with him. Later. When he was not kissing her so sweetly, as if she were precious to him, his lips feathering over hers in a series of gentler kisses, giving more than they took. His kiss was velvet and silk, strength and heat and power, the forbidden and the delicious.

Just as he was.

Part of her longed for him so desperately, it seemed she could feel the ache in the marrow of her bones. And another part of her knew that wanting and loving him was utterly foolish, supremely useless. He was a law unto his own. No woman had ever tamed him or claimed his heart.

None would.

She knew all that, just as she knew at any second, their interlude could be interrupted. Her reputation could be blackened forever. Yet still, she kissed him. Still, she stayed in his arms where she could not help but to feel she belonged, clinging to him, wanting him. Being his fool once more.

Nothing mattered but Montrose's kiss.

His lips left hers, but he stayed close, his breath falling hot upon her mouth in a lingering caress. "I missed you."

His low pronouncement should not send a frisson of desire down her spine. Nor should it tighten the knot of yearning in her belly.

And yet, it did both.

What a fool she was, clutching him to her rather than

pushing him away, longing for one more kiss. "More of your rakish charm."

"Truth." He kissed the corner of her lips, then her cheek, before burying his face in her hair and inhaling. "Tell me I am not alone. Tell me you missed me, too."

She had not even seen him in the crush. He must have arrived late, as he so often did. Her heart beat faster. "Montrose, we cannot be alone like this. If anyone should happen upon us, I will be ruined."

He kissed the opposite corner of her mouth, then her jaw. "If you are ruined, you will have to *marry* me."

He sounded pleased by the notion.

She struggled to summon up some restraint. But then he kissed her ear, and all efforts at resisting him faded like the stars in the night sky when the sun rose. "I have not changed my mind."

"Your kisses say otherwise, darling," he murmured.

When he caught the fleshy lobe of her ear in his teeth and gently nipped, liquid heat pooled in her core. "You are an experienced rake. Of course your kisses are pleasant. Anyone would find them so."

"Ah, but I do not want to kiss anyone, Hattie." He licked the hollow behind her ear. "Only you."

*Only you.*

She told herself these were more practiced words of seduction from a man who had made a career of collecting bedmates. She told herself he did not mean them.

But the hot glide of his tongue was turning her knees to jelly.

"Montrose." Her voice was weak. She did not flee his arms. Instead, her fingers had somehow found their way into his hair.

How luxurious it was, sleek and smooth and thick. Touching his hair was not helping her predicament one whit.

DUKE OF DEBAUCHERY

She would stop.

In a few seconds.

Or mayhap a minute.

"Mmm?" He made a noncommittal sound as he pressed a string of kisses to her throat.

She fought to keep her wits about her, to remember how very wrong this was. "You must cease this at once."

There was precious little determination in her voice.

Because all she wanted was more.

"I dislike balls," he said against her skin, kissing the tops of her breasts exposed by her gown's décolletage.

So incendiary was the touch of his lips upon her there that it took her a moment to even realize what he had just said. And further, that the words made precious little sense. What had Montrose's dislike of balls to do with kissing her? Or sweeping her into a deserted room and dismantling all her defenses?

"Pardon?" she managed as he worked his way back up to her neck.

"I do not like courting." Another kiss, this time on the mad flutter of her pulse. "I do not like propriety." Another. "Or rules." Another. "Driving on Rotten Row makes my teeth ache." His lips had traveled all the way back to her ear. "Not being able to touch you makes my cock ache."

The wicked word made her gasp. He was ravishing her in the midst of a ball. Speaking in a fashion a true gentleman would never speak to a lady.

She should not like it.

His iniquity should not make want unfurl within her.

"You should not say such things, Montrose," she forced out, but as she admonished him, she arched her neck, giving him better access. "It is sinful."

"You should not make me suffer," he countered, kissing the whorl of her ear. "Refusing to wed me is the true sin."

She shivered, and still, she made no move to escape him. "You do not want to marry me. Not truly."

"Believe in yourself, Hattie," he whispered, drawing her closer to him, so their bodies were aligned from breast to thigh.

How perfectly they fit together.

"I believe in my common sense," she countered breathlessly. "My wits. My pragmatism."

He raised his head, at last granting her a reprieve. Except, when the all-too-handsome Duke of Montrose was gazing down at her, his eyes glittering with want, it was not a reprieve at all. Because seeing the way he was seemingly affected by their embrace made her yearn for more.

For everything.

Made her want to give in. To tell him *yes*.

She must not do so. This was a passing fancy. Montrose was easily distracted, forever in search of diversion.

"I need you, Hattie." He trailed the backs of his fingers over her cheek in a tantalizing caress that was so tender, her heart could not help but to be affected. "Do you not see? For you, I have attempted to become respectable. I only imbibe spirits at my club in the evenings. I am trying to win you every way I know how."

His impassioned speech was so very Montrose. She had to admit, she had believed he would tire of this game long ago.

But he had not. He was still standing here with her, after pursuing her for so long. She stared at him, searching his expression, his eyes. She would have asked him if he was in his cups, but he tasted of wine, and he did not seem bosky.

He seemed intense. Determined.

He was still the same wild Montrose who did as he pleased. But he was also different. He was the same Montrose she could not help but to love. She told herself her unwanted feelings for him were the reason for her untenable susceptibility where he was concerned.

"Why?" she asked, needing to know the answer.

If there was something more than his guilt…

*Nay.* She did not dare entertain such a foolish notion. He did not fall in love. He seduced. He courted excess. He was a sybarite. He was notorious.

*You love him* said that horrid voice within. *He could be yours. Tell him you will marry him. Say yes.*

But if she was expecting an impassioned declaration of love, she was to be sorely disappointed.

"I need an heir," he said. "You need a husband. Whenever I kiss you, you turn into flame. What other reason need either of us have?"

Only the most important one.

And the absence of it was just the reminder she needed.

Hattie extricated herself from his embrace. She had to leave this room, leave his intoxicating presence, before he ruined her. This was not the privacy of her bedchamber at Torrington House. There were hundreds of other guests, all the toast of polite society, making merry just down the hall.

He was still the man who had the power to break her heart. She must not forget.

Hattie rubbed her hands over her arms, as if she could remove the imprint of him from her palms. "Those reasons are not enough for me, I am afraid. I do thank you for the honor, Montrose. But it would be best if we keep our distance from now on."

"Hattie," he protested, striding toward her.

She moved faster, blindly, in a panic. If he touched her again, she would be at his sensual mercy once more. And she could not afford to take such a risk.

"Please, leave me alone, Montrose," she managed before

yanking open the door and stepping into the hall, closing it soundly at her back.

The hall was mercifully empty.

She did not dare wait to see whether or not he would emerge, further endangering her reputation. Instead, she moved as swiftly as she could in the direction of the ballroom. There was no way he could waylay her in the midst of all the guests.

\* \* \*

Monty stared at the door Hattie had just fled through, bemused, prick hard as iron.

*Beelzebub's earbobs*, where had he gone wrong? The echo of her impassioned demand still seemed to reverberate in the empty chamber, mocking him.

*Please, leave me alone, Montrose.*

*It would be best if we keep our distance from now on.*

Like bloody hell he would leave her alone and keep his distance. Who did she think she was fooling? He would wager everything he had that if he had raised her skirts and found her cunny, she would have been dripping for him. The passion between them was as hot and undeniable as the sun in the summer sky.

Where, then, had he gone wrong?

He had been doing his damnedest to earn a yes from the lady's lips. And all she did was kiss him as if her life depended upon it and then tell him to go to the devil.

Which was decidedly where a rotten scoundrel like him belonged, but that was another matter entirely. Of course, he did not deserve Hattie Lethbridge as his wife. That went without saying. He was damaged. She was innocent. He had made a muck of most of his life. He had almost killed his friend with his recklessness. He had spent more years of his life sotted than aware of what was going on.

He had devoted himself to pleasure and distraction, an endless procession of quim, an eternal fountain of drink. Then, there was the laudanum, which even now slithered through his veins with the delicious torpor of a serpent. The laudanum negus he had consumed prior to his late arrival at the Whitley ball this evening was belatedly having its effect upon him.

But he remained determined to have her.

She would be his.

He waited for as long as his patience would allow, giving Hattie time to go back to the ball. Finally, when he could stand no more of the silent recriminations haunting him in the shadows of the study, he quit the room.

And nearly ran into Searle.

His cousin raised a brow, casting a pointed glance to the closed study door behind him, as if he knew what had happened within not long ago. "Up to the devil's mischief again, Monty?"

*God's fichu*, what had he seen?

"I was looking for blue ruin," he lied.

"You will not find it in Whitley's study. He is a whisky man. Always has been." Searle paused, giving him an assessing look. "That is not truly the reason you were hiding yourself within the study, is it?"

His cousin was ever too perceptive for his own bloody good. But Monty had no wish to tell the truth. He felt strangely protective of Hattie. As if she were already his.

*Because she is mine.*

He banished the voice within, which was wrong. Hattie had yet to give him the only word he wanted to hear from her pretty, pink lips.

"You sound like a protective mama, clucking over her

debutante," he mocked instead, keeping his tone light. "Why so suspicious of me, cousin? You ought to know me better than to think I was wetting my prick in Whitley's study whilst a ball raged on. By the good Lord's chemise, I am almost a betrothed man."

"You and your nonsensical curses." Searle shot him a rueful grin, not even flinching at Monty's crudity, which had been meant to distract. "How is the ankle?"

"It pains me."

That was not a lie. It was also an excellent reason to continue adding drops of laudanum to all his beverages. Or at least, that was what he told himself.

"How goes the plan to make Miss Lethbridge your bride?" Searle asked next.

Another sore subject, as it were. "Has my betrothal been announced yet, Searle?"

His cousin's lips twitched, as if he struggled to suppress his mirth. "No."

"Then that is how the plan bloody well goes," he growled. "Do you intend to stand here in the hall, Searle? I cannot imagine your marchioness will be happy at being abandoned for so long. Moreover, she will undoubtedly be beset by partners."

Searle's jaw clenched. "None of these fops are worthy of dancing with my wife."

And neither were any of them worthy of dancing with Hattie.

Alas, he could not claim her for every set as he longed to do. Such a strange reaction, that, from a man who did not even like to dance. He would fret over the implications later.

"Let us return to the festivities, shall we?" He started in the direction of the ballroom, where the strains of the orchestra emerged.

"Quite right," Searle agreed, walking with him. "I cannot allow the pups to slaver over Lady Searle."

"No, you cannot," he agreed. And neither could he bear the thought of anyone leading his Hattie about the ballroom. He would glare daggers at them until they fled if need be. "Searle, have you any sound advice for persuading a lady to accept a proposal of marriage?"

"Oh, ho." His cousin laughed because he was enjoying this, the blighter. "I never thought to see the day. The Duke of Montrose, greatest scoundrel in London, has been laid low by love."

"It is not love," he was quick to deny. "You know I do not believe in such a foolish emotion. For myself, it is not possible. It is merely a need. I require an heir. I also seek to make amends with her brother. The lady in question is in need of a match."

"All excellent motives," Searle agreed as they entered the ballroom. "But I do think you may be surprised to realize everyone is capable of love, regardless of how great an implausibility such a tender emotion seems. When I was in the depths of my despair, revenge the only thing spurring me to live another day, I never could have imagined what I would find with my Leonie."

The lovesick expression on his cousin's face set Monty's teeth on edge. He well remembered the dark days when his cousin had been lost at war and had been presumed dead. "Thank Christ you are here now. Maudlin sentiments and maggot-laden brain aside."

"Love is not a maggot, Monty."

Monty's gaze was already searching the assemblage, seeking Hattie. Where the devil had she fled to? Perhaps she hid behind the potted palms once more, and he would need to rescue her. If any of the witless chits present were gossiping about her, he would deliver them the most crushing setdown he could fathom.

"Romantic love is absolutely a maggot," he countered, glancing back at his cousin once more. "It will inevitably spoil whatever it has infected."

"With such romantic sentiments, one must wonder at your difficulty in ensnaring Miss Lethbridge," Searle said cuttingly. "I would have expected her to be swooning at your feet by now. Whatever is the matter with her?"

"To the devil with you," he said without heat. "You do not think me fool enough to call love a maggot to her directly, do you? Despite my opinion of such an impossible emotion, I will not lie to her. I am who I am, and she knows it. Indeed, I expect that is the reason for her reluctance."

"Her reluctance or her refusal?"

Searle was knowing. *Damn him.*

"Both," he bit out.

Where the hell was she? Still no sign of her. Not even a hint of her dark hair and ivory gown. To be fair, there were a host of ladies in ivory gowns, whirling with partners, chattering on the periphery of the glittering spectacle, rendering it difficult to discern one from the next, at least initially. But his gaze made short work of them. None was Hattie. None could hold a candle to her beauty.

Each time he saw *her*, each time he held her, her allure only increased.

She was the opposite of every woman he had ever known. Past conquests had lost their luster when they had melted in his arms. The moment he had kissed a lady and known her willing, his interest had begun to wane, so that by the time he and his bedmate had finished, he was ready to leave, never to think of her again.

But Hattie haunted him. He kissed her and hungered for more. He touched her, and she seemed to brand him. He inhaled her scent, and the ghost of those sweet, exotic notes mocked him. He spent every night grasping his cock until he spilled to thoughts of her.

Her alone.

Even as he inwardly railed against such a dependence. He was the Duke of Montrose, *for God's sake*. He attached himself to no one. Better to spend his life flitting from one lascivious entertainment to the next than ever tell anyone the truth about his past. The sins he indulged in were designed to drown the sins that had been visited upon him.

Only Torrie knew about those, and his knowledge had been obliterated by the phaeton crash. Monty had told no one else. Not even Searle.

"Monty?" his cousin's voice sliced through his tumultuous thoughts. "I see Lady Searle just over there. Perhaps she has an inkling of where Miss Lethbridge has gone. They have become friends, after all."

Hattie was friends with Lady Searle? Monty frowned. "They have?"

"Of course." Searle flicked at the impeccable sleeve of his coat. "She, Lady Catriona—er, Lady Rayne now, I suppose—the Duchess of Whitley, and Lady Frederica, have all been getting on quite well. Leonie was the one who drew them all together. Of course, now that Lady Rayne is *enceinte* and rusticating at Marchmont—"

"Does everyone know I am to be an uncle but me?" he interrupted, irritated that even Searle was aware of Catriona's delicate condition when he himself had been in the dark.

"There is to be a new addition to the family," Searle said good-naturedly. "Of course, I was informed by Aunt Letitia first, and then Leonie received the happy letter from Cat herself."

Again with the bloody letters.

He must have muttered something aloud.

Because Searle's brows instantly hiked upward. "You have not been reading your correspondence, have you, Monty?"

His ears burned. He would get to the damned epistles. He would. But now that he could only drink gin in the evening, he often ended the night with a drop of laudanum as well, which put him into an excellent state for slumber. He could sleep, for the first time in years, without the nightmares coming to claim him.

"I have yet to find a suitable secretary to replace the last fellow." Who had left Monty's employ of his own volition after Monty had punched him in the eye. In Monty's defense, it had been a horrid accident brought on by a combination of drink and one of his insufferable nightmares.

"I do not suppose you would have read your correspondence yourself in the absence of a secretary," Searle said, his voice wry.

"Of course I would," he snapped. "I have merely been busy in the wake of my accident."

"Busy drowning yourself in swill." His cousin's countenance was all hard angles of disapproval.

"Busy attempting to gain Miss Lethbridge's hand," he corrected coolly. "And heal my ankle so that I can walk once more without pain."

Even if his cousin was correct, that did not mean Monty wanted to hear his judgment. He had enough of that from his cursed mother, thank you.

"Ah, yes. Of course." Searle's voice made it plain he did not believe him. "How could I forget?"

"You are growing tiresome," he muttered, tugging at his too-tight cravat as he searched once more for Hattie.

In vain, *damn it all.*

"Come. Lady Searle has caught sight of us," Searle said, ignoring his ill-tempered grumbles.

Monty allowed himself to be shepherded toward the icy-blonde beauty his cousin had married. Once known as Limping Leonora for a childhood incident that had left her with an unsteady gait, she was no longer mocked or scorned. A bold, undeniable beauty, she held her head high instead of attempting to hide in the shadows. Monty admired her, and he was impressed by her genuine devotion to Searle.

For the moment, however, all he wanted was to know whether or not she had seen Hattie.

He and Searle reached her side at last, deeper in the crush where the glow of the chandeliers was even hotter. Formalities were observed—just barely—before Monty led the way of the conversation.

"Have you seen Miss Lethbridge, my lady?" he asked, doing his best to snuff the need burning through him and keep it from his voice. It would not do to seem desperate, after all. "Searle tells me you and she are fast friends."

"Oh, yes," Lady Searle said, smiling. "Miss Lethbridge is wonderful. We share a love of reading, and she has been a dear with Lady Georgina. I do think she would make an excellent mother one day."

Lady Georgina was a wee bairn. Monty had been there with Searle on the day of her birth. He had seen her on a handful of occasions when visiting his cousin, and he had to admit, he was ever suspicious of squalling children. He recalled a cherubic face, two tiny hands, and the need to flee after Lady Georgina had begun to cry with displeasure over a delay in her next meal.

But there was something about the thought of Hattie as a mother—it took his breath. He could see her, a Madonna, his child growing within her. And all through him crashed a wave of possession so sudden and so fierce, he had to grit his teeth just to maintain control of himself.

He cleared his throat, mindful of the fact that Lady Searle

had failed to answer his question. "Indeed, I have no doubt she would be an unparalleled mother one day. But have you seen her this evening?"

"She has gone home early with her mother, I am afraid," Lady Searle said, giving him a sympathetic smile, as if she could read the wretchedness roiling within him. "Something about a megrim, I believe."

*A megrim.*

*Beelzebub's stays*, he was willing to wager he was the megrim in question. Or at least the reason for it. The realization quite nettled.

"I see," he managed, attempting to look unconcerned.

"Monty has been desperate to convince poor Miss Lethbridge to marry his sorry hide," Searle said then.

Monty skewered him with a glare. "Desperation is not my style."

Except, when it came to Hattie, it was.

"You could not find a finer lady to be your duchess," said Lady Searle, looking like the cat who had gotten into the proverbial cream. "Have you offered for her, then?"

Monty's lips flattened. This was not the manner in which he had intended to spend the evening, damn it. Hattie had fled. Here he stood at a ball, that infernal societal torture device he loathed, making conversation about wanting to marry a lady who refused to accept his suit.

What had his life come to?

And yet, some part of him—the part without pride, it was certain—wondered if perhaps Lady Searle could offer him some aid.

"I have," he found himself admitting, much to his shame. "And she has not been…receptive."

"Fancy that," Searle jibed. "The most successful rakehell in London, the man who can get dozens of ladies to fall into his bed with the crook of an eyebrow, cannot convince a lady to wed him."

"Stubble it," he growled at his cousin. For he was not wrong, blast him.

"You must pay my husband no heed," Lady Searle said, sending a lovesick smile in Searle's direction. "If he is finding joy in your inner torment, it is only because he loves you and wishes to see his cousin happy. One cannot forget his attempt at getting me to marry him consisted of ruining me and forcing my hand."

Searle's grin faded. "If I could do it all over, my love, you know I would change—"

"I know, my darling," she interrupted before turning her attention back to Monty. "What I mean to say is that if you were soliciting advice from Searle, you must recall the manner in which he won my hand."

"Are you suggesting I compromise Miss Lethbridge?" he asked.

"Of course not," Lady Searle hastened to say. "Ruining the lady you love—compromising her—is not the way to proceed, as it will only lead to unnecessary complications."

"Here now, no one said anything about love," he felt the need to point out. "I greatly admire the lady, and I respect her, but I do not love her."

Also, he desired her more than he wanted his next breath. More, even, than his next taste of opium.

"If you do not love her, then why do you want to marry her?" Lady Searle asked.

Confound her.

"For the ordinary reasons," he mumbled, tugging at his deuced tight cravat yet again. "Heirs, etcetera."

Because if he did not make her his, he would soon perish with wanting. Wisely, he kept that bit to himself.

"Hmm," Lady Searle offered, noncommittally.

"Hmm," he repeated. "What the devil does that mean?"

"Monty," Searle warned. "You are speaking to my wife."

Yes, and he ought to have afforded her greater honor. Spoken to her with more respect, it was true. Also, he never should have sworn. But he was the Duke of Debauchery for a reason, and he could only change so much of himself.

"Forgive me," he offered. "What the devil does that mean, *Lady Searle?*"

"Thick-headed coxcomb," Searle said without rancor.

"Damned right I am," Monty returned, but he was quite sure he and Searle were speaking of different heads altogether.

"Monty!" The protestation came from Lady Searle rather than his cousin, however. Twin flags of color darkened her cheeks.

He gave her an innocent look. "Yes, my lady?"

He saw her waging an inner battle. She could hardly say that she had understood his double entendre. In the end, she simply sighed, shaking her head as if he were a hopeless cause. "Surely you realize that a lady wants to be married for more important reasons than the procuring of heirs."

"Those who believe in romantic folderol, yes," he agreed. "Those who are practical? I think not."

"Perhaps Miss Lethbridge is not as practical as you suppose," she said quietly.

Hattie? Impractical? Hattie *a romantic?*

He had never imagined she was.

The suggestion gave him pause. Did she want to be wooed? He had been attempting to court her properly. Was that not good enough? Was there a difference?

"What are you suggesting, Lady Searle?" he asked.

"I am suggesting that perhaps there is a reason why Miss Lethbridge has not accepted your proposal of marriage," she said sagely. "No lady wants to be told she is being married so she can be a broodmare, you understand."

Of course not. Nor had he suggested such a thing to Hattie. But neither had he declared his undying love for her. Nevertheless, he grew weary of the crushed ballroom, the lights, the whirl of dancers, the eyes upon him.

All he wanted was to marry Hattie. But accomplishing such a feat seemed more out of his grasp by the day. She kissed him so sweetly. Her body responded to him. Their attraction was undeniable. And yet, still she resisted.

"Lady Searle, rest assured I did not make such a proposal to Miss Lethbridge."

"Of course you did not, my dear." She patted his arm in a maternal fashion. "But that does not mean Miss Lethbridge was not able to infer, all the same."

"Bloody hell," Searle interjected then. "I never thought to see the day my wife would be instructing you on the proper means of securing a wife, Monty. How the wicked have fallen."

He *was* wicked. And he had always been fallen. But he was also determined. Hattie was his chance to make a change. She could not remove the blemishes upon his soul. She could not erase the stains of his past. But he could not shake the belief that she was for him. That she belonged with him.

That she was his. And he was hers. Whatever that meant.

He met his cousin's gaze, unflinching. "She is the woman I want at my side. The one I want as my duchess. It is to be her or no one else."

As he said the words, he realized their truth. Marrying anyone other than Hattie was an abomination to him.

"You are truly in a bad way," Searle observed. "I have never seen you like this, other than when it came to drink."

It was true, he craved Hattie in the way he had chased his

next sip of oblivion. He was not sure if he should fear that knowledge or embrace it.

"I know what I want," he said. "And it is her as my wife."

"You are sure about your feelings for her, Monty?" Lady Searle asked then.

He was sure of the fire burning inside him. It was Hattie's. But he could not say that. Not aloud. Not to anyone.

"I am sure I want her as my duchess," he said simply instead. All he could offer. He did not dare humble himself any further. "Any advice you could offer me would be appreciated, my lady."

"There is one thing I know for certain about Miss Lethbridge, and it is that she loves her brother dearly." Lady Searle paused, seeming to consider her next words with care. "I understand Lord Torrington was involved in the accident which saw you injured as well, and that he is no longer quite...himself. However, in spite of that, have you gotten his approval of the match?"

He had not approached Torrie. Given his friend's loss of memory, their interactions in the wake of the accident had all proved deuced awkward. He still held out hope the old Torrie would return. In time.

"I have not," he said.

"Perhaps you might begin there," Lady Searle suggested. "If you have her brother's approval, I have a suspicion Miss Lethbridge will be far more amenable to your suit. Indeed, it is entirely possible she perceives you responsible for her brother's current plight. However, if Lord Torrington approves..."

*The good Lord's chemise*, why had he not though of such a tactic? It was brilliant, and it made perfect sense.

"If Torrie approves, Miss Lethbridge will not be so convinced she must tell me nay," he finished, grinning as a surge of hope shot through him. "Thank you, my lady. You are a godsend."

"Yes, she is," Searle agreed, giving his wife a lovesick look. "Truly."

Lady Searle smiled back at him. "I merely want to see all my friends as happy as I am."

Monty was not certain he was capable of making anyone happy. But he wisely refrained from saying so. Instead, he began plotting the means by which he would win Hattie Lethbridge's hand. At fucking last.

## CHAPTER 7

⁂

*H*attie stabbed viciously at her embroidery, and for the third time in the last quarter hour, she stuck her thumb with the needle.

On a pained hiss, she set her needlework aside and rose from her seat. She needed to distract herself from thoughts of Montrose. Had she truly almost allowed him to ruin her at a ball the evening before?

Her foolishness where he was concerned knew no bounds, it would seem. By the grim light of day, without the evening's dark seduction to lure her into disaster, she was forced to be honest with herself. Her ability to resist Montrose diminished with each moment she spent in his presence.

With each delicious kiss.

Every decadent touch.

But the folly of falling ever more beneath his spell was not lost upon her. Although he was the most attentive suitor she could have imagined, and although in his arms was where she longed to be, she knew he was still Montrose. He was a rakehell, wild and unbridled.

She had scarcely slept last night. His scent had seemed to linger on her even after she had fled him, and long into the night, she could still catch the clean, sharp scent of his soap. Her lips had still burned with the pleasure of his kiss. She had throbbed with unquenched desire. And her heart had been heavy with the knowledge that she yearned for him more and more.

She had spent years admiring him from afar. Guarding her heart had been easy before, when he had never noticed her. When he had not pressed his suit, when he had not touched her or kissed her or appeared in her chamber like the wicked rake she knew him to be.

Something was wrong with her.

Because regardless of his carelessness, his madcap behavior, despite the part he had played in Torrie's accident, and in spite of the fact that she knew him to be a heartless rogue, she could not stop thinking about him.

Oh, drat him. Drat his rotten, miserable hide. Why could he not have left her alone? Why did he need to be so persistent in his wrongheaded insistence they wed?

A flurry of movement on the threshold of the room caught her eye.

She spun about as awareness slammed into her.

Montrose stood there, tall and handsome.

Wicked.

Heat burst inside her. He was here. Prowling toward her with a confident air.

And she was alone. No lady's maid to protect her.

"Montrose." Belatedly, she dipped into a curtsey. "What are you doing here?"

She should have known her fleeing the ball last night would not have gone unanswered.

He stopped when he reached her and sketched an elegant bow. "I came to have an audience with Torrie."

His words settled over her, piercing her with shock. "Surely you did not tell him..."

He flashed her a grim smile. "Your opinion of me is not high, is it, Hattie?"

Her opinion of him was that she did not dare trust him.

"You do not exactly inspire a great deal of comfort in me," she said, particularly since she was unchaperoned with him.

*Again.*

This time was every bit as dangerous as last night at the ball and when he had come to her in her chamber. Anyone could happen upon them. All it would take was her mother, brother, or a servant to leave her with no choice but to marry him.

"I am wounded." His smile deepened, revealing fine lines around his dark eyes. He helped himself to one of her hands, taking it and raising it to his mouth for a kiss.

She watched, mesmerized, as his lips touched the top of her hand. She felt the contact all the way to her toes. What would it be like, she wondered, to feel that mouth everywhere?

She struck the unwelcome thought from her mind, for it would do her no good. Nor would it aid in strengthening her defenses against him. "I know you, Montrose."

"Ah, but you do not know me nearly well enough yet, darling." He turned her hand over, having yet to relinquish possession of it, and frowned. "What is this? You are bleeding."

So she was. Blood had pooled on her thumb and streaked down her palm. She had not even noticed because she had been so distracted by *him*.

"I was doing needlework," she said, trying to ignore the visceral reaction his touch had upon her.

*He is only holding your hand. He is only a man.*

Only the man she had watched and wanted for years.

*He is noticing you now.*

*Because he feels obligated*, she reminded herself.

"You were doing needlework?" He reached into his coat. His eyes burned into hers as he extracted a handkerchief and dabbed at the blood. "It hardly seems like you to be so careless as to do yourself injury."

He was right. Ordinarily, she took great care with her embroidery. She had a talent for it, and she found it soothing.

"I was distracted." She tried to tug her hand from his grasp, but he held fast.

The drop of blood upon the white square was a stark, poignant contrast. She had sullied it, made her mark upon his monogram in a desperate irony.

"What distracted you, sweet Hattie?" he asked in that silky rake's voice.

The one that said he knew precisely what had been distracting her.

Him, devil take his hide.

She said the first thing that came to her mind. "A horse."

"A horse." He took his time, inspecting her hand for further injuries, before raising her thumb to his lips. "I did not think you horse mad."

She was mad, all right.

"A horse's arse," she elaborated, trying to strike the frisson of desire rolling through her.

Any lingering sting she had felt there, however slight, had been banished. All she felt was heat. Heat that shot up her arm and settled between her thighs.

"You were thinking of me," he guessed. "My darling Hattie. I did not take you for a hopeless romantic."

"I was being facetious," she told him. "Give me your handkerchief, and I shall see it laundered or replaced."

He was considering her, and it was once more that speculative rake's regard. "Do you ever allow anyone past your defenses, Hattie Lethbridge?"

"Not you," she was quick to say. Not if she could help it, anyway. She did not dare allow him any further than he had already trespassed. "The handkerchief, Montrose. My blood is upon it, and I wish to rectify the matter."

"Surely you do not think me such a wastrel that I cannot afford a hundred more just like it tomorrow?" He tucked the scrap back into his coat. "No indeed, I rather relish the notion of carrying a piece of you close to my heart."

She snorted. "Spare me your rakish wiles, Your Grace."

Because she could not afford to fall prey to them. And her pounding heart and the need deep within warned her she was tottering on the edge.

"Do you think I have ever asked for another lady's hand, Hattie?" He was being serious now.

His stare made her falter. He was looking at her almost tenderly. As if he felt something more for her than the guilt that was compelling him to continue making his offers.

"Have you?" The question fled her before she could snatch it back.

His answer should not matter.

"Of course not." He raised her palm for another slow, deliberate kiss.

This one, she felt as a pang deep inside. In her core. In the place he would fill, if he were her husband...

If?

What was she thinking? This gorgeous rake, this scoundrel, would tear her heart to shreds if she let him.

She must never, ever let him.

"Do not try to make me believe your proposal is motivated by anything other than your guilt," she snapped, hating him for the way he made her feel.

He kissed another place on her palm. "Have you ever heard of palmistry, Hattie?"

Of course she had.

"Stuff and nonsense," she dismissed.

"Is it?" He was still holding her hand, head bowed. With his forefinger, he traced over the longest line bisecting her palm. "I am not so certain."

She tried to ignore his scent that washed over her, making her yearn. "Do not pretend you are an authority on it, Montrose. I was not born yesterday."

"You are yet a babe wet behind the ears," he said in a teasing tone. "This line here." He stroked again. "It says you will marry a man you already know. A friend of your brother's. He will give you everything you want, kiss you senseless as often as possible, and make you his duchess."

She forgot to breathe. He was stroking her hand softly. Nothing more. And she was on fire for him. Aflame from the inside. Longing clawed at her. Old longing, deep-seated longing. The kind she had alternately nurtured and quashed for years.

Ever since she had met him, though Montrose had not yet been a duke. He had been the Marquess of Ashby. His father, the duke, had still been alive. Montrose had come to visit their country estate for the hunt. How avidly she had watched him, riding alongside Torrie. He had cut a dashing figure even then.

"Montrose," she protested. "Please cease this."

"I cannot." His fingers tightened on her hand as his gaze met hers once more. "I asked Torrie for his permission today. To wed you, Hattie. He has given us his blessing. All I need is one word from your pretty lips."

Her brother had given his blessing.

Or rather, the shell her brother had become.

She could not forget. "Torrie does not have any recollection of you, thanks to your careless, drunken ways. He does not remember how much of a wicked, unrepentant rake you are."

Regret shadowed his handsome face. "You do not need to remind me. If I could return to that night and talk him out of the race, I would do so, and gladly. I wish it had been me rather than him, a thousand times over. But it was not, and I cannot change the decisions I made in the past, however poor or lamentable they are. All I can do is strive to do better now and in the future."

She wanted to strike him for his arrogance. "Damn you, Montrose. I have already told you I will not be your sacrificial lamb. Marrying me will not change anything either. You do not want a wife. You want a mistress and another bottle of gin."

Her words were cutting. Harsh.

He flinched as if she had indeed struck him, and she wished she could recall them. Unspeak them. Undo all the feelings for him she did not want to have. But she could not any more than he could return to the night he and Torrie had drunkenly raced their phaetons.

"I am not worthy of you, I will own," he said at length, releasing her hand. "If the prospect of me as your husband is abhorrent to you, you need only say it."

The color had fled his face, and she could not credit it, but all indications suggested she had hurt him. She, the spinster wallflower, younger sister of his closest friend, the woman he had never spared a second glance whilst he chased after half the skirts in London, had wounded the mighty, beautiful Duke of Montrose.

She hated that she had caused him a moment of hurt.

Hattie reached for him, but he slipped from her grasp.

He was stalking away, leaving her, his broad back mocking her with the promise of all that could have been. All she had ever wanted without ever daring to hope for. All she knew she should never have, for marrying this man would break her.

It would break her heart.

Break her spirit.

Ruin her.

Because she loved him. She had always loved him. But he could never find that out.

"Montrose," she called out. "Wait."

He stopped, remaining still for so long, she feared he would never turn.

Until, at last, he did. His countenance was stark. Needy. Gone was every trace of the polished rake. She could not shake the feeling she was seeing him, the real him, for the very first time.

He looked lonely in that moment. Powerful, gorgeous, and utterly alone.

"What is it, Hattie?" His lip curled, almost a sneer. "A man can only bear so much rejection before his pride forbids him from making himself into an even greater fool."

"Why do you want to marry me?" she asked. For his answer mattered.

His answer would decide her future.

"Because I need you."

His raw statement sent her reeling, but she gathered her wits. "Why?"

"What do you want from me? Do you want me to tell you I love you? To whisper sweet nothings in your ear? To tell you I will be faithful and true until my dying day?" He stalked back toward her. "Do you want me to tell you that you are the one who will rescue me, the one who will change me? Because if that is what you are asking, I cannot give it."

It was her turn to flinch. Of course, he could not give her what she wanted. She knew it. She had always known it, which was why keeping him at a distance had been so paramount.

But it was what he had said originally, his initial answer, which lured her now. The spark of hope ignited, however foolhardy.

"Why do you need me?" she asked.

"Because." He raked his fingers through his dark hair, leaving it rakishly disheveled.

She was not going to allow him to escape so easily. "That is not an answer, Montrose."

"Damn you," he growled. "Because I want you, your innocence, your body, your kiss. I want purity. I want what has not been despoiled or jaded or destroyed. I want the way you remind me of who I ought to be rather than who I am."

Here, she thought, at last, was pure, unadulterated honesty from the Duke of Montrose. A rare gift indeed. For he excelled at playing the role of scandalous devil-may-care. All his reasons were selfish. That she believed as well.

Strangest of all, it made sense. Montrose wanted her because she was the opposite of him. He was a jaded rakehell, whilst she was a lady who had only ever kissed one gentleman aside from him.

"There you have it," he snarled. "The hideous truth. That was what you wanted, was it not? Fear not, madam. I will take my suit elsewhere. You are not the only unattached female in London."

Fear and pity roiled within her, along with a desperate, surging, searing longing.

He was about to turn away from her again, when she blurted the words she knew she would come to regret.

"I will marry you, Montrose."

He stilled. His expression was unreadable. "You will?"

The Lord knew she should not.

DUKE OF DEBAUCHERY

Every practical, intelligent part of her also knew she should not.

The rest of her? The rest of her was weak for him. Weaker than ever. The rest of her knew she could not allow him to walk away from her and marry another. Because she, too, was selfish. The Duke of Montrose was the one thing she had always wanted. The one thing she had never dreamed she could have. The one thing she had always known would be her destruction.

*He needs me*, she thought.

And mayhap, she needed him too.

"Hattie," he prodded, expectation lacing his tone. "Will you marry me for certain? Promise me this is not some game of yours, that you will not change your mind thirty seconds from now."

Here was her chance to defect. To embrace reason. To save herself.

She took a deep breath. "I will marry you."

Those words, as they left her, felt right. She could not feel remorse for them now, even if she knew it highly likely she would later.

She was in his arms then, and she did not even know how. His muscled strength banded around her, holding her to him. His body leaned into hers. Something rigid pressed into her belly, and she knew what it was. Oh, yes, she knew well enough. That most masculine part of him, the part he would use to claim her. Catriona had assuaged her curiosity in her letters in some ways. But Hattie knew there was much to explore.

Exploring it with Montrose held impossible allure.

Danger, too.

But the allure itself was intoxicating. She clung to that feeling, to the pulsing, buoyancy of hope. Of wonderment. Of desire. Because she had thrown herself headlong into the flames, and it was only a matter of time before she was burned.

She knew it, even as his lips slammed down on hers, hard and claiming. She knew it even as she answered his kiss with all the banked desire deep within her. With all the wonder, the need, the anguish. Part of her wanted to believe there was a future for a drunken ne'er-do-well and a wallflower. The other part of her knew there would be no happiness in this union. At least, not for her. For Hattie, there would be only the inevitable pain.

She kissed him back with everything she had, hoping he would be worth it. Hoping she could withstand the dance through the flames.

It was only the clearing of a throat that brought her back to reality, tearing her from Montrose's kiss. Flushing furiously, shame sweeping through her, she extricated herself from the duke's embrace and stepped away. Her brother, the stranger, stood at the threshold of the salon.

"You asked for a moment alone, old chap, but this is beyond the pale," Torrie said, addressing Montrose. "At least, I think it is. I have forgotten a great deal, but I do remember that it is unseemly for a gentleman and lady to be alone, unchaperoned."

"Forgive me," Montrose said, but his gaze had never left Hattie's. "I lost my head."

"As did I," Torrie quipped, laughing.

But his levity was brittle. The joke was lost upon them all. And though Montrose was looking at her as if he wanted to devour her, and although she had just consented to be his wife, Hattie could not summon up a modicum of hope.

Misgivings flooded her. What had she done?

CHAPTER 8

*M*onty was in finest bloody spirits. He finally, at long last, had everything he wanted within his grasp.

He was seated across from the Marquess of Searle at The Duke's Bastard. He had a gin at his side, the residuals of his morning laudanum humming through his veins, and a special license to wed Hattie.

Life, he decided, was good.

Damned good.

*Too* damned good?

Never mind that. He took a sip of his drink, enjoying the burn of it settling deep in his belly. "Have you any advice for me, Searle? I shall soon be a married man. Victim of the parson's mousetrap, and all that claptrap. Your marchioness seems reasonably happy. How does one please a wife?"

Searle sent him a wicked grin. "In the same manner one pleases any woman, I expect. Surely you know how to do that by now, with your reputation."

"Devil take you, Searle." He took another sip of gin. "I did not mean in bed. I have been swiving since I was a lad."

Searle raised a brow. "Did I say anything about a bed or swiving?"

Monty snorted. "Do not act as if you are not bedding Lady Searle to within an inch of her—"

"Monty." Searle's tone was rife with warning. "You are speaking of my lady wife."

"Yes, well. Lady Searle recently had a bairn, which is ample proof you have been bedding her," he could not help but point out, though he knew it would do nothing to further his cause. "I would not say you have been chaste as a monk."

"Damn it, Monty. I do not know whether to laugh or rail at you for your insolence." Searle took a sip of his claret.

*Claret.* Since when had Searle chosen claret over whisky or gin? Next, he would be asking for orgeat. Or his mother's milk.

Was that a flush staining his cousin's cheeks?

*The good Lord's chemise.* What a development. Did marriage turn one into a maudlin, sentimental milksop?

He hoped not.

"What insolence?" He lifted his glass back to his lips. One more tipple. "Consider it honesty. A forthright nature. I am getting married, old chap. Not turning into a parishioner. You cannot expect me to change my ways."

"Your wife may expect you to do so," Searle said, his tone stern. Chastising, almost. "Indeed, I cannot think she will be pleased for you to carry on as you have these last few years. Miss Lethbridge seems a lady of reason. It is astounding an intelligent female such as she would deign to accept your tattered hide as her husband."

"To Hades with you," he snapped, for he did not like the notion of Hattie wanting to change him. He was himself. Always had been. Always would be. He was damaged. His scars were on the inside. Carnal distraction, spirits, and opium were the balms for his soul.

And Hattie's mouth.

And her breasts. *Dear God*, her nipples. Those responsive, pink buds the color of her lips. To say nothing of her cunny, which he was certain would be equally exquisite. If the rest of her were an elixir, he had no doubt that sliding home inside Hattie's body would be the ultimate tonic.

Until he tired of her, of course. Which would inevitably happen, just as it always did with the ladies of his acquaintance. He could not be so fixated upon a single woman as Searle was with his marchioness. One woman, for Monty, forever? Impossible.

"Marriage requires compromise, Monty," Searle told him. "You and your bride must meet each other on common ground. It is not a journey either party can undertake alone and succeed. Trust me. My marriage did not begin as it should have, and it will be my eternal regret."

"Ballocks. Compromise is for spinsters and dowagers." He scowled at his cousin, who was rather being a supercilious arse about the matrimony folderol now that he thought upon it.

God knew he certainly had no intention of compromising. He knew from experience with his mother and his sister that females sought to change him. They fretted over him. Told him he drank too much. Told him he would get the pox if he did not curtail his insatiable appetite for bedding an endless string of women. Upbraided him for knocking over statuary and punching footmen and pissing on the carpet.

It was true, the last had not been one of his finer moments.

But still. He would not be hen-pecked and nattered.

Searle raised an imperious brow. "On the contrary.

Compromise is for men who wish to live contented lives with happy wives whom they love."

Monty snorted at such rot. "Ah, there you have it, Searle. I am not in love. I shall live as I wish. As my duchess, Miss Lethbridge's general happiness will be my goal, but do not cast me as a reformed rake in the next great tragedy just yet. I fully intend to carry on as I always have."

Which meant he would bed Hattie until he exorcised this unholy need for her from his body. He would also be doing his best to make amends for his part in Torrie's accident by seeing to it that his spinster wallflower sister became a wife after all. Monty's guilt would be ameliorated. His life settled. He could get an heir on her for his troubles and go to the grave a sated man.

"You cannot mean to continue on as you have when you wed." His cousin's voice, a cutting blade of disapproval, slashed through his thoughts.

Of course he would.

"Nothing need change." He took another sip of gin. "Miss Lethbridge already knows what I am about. I have warned her. Nevertheless, she has chosen to accept my suit."

He *had* warned her. Reasonably. He had told her he was not changing. He had been a damaged sot ever since he had been a stripling. Time had not healed him. Neither would wedding Hattie Lethbridge. But seeking solace between her pretty thighs would not hurt, either. He could not recall wanting a woman as badly as he yearned for her. Ever since sneaking into her chamber, he had been slavering over her as if he were a mongrel in heat.

This urgency and voracious hunger within him, however, would pass. He was certain of it. Nothing in his life had ever been enough. And so, he was doomed to repeat the endless cycle of perennially wanting more.

"I want you to know the happiness I have experienced within my marriage." Searle's expression was stern.

Almost bloody sad.

More maudlin sentiment.

"I have all the happiness I need," he told his cousin, and then he poured the remainder of his gin down his gullet.

"Gin cannot make you happy the way a woman can, Monty." Searle was looking at him with something akin to pity now.

"And one woman cannot make me happy the way many can," he countered.

For all his reckless, restless life thus far, that had been invariably true.

He did not expect Hattie Lethbridge to be any different.

\* \* \*

HATTIE'S MOTHER, who had been a bastion of propriety all her life thus far, had suddenly decided to ignore society's dictates. Which meant that when Montrose called upon her quite unexpectedly in the days following her precipitous acceptance of his proposal of marriage, Mama fled the small morning room in which they had been seated. Not only had she left Hattie and the duke unchaperoned, but she had closed the door.

Hattie glared at the door now as she offered Montrose a curtsey.

He bowed.

No walking stick today either, she noted. He certainly seemed hale, aside from his complexion being somewhat pale. Dark shadows marred the flesh beneath his eyes as if he had not slept. She could not help but wonder if she looked the same.

For she had scarcely slept a wink for the past several nights.

Misgiving had turned into second thoughts, and by the faint strains of dawn tracing the sky, she had been convinced she must cry off. That Montrose had cast some spell over her to persuade her to wed him.

The spell had consisted of his words. His need. And her stupid, wretched heart.

He bowed in most elegant fashion, his fathomless brown gaze assessing. Alert. "Hattie, darling. You look lovely."

Despite her best intentions to don her armor and treat him as she would any enemy about to storm her castle, a flare of warmth sparked to life within her at his use of the words *darling* and *lovely*. Ruthlessly, she doused that incipient longing, telling herself these were words he likely used upon all his women. He was a practiced rake. A devious flirt. A rogue.

Too handsome for his own good.

And too reckless, too.

She forced herself to greet him in turn, careful not to show the slightest inclination of pleasure at his sudden appearance after so many days had followed his proposal without a call from him. "Your Grace. I did not expect you today."

His lips quirked into a wry half grin that only served to enhance his raw masculine beauty, blight him. "Is that chastisement I detect in your lovely voice?"

Yes, it was.

She took a deep breath and moved to the window, where she might distract herself with a view of the street below. All the better to avoid looking at him. He was her own personal Medusa, but instead of turning her to stone, he turned her into a fool.

## DUKE OF DEBAUCHERY

Hattie Lethbridge was no fool. Which was why she turned her attention to the rumbling carriages beyond the paned glass instead of the wicked rake behind her.

"It is an observation, Your Grace." She forced her voice to remain mild. Unperturbed.

"Such formality." His footfalls heralded his proximity even before a rush of awareness swept over her. "Hattie, will you not look at me?"

*That touch.*

It was like a brand and a knife to her heart, all at once. Because oh, how she wanted it. Oh, how she wanted *him*.

Why had she agreed to marry him?

"Why have you come, Montrose? You have already gotten what you want, have you not? Surely there is no need to tarry with me now." She closed her eyes briefly against a rush of shame for the bitterness she had allowed to seep into her voice.

"You are angry with me."

His steady observation only served to heighten her irritation and her ire with herself. She turned and instantly regretted the motion, for he was far nearer than she had realized. She lost her balance and fell against him, making their bodies flush. Her palms landed on his chest.

Rigid, warm, solid male muscle greeted her greedy touch.

His hands were on her waist. She was tall, but he was taller. She was strong, but he was stronger. She could escape his hold, but only if she wanted.

Hattie found herself strangely reluctant to move away, to sever the connection.

She swallowed and tried not to look at his lips or to recall the way he had kissed her. "You did not answer my question, Your Grace."

"I have come because you are my betrothed." His gaze

scoured her face, settling upon her mouth. "I will own, I expected a different sort of greeting altogether."

A different sort of greeting? Was she to throw herself into his arms? What manner of females did Montrose ordinarily charm?

Strike that question—for she already knew and loathed the answer.

Jealousy curdled within her. A jealousy she had no right to feel. Montrose had already warned her, had he not, what to anticipate from him? Had she believed he would come to care for her? To love her?

*Foolish, foolish Hattie.*

"You are fortunate you are getting a greeting at all, Montrose," she told him frostily then. "You asked me to marry you, and then you disappeared."

His jaw tightened. "I asked you to marry me on multiple occasions and met with your refusal each time."

She recognized the stubborn expression on his face, and she wished she did not find it quite so handsome. "You know the reason why."

"*Reasons.* As I recall, there were many." His fingers tightened upon her waist, perhaps in warning.

Or in possession.

Her heart beat faster. "I was a challenge to you, then, Montrose? After I capitulated, you grew bored."

"I have hardly gotten what I want from you, *Miss Lethbridge.*" He used her surname mockingly, and she knew it was because her clinging to formality vexed him.

Good. Because *he* most certainly vexed *her*.

She ran her tongue over lips that had gone dry. His gaze followed the movement.

Her awareness of him shifted, turning into something else. Deep inside, a molten sensation of excitement burned through her. His scent teased her senses. Musky, male, shaving soap, the crisp freshness of a spring day. Delicious.

How could a cad smell so divine?

How could a woman who prided herself upon her intelligence be so weak when it came to this bold scoundrel? This thief of hearts?

Surely hers was not the only one he possessed.

How she hated the thought.

His words hung between them, poignant. Heady. "What else do you want from me, Your Grace?"

His head dipped, until his lips were so near, she could feel his breath, hot and tempting, upon her mouth. "You as my wife, to begin. And then more. So much more."

*More.*

Too vague.

Her curious mind railed against such a travesty. She wanted specifics. Details. Action. Touch.

Her cheeks flushed. She was sure she was as red as an apple. "I thought you had changed your mind," she said, determined to change the subject.

To regain a modicum of control.

"Never." He flashed her a brief, grim smile. "Have you?"

He tensed, as if he dreaded her response.

How odd. Emotion was not what she expected from him. Unless she was mistaken, and it was merely pride reflected in the shadows of his chocolate eyes?

"Hattie," he pressed when she did not answer.

"Yes," she admitted. "I have."

He flinched as if she had struck him. "You no longer want to marry me?"

Part of her wanted to marry him more than she had ever wanted anything else. Part of her did not dare. He was a rake. A scoundrel. He was the Duke of Debauchery, for heaven's sakes.

And he was watching her with his predatory eyes, his expression harsh. If looks could cut, he would have sliced her to ribbons.

She took a deep breath, which was a mistake, for it filled her with his intoxicating scent. "I am not sure if it would be wise. I have been plagued by misgivings ever since agreeing to it."

His jaw tightened. "Because I have not danced attendance upon you in the last few days? Is that it, Hattie? I did not take you for an empty-headed chit who needed to be flattered and fawned over."

That stung. "You are being unkind, Montrose."

"As are you, madam." His fingers flexed on her waist. "Do not play games with me."

"This is no game." Her pounding heart told her so. As did the longing. "I have been thinking. If we are to wed—"

"*When* we wed," he corrected, lowering his head a fraction.

Bringing his sinful mouth nearer to hers.

She swallowed. "If we are to wed, we need to have rules, Montrose."

"Rules." One of his hands moved, navigating up her spine in a delicious caress. He traced his way to her nape, his fingers sifting through her chignon to cup her head. "Perhaps you have me confused with one of your milksop suitors, Hattie. I do not believe in rules."

"My milksop suitors?" She struggled to concentrate. To stop looking at his lips. To stop longing for them upon hers.

"Lord Hayes," he growled. "The Earl of Bloody Rearden. Milksops. Both of them."

As a wallflower, she could not boast legions of suitors, but Lord Hayes and Lord Rearden had been amongst them. Strange to think Montrose had noticed. He had mentioned Rearden to her once before, she recalled now.

"They are not milksops, Montrose." She would cling to her resolve. Remain firm. "And rules are necessary. Imperative, I believe, to the success of a union between us, if one is to come to fruition."

"I am in possession of a special license that says it damn well will come to fruition. And soon." His gaze dipped to her lips. His head lowered another fraction. "I want you in my bed, Hattie. I will be damned if I have to climb another tree to get to you."

He wanted her.

In his bed.

What a wicked thing to say.

So why did it make her feel so wonderful?

She struggled to consider his words, to avoid thoughts of beds and the Duke of Montrose altogether. "You obtained a special license?"

"I set myself to the task immediately after you agreed to become my duchess." One more incremental lowering of his head. His breath fell over her lips.

She felt suddenly as if she had drunk too much wine. Her skin was buzzing. Warmth suffused her. "Montrose…"

"Hattie." His mouth was finally upon hers then.

Not a ravenous claiming as she had anticipated but a soft, gentle seduction. An exploration of her lips. There was such tenderness in his kiss. His lips were full, skillfully settling over hers, coaxing hers to respond. He cupped her face, held her still. Her hands slid around his neck. She did not feel trapped.

She felt as if she wanted to moor herself to him. To stay in his arms forever.

When Montrose kissed her, she could forget about everything else. The world fell away, all her concerns, his storied past. She could ignore the day he had proposed to her, when he had smelled of gin. She could tamp down the fear he would inevitably break her heart.

There was not a trace of spirits on him now. Nor the scent. Nor the taste as his tongue traced the seam of her lips before slipping past them. She opened for him, her tongue meeting his.

Velvet and heat. Seduction and sweetness.

"You want me," he said against her mouth.

She did not dare say yes. Did not dare to give him that power.

Instead, she tipped back her head, severing the kiss with great reluctance. "I want *rules*, Montrose."

"Marry me tomorrow, and I will agree to them all." He kissed her again.

Marry him tomorrow?

Was he mad?

She would have asked him, but his lips on her obliterated all sensible thought. His body was hard as she pressed herself against him, seeking more contact. And that was when she felt the most masculine part of him once more. Long and hard and pressing into her belly.

She tore her mouth from his. Their eyes met.

The grin he gave her was positively carnal. "Have I shocked you, darling?"

Deep in her core, a new ache throbbed to life. A desperate longing.

"You are indecent, Montrose." Her voice was irritatingly breathless, her accusation lacking any real censure.

"Always."

But perhaps she was indecent as well, for she did not want to move. Indeed, her instinct was to get closer. "I cannot marry you tomorrow."

"Of course, you can." He gave her another kiss, this one slower. More deliberate.

He was attempting to woo her with kisses. To make her forget about her doubts, about her rules.

It was working.

She broke the kiss. "If we marry in haste, everyone will assume the worst, Montrose."

"If you marry me, everyone will assume the worst even if we take three months to wed." He kissed the corner of her lips. Her cheek. Her jaw. Her ear, where his lips hovered. "Marry me tomorrow, Hattie. To the devil with your second thoughts and your list of rules. I want you. You want me. That is all that matters."

How easy it would be to agree. She understood his reputation now. He was a master of seduction. He had chipped away at her resistance with his lips and his touch. Was this what he did to all his women?

The question nettled enough to remind her of her rules.

"I want rules, Montrose," she insisted.

But he was kissing her neck now. He found a particularly sensitive place and bit gently, then soothed the sting with his tongue. "Stuff your rules."

Oh, he was good.

Her knees were turning into jelly.

"Montrose." Her traitorous head tipped back, granting him the ability to move his mouth lower.

To find the hollow at the base of her throat. Then her clavicle.

"Darling." He said the term of endearment against the swell of her breast, just above the edge of her bodice. He kissed the top of her left breast first. Then her right.

She forgot to breathe.

He was better than good.

How could she possibly survive a marriage to him? And yet, how could she want anything else?

"Fidelity," she managed to say.

His fingers were tugging on her bodice, lowering it incrementally. He stilled. "Pardon?"

"Fidelity." She clutched his shoulders, telling herself she would push him away in a moment. Telling herself she was most certainly not clutching him nearer. "It is one of my rules."

## CHAPTER 9

*If* there was one word in the vast lexicon which ought to have wilted his prick, Hattie had just said it.

Twice.

*Fidelity.*

One of her blasted rules.

*God's fichu*, why did she suppose he could be faithful to one woman for the rest of his life? He was sure he was incapable of such an impossibility. Moreover, why the devil was his cockstand still straining against the fall of his breeches, as if such a despicable word had never been dropped like an anvil between them?

He needed laudanum.

Or gin.

Oblivion.

He also needed Hattie in his bed. The ache for her was unbearable. His body hungered for hers.

But fidelity?

"No rules," he said firmly, his decision made. He could have her without them, he was sure of it.

Her hands were on his shoulders. Pushing.

"Then no wedding."

That gave him pause. He straightened to his formidable height. He cupped her cheek in his palm. "I am only sparing you disappointment, Hattie. You already know who and what I am. I will not lie to you."

Her lips tightened, and the glaze of passion vanished from her gaze. "I am firm on this rule, Montrose."

And he was firm, too. That part of his anatomy was still pressed into her gown, nestled against the softness of her belly. Begging to be inside her.

He sighed. "I cannot make such a promise to you."

Her chin lifted. "Then I cannot make one to you either."

The thought of another man touching her produced a strong, unprecedented reaction in him. He had never before been jealous of a paramour.

He thrust the unwanted response aside in favor of pragmatism. "You will not take a lover until you bear me an heir, as is the way of such arrangements."

She stiffened at his mentioning of an heir. But of course, this was the standard union for men and women of their class. She hardly ought to be surprised. They married. The heir was secured. They went their separate ways.

"Fair enough, Montrose." Her countenance was still a study in strain. The lushness was gone from her lips. "I will remain faithful to you until I bear you an heir, and you must do the same."

That did not seem nearly as impossible.

But Hattie taking a lover in the future... His mind refused to contemplate such a notion. *Mine*, said something deep within him. *This woman is mine.*

And he would do anything to have her.

Including agreeing to her damnable rules, it would seem.

"I agree to your rule." He moved to kiss her again, but she slipped from his grasp, flitting across the chamber.

He mourned the loss of her warmth. Her curves. Her scent. Those bewitching eyes, snapping into his at such proximity.

"I have more rules," she told him.

Of course she did.

She was Hattie.

"Name them," he gritted.

"I am bringing Sir Toby," she said.

*Beelzebub's earbobs.* The feline. He still needed to find out the creature's namesake.

"It has to sleep in the mews," he told her.

"He will sleep in my chamber just as he always has," she countered.

His cock was still hard as marble. And he was no closer to getting what he wanted.

"He may sleep in your chamber unless I am visiting you. Then, he must go elsewhere." By God's breath, he would not fuck his wife with a feline for an audience every night.

Every night?

And afternoon.

Morning, too.

Anticipation surged. By this time tomorrow, he could begin introducing her to the many pleasures of the flesh. He began envisioning all the places at Hamilton House where he could tup her.

"That is fair enough, I suppose," his future duchess allowed. "How often do you think you might anticipate…visiting?"

He almost swallowed his tongue. At this rate, once every hour. What was wrong with him? He was not even in his cups, and the laudanum-laced tea he had consumed that morning was not enough to dull the throbbing ache of desire that haunted him whenever he was in her presence.

Or whenever they were apart, for that matter.

If he did not have her soon, he would go mad.

"As often as we both would wish," he managed when he had finally found his voice.

It was thick with lust.

He moved toward her again, unwilling to allow so much distance between them. The sunlight streaming in the windows behind her cast her in a glow, lending her dark hair a lustrous sheen. He could understand why those insipid chits had been gossiping about her that night when she had overheard their jealous vitriol.

She was glorious. Unique. She was simply Hattie.

"Stay where you are," she ordered him, holding up a staying palm as if she possessed some magical power that would overwhelm him and force him to halt.

She did not.

Monty kept right on walking.

He stopped only when her decadent violet scent hit him. And then, he slid an arm around her waist, hauling her against him. She did not protest, other than to make a husky sound of surprise. "What other rules have you?"

Her gaze had settled on his mouth. She blinked, looking adorably befuddled. "Rules?"

Ah, she was not as unaffected as she pretended. How easily he could make this particular kitten purr. "The rules that will enable me to marry you on the morrow."

Her dark lashes fluttered once, twice. "I did not agree to marrying you tomorrow, Montrose."

"You said I needed to accept your rules." He gave her a slow smile, the rake's grin that had never failed him in getting beneath a lady's skirts in the past. "I have already accepted two. Have you more?"

"You agreed to a *compromise* on two." A frown creased the creamy skin of her forehead.

*Beelzebub's earbobs*, this was the conversation with Searle all over again.

What was it with everyone else and that horrid word?

He suppressed a shudder, turning his mind instead to the delicious feeling of Hattie in his arms. He longed to kiss her again, to claim her mouth with his. But this was serious business. If he wanted to be a married man this time tomorrow, he had to tread with care.

"You agreed as well, darling." He could not resist tracing the fullness of her lower lip with his forefinger. "I would say we both compromised on two rules. Name your other rules."

She stared at him.

And he suspected there was not more than two. That she had been blustering her way through this interview. But why? She had already agreed to marry him. What had changed her mind? He traced the bow of her upper lip before trailing his touch to her smooth jaw.

"I cannot think of any others at the moment." She swallowed, and he absorbed the slight vibration through his fingertip. "I require more time to compile them. As I am marrying a wicked rake, I shall need to gird myself well."

She thought him a wicked rake? Was it fear that propelled her, then? Fear of what, however? What could he possibly do to her, aside from marry her, bed her, make her a duchess and a mother, and allow her to live her life as she chose when his heir was secured?

She was ever a cipher, Miss Harriet Lethbridge.

There was one thing of which he was certain, however. If he gave her more time to concoct additional rules, she would simply continue talking herself out of wedding him. That was not to be borne. Now that she was within his reach, he could not stop until she was his.

"No more time, Hattie." He shook his head slowly, his gaze devouring her face. Why had he never noticed how unique, how lovely she was? How different from the typical English beauty, the tired roses in full bloom that were his ordinary fare? "We will wed tomorrow, and that is that. I accept your rules."

Her verdant gaze shot to his. "I have not planned a thing. We have no guests. I have no dress."

He admired the way this particular gown emphasized her bosom. "Why not wear this one? You look fetching in it."

"Fetching." Her frown had returned.

He had said the wrong thing. Again.

"Beautiful," he clarified. Beddable. Delicious.

Her eyes narrowed. "Do not use your flattery upon me, Montrose. I am inured."

Prickly Miss Lethbridge. He would take great pleasure in kissing all the starch from her sails. Licking, too.

*Patience, Montrose. Patience and persistence.*

"Speaking the truth is not flattery." He found a dark wisp of hair that had come free of her coiffure and tucked it behind her ear. "We have been alone for far too long already, Hattie. At any moment, someone will swoop down upon us, putting an end to this. I will have your answer. Will you marry me tomorrow?"

"Tomorrow," she repeated faintly, as if he had asked her to travel to the moon instead of become his wife.

"Yes," he persisted. "Tomorrow. I have already compromised on two massive points, faithfulness and felines. Now it is your turn."

"I do not know what to say." Her breathlessness had returned.

Perhaps because he had trailed his touch over her décolletage, not stopping at the edge of her bodice, but descending lower. To the hardened bead of her nipple. Though layers separated him from the prize he sought, the hitch in her breath and her body's hunger sent longing arrowing to his groin.

"Say yes," he told her.

And then, he could not resist catching that responsive bud between thumb and forefinger, plucking.

She inhaled sharply, her lips parting. "Montrose."

He rolled her nipple, pinched it lightly until she gasped again. "Hattie. Marry me tomorrow. I cannot spend another night beyond this one without you."

As the last words left him, he realized they were common. Simple, false flattery. Reassurances he had given other women without hesitation. They would not do for Hattie.

"I want you as my duchess," he said, trying again. Hattie was not every woman who had come before her. She was different. Special. She was Torrie's sister, by God. He could not treat her as he had all the rest. "I want you at my side. I need you, Hattie."

Still, she said nothing.

Not a word as he cupped her breast, his fingers tightening over the deliciously rounded swell. He was staking his claim, it was true. He could not resist. It seemed impossible to him that he had gone so many years without touching this glorious woman. Without making her his.

Tomorrow would be the day.

He would make amends for all the time he had failed to see her.

"Montrose," she whispered, her voice dripping in reproach. But her body spoke a different language entirely, her back arching, thrusting her breast into his palm.

Mayhap she needed him, too.

Perhaps he was the man who could unlock all Hattie's sensuality. There was a passionate woman burning beneath her prim, proper exterior. He could sense it.

"No more second thoughts," he told her. "No more doubts. One word is all I need from you, Hattie darling."

For a long, heavy moment, she remained silent. Her verdant gaze burned into his. Her lush body curved into his as if it belonged.

*Because it does*, said a voice deep within him.

"Yes," she said, at long last.

Satisfaction swept over him, along with relief.

The door opened, and Lady Torrington cleared her throat. "Do pardon me for my scattered wits, Your Grace. I have finally found my needlework."

Fortunately, his back was to Hattie's mother, thus blocking her view of his hand upon her daughter's breast. He released Hattie and spun on his heel with a ready smile.

The smile was real, even if his delight at her entrance was feigned.

It was the smile of a man who had just secured what he wanted.

"Lady Torrington," he greeted. "How fortunate you have arrived. Miss Lethbridge will be needing your aid in arranging the particular details of our impending nuptials."

Torrie and Hattie's mother faltered, her gaze darting to Hattie, who still stood behind him. "We shall have several weeks to plan, of course. Never fear, Your Grace. It promises to be the event of the Season."

To the devil with the Season. To the devil with ceremony and circumstance.

He wanted Hattie.

And he wanted her now.

"My dear Lady Torrington," he said, tempering his words with a kind, if pitying, smile. "Having conferred with my betrothed just now, I cannot help but to deem such a wait altogether impossible."

"Forgive me, Your Grace, but we shall need proper time

to prepare." Lady Torrington's lips compressed with obvious displeasure. "Surely you can see that, as a gentleman of reason."

*Ha!* When had she ever known him, in all his years of being Torrie's most disreputable rakehell friend, to be a gentleman of reason? What tripe.

Hattie's mother wanted a grand wedding—an event of the Season, as she had put it—for her own gratification, not for her daughter's. Monty could see through her ploys. Moreover, he did not forget the evening Lady Torrington had all but begged him to take her to bed. Her husband had been in the grave some five years, it was true, but he was her son's *friend*.

He had been preyed upon enough in his lifetime.

He turned back to Hattie. "Miss Lethbridge, do you desire a lengthy courtship, or would you prefer to wed me on the morrow?"

He held his breath, awaiting her answer, horridly aware she could change it at any second. Willing her not to do so. His eyes met hers. Their gazes held.

It seemed to him, in those frozen seconds, that a wealth of information passed between them. A windfall of understanding.

At long last, she jerked her gaze away, her stare flitting to her mother. "I am wedding His Grace tomorrow, Mother. I do not require a society event."

"But—" Lady Torrington sputtered as if all her dreams and plans had been torn from her grasp.

Too bloody bad.

He bowed, ignoring her protests. "If you will excuse me, Lady Torrington, Miss Lethbridge. I must take my leave, as I have much to arrange."

CHAPTER 10

The Duke of Montrose was a clever, persuasive, handsome scoundrel.

Somehow, he had convinced Hattie to give him nearly everything he had wanted.

Very well—he had convinced her with his kisses and his knowing hands, his tongue, his handsome face, his deliciously masculine scent, his everything. Every part of him. His deep voice. Those dark eyes.

What a fool she was.

And he was…well, he was her gorgon.

Her lady's maid finished brushing out her hair.

"There you are, Miss L—Your Grace," said Lansdowne.

She could not fault Lansdowne for confusing her title. It was new and sudden to Hattie as well. Almost impossible, in fact, as she stood, surrounded by the duchess's apartments in Hamilton House. The appearance of them was not shabby by any means, but it was clear they had not been inhabited for some time.

The wallcoverings were crimson flock damask, quite elegant but faded from dozens of years of sun. Perhaps better suited to the last duchess who had chosen them. The furniture was luxurious satinwood, but this, too, bore the hallmarks of the previous century in its styling. Indeed, it was as if the room had been held in waiting for a generation.

Being here now felt strange.

Wrong.

Thrilling.

All of those feelings, all at once, in truth.

It was difficult to believe she had, in fact, married the Duke of Montrose that morning in a small ceremony. Not even her dearest friend Catriona had been able to attend, for she was lost in the countryside with her new husband and their growing family.

"Thank you, Lansdowne," she forced herself to say at last, ashamed at how her mind had been wandering.

She could only ascribe it to the strangeness of the day.

Of marrying the most notorious rakehell in the realm.

The man she loved.

The man she had loved in secret for years.

But never mind *that* source of burning shame.

"Will that be all, Your Grace?" her lady's maid asked.

Hattie wore her dressing gown. Beneath it, a plain night rail—her best, of course. She had not had the opportunity to commission a fresh wardrobe. She had brought precious few belongings along with her to Hamilton House. More would follow tomorrow.

Her packing had been frantic. Unsettled. Fraught with worry.

And wanting, too.

She could not forget that.

Her mother's warnings to her had been frantic. Dire.

*The Duke of Montrose will not settle with one woman alone, Hattie. You must resign yourself to that fact now, before your heart becomes involved.*

*Oh, Mother*, she thought now.

Too late for that.

Far, far too late.

"Your Grace?" Lansdowne persisted. "Do you require anything else?"

Her lady's maid was eager to make herself scarce, and Hattie could not fault her. She was on edge herself, knowing that at any moment, she could expect the knock on the door adjoining her chamber to her husband's.

Her husband's.

What a strange phrase.

Stranger word.

Strangest of all—the notion she had married him. Hours before, they had exchanged vows, observed by their mothers and a most solemn Torrie and no one else.

"That will be all, Lansdowne," she told her lady's maid at last, grateful she had followed her from one household to the next.

Although Montrose had introduced her to his staff, and his domestics had seemed welcoming, she was grateful for a familiar face within these strange walls. For someone she knew she could trust.

Because one thing was certain, she could not trust her husband.

The man she had married was rife with secrets. And she could not be certain he would ever deign to share any of them with her.

"You look lovely, Your Grace," Lansdowne said. "You will steal His Grace's breath."

"Thank you, Lansdowne." She was grateful for her maid's praise. Truly, she was. "I bid you good evening."

But she was also painfully aware that her husband had boasted some of the most beautiful women in England as his paramours. Not that she had been paying his conquests any mind...

Very well. She had been paying them heed. Montrose was connected to ladies who were gorgeous, sure of themselves, experienced, worldly. Ladies who were nothing like wallflowers, who did not even know how to choose a complimentary color in her evening gowns, if the scurrilous gossip of those two shrews was to be believed.

As she fretted inwardly, her maid quietly took her leave from the chamber.

Hattie was alone.

Alone with her thoughts.

Her eagerness.

Her misgivings.

*Dear heavens.*

Lansdowne had scarcely even been gone when a knock sounded at the door adjoining her apartment to the duke's.

To *his*.

Montrose's.

Her *husband*.

What had she done?

"Enter," she called out, for what else could she say?

The door opened.

There he stood.

He was dressed in a banyan. His hair was damp from a bath. And he looked like sin personified. He was the most beautiful and terrifying sight she had ever beheld.

There was no way she could allow this man into her bed.

"Montrose," she said, trying to control the odd combination of eagerness and fear battling for supremacy within her.

"Hattie." There was no denying the approval or the hunger vibrating in his voice, echoed in his heated stare. "Now that we are husband and wife, perhaps you might call me Monty, as everyone does."

Her brother called him Monty, or at least he had, before the accident. She had heard others do so as well. But something about his request felt wrong. Hattie tried to temper her nerves as he sauntered deeper into the chamber, nearing her.

"I should like to call you by your Christian name," she managed to say past the nerves tangling her up in knots. "To everyone else, you are Monty."

He stopped before her, his gaze traveling hungrily over her. "I never liked my Christian name, but if you prefer, I suppose Ewan will do."

Of course, she knew his full name, Ewan Christopher Hamilton, Duke of Montrose. But garnering his permission to call him Ewan felt intimate. Warmth blossomed inside her.

"Ewan," she repeated. "Why do you hate it? It is a beautiful name."

*A beautiful name for a beautiful man*, she thought. But she kept that part to herself.

"It sounds much better when you say it." His gaze flitted to her lips.

How she longed for his mouth upon hers. The urgency rising within her took her by surprise. She must distract herself. Part of her felt like the hare being hunted. Part of her wanted him more than she wanted her next breath.

"Ewan," she said again, testing the name. Her heart pounded. Heat pooled in her core, throbbed from her center. Her reaction to him was dangerous. He was dangerous. She needed to proceed with caution. To go slowly.

She wanted his claiming. His kiss.

And he gave her what she wanted.

But not as quickly as she anticipated. Rather, he took his time. His gentleness disarmed her. He cupped her face in his hands, tracing her cheeks gently with the pads of his thumbs.

"You are glorious, Hattie." His voice was soft. There was

no doubting the admiration glinting in his gaze or imbuing his rich tone with a husky quality.

More heat unfurled within her, along with a rush of tenderness she had previously not allowed herself to feel for him. He was her husband now, after all.

"Thank you," she said, giving him a tremulous smile she knew would make it obvious just how fraught with worry she was on the inside.

With fears and doubts.

She was married to a reckless rake. And he owned her heart. But a voice inside her pointed out he had not been so very reckless over the course of the last few weeks. No rumors concerning him had reached her. Since the day she had smelled gin upon his breath during his proposal, she had not scented it again. Instead, his kisses tasted of only wine or tea.

Still, she knew it was too much to hope he had reformed with such ease. He was still the same wild rake he had always been. The trouble with Montrose was that there were moments of such incredible kindness. Gestures, words, and deeds that made her forget all the rest.

Until whatever prompted him in his hedonistic ways resurfaced, of course, and he was at it again.

"No, Hattie," he said, interrupting her tumultuous thoughts as he tunneled his fingers into her hair. "Thank *you*. Thank you for marrying me. Thank you for becoming my duchess. I do not deserve you; it is certain. But I will do my utmost to be the best husband to you I can."

She understood that this was as close to a declaration as she would get from Montrose. Scratch that—from *Ewan*, for that was how she must think of him now.

To that end, she worked up the courage to touch him as well. She settled her hands upon his shoulders first. They were broad and firm. Warm, too. Shielded from her for the first time without his many layers. Belatedly, she noted he appeared nude beneath the banyan, which parted in a vee to reveal a swath of his chest. Stippled with dark hair and lean and firm, and so very masculine. So very intimate.

She inhaled, dragging his scent into her lungs. "I will do my best to make you happy as well, Ewan. I am not accustomed to being a wife, after all."

"Ah." He smiled. "Nor am I accustomed to being a husband. On that, we are well-matched, darling."

When he called her *darling*, and when he was standing so near, and when his fingers were beginning to massage her scalp, and when her hands were upon him, all the anticipation coiling within made her weak. So weak.

"Ewan," she said, breathless.

A slight frown furrowed his brow, and she supposed it was because he was unaccustomed to being called his given name. "Yes, Hattie?"

Her hands crept up his neck. She cupped his head, her fingers sinking into his thick, dark hair. It was so luxurious, so soft. She had never dared to caress him thus without him kissing her before. But it felt good to explore him now. To touch him freely, boldly, and as she wished.

She summoned the rest of her daring. All she had left. "Will you kiss me again?"

"With pleasure, my darling." His frown was gone, his brow smooth, his countenance unfairly handsome as he lowered his mouth to hers once more.

Their lips met. Hers parted naturally. The fit of their mouths was right. Perfect. This kiss was more demanding than the last. And yet, it was still slow. Exploratory. Their tongues met. The kisses they had shared before had been the prelude to this masterful seduction. He was heat and strength and desire. He was sin and temptation and power.

Intoxicating.

That was what he was.

She kissed him back, grasping handfuls of his hair, holding him to her. He made her feel ravenous. He made her understand all the women who had fallen beneath his spell. There was something about the way he kissed, the way he touched a woman, that made her feel as if she were the rarest treasure laid before him.

He kissed her as if he wanted to devour her and as if she were a goddess to whom he paid homage. Long and deep and slow. He took his time. And she took hers as well, tipping back her head, opening wider.

They remained locked in each other's embrace, their mouths fused, until at last he withdrew. His breath fell hot upon her lips as he tipped his forehead to hers. Their noses brushed. The moment was strangely intimate. Perhaps the most intimate of any of their encounters, even though their mouths no longer clung.

"I am trying to pace myself. To seduce you. But you are the one who is seducing me."

The tip of his nose grazed the bridge of hers. The act itself was innocent enough. It should not have robbed her breath, and yet, somehow, it did. Or perhaps it was his words. The notion that she, Hattie Lethbridge, could possibly seduce the Duke of Debauchery, why it was…

Ridiculous.

Unbelievable.

*Delicious.*

There was something raw and real, resonating in his voice, in his touch. Tonight was different. Something between them had shifted. Whatever it was, it gave her a new sense of determination. She wanted to wrap herself around him and never let go.

She rubbed her nose against his. "How can *I* seduce *you?*"

He laughed softly. "London's greatest sinner, yes? You are no fool, Hattie. You must know my reputation—"

No, never mind all that. She did not want those reminders. Did not need those ghosts coming between them.

She pressed her mouth to his instead, staying the rest of his words. Whatever he had been about to say, she knew it was not something she wanted to hear. Because all she did want now, in this moment, was him. Not words. Not reasons. Not excuses. Not explanations.

Just action.

Pure, unadulterated need. Hers for him, his for her. He kissed her back with all the passion burning inside her, with all the fiery need. This kiss turned voracious, possessing none of the pretty hesitance of its predecessors.

Her kiss had ended his attempts at being a gentleman. He was wild now. But that suited her fine, for so was she. His tongue plunged into her mouth, one of his hands fisting in her hair, angling her head to where he wanted it. There was no doubt who was in control now.

It was not Hattie, who had begun this with her kiss. It was Ewan. All Ewan. And he was determined to show her. To seduce her. To shift the power balance between them, back to where it had been.

She fell headlong into that kiss, into him. Greedy. Needing. It still did not feel real somehow, that the man she loved was in her arms. That he was hers. And perhaps that was because she knew—oh, how she knew—whatever happened between them must be temporary. This would not last. It was transient.

No one could ever contain the Duke of Montrose, least of all her.

But mayhap that was what made kissing him, joining herself with him, all the sweeter. Or all the more bittersweet. Their tongues battled. Their kisses grew harsh. Uncontrolled. The heat within her rose to a crescendo. So, too, the longing. The desire. The need.

"Hattie," he murmured against her lips. "My sweet, beautiful, Hattie. You do not know what you are asking for."

"Perhaps I do," she said before thinking better of her words.

His head jerked back, gaze searching hers. "I want to be gentle, darling. To ease you into lovemaking. I have never... I do not know how to please a lady."

A virgin, was what he meant. For certainly, he had seduced and bedded more ladies than she cared to count. The rumors and the gossip had cut her. She could not deny that. But it had no place here and now. Tonight was about Hattie and Ewan, not about a wallflower and the Duke of Debauchery.

"I just want you, Ewan," she told him honestly. Earnestly. "Not gentle. Not anything other than you, just as you are. You are the man I wed. You are the man I want."

"Christ." The epithet hissed from his lips, out of place in this moment of carnal surrender. "You do not even know me."

No, she did not, not in the Biblical sense.

But she knew enough. She had known him for years as her brother's trusted friend and confidante, after all.

"I do," she countered, meeting his gaze, doing her best not to fall headlong into it. "I know you are my husband. I know your kisses. Your touch. I know I want you. How can you doubt it?"

"*God's fichu*, Hattie," he growled. "How did you get to be so bloody perfect?"

And then, he was kissing her all over again. Stealing her breath as well. Making her heart pound. Making her longing for him grow until it was a raucous clamor within, drowning out caution and fears. Silencing everything but the desire.

How did *he* get to be so bloody perfect? That was what she wanted to know.

But words were beyond her and unnecessary now. Because he was kissing away everything else. And his hands were busy removing all the rest. Her dressing gown parted to reveal the night rail she wore beneath. Prim and ivory, it was a garment for modesty. Her husband did not seem to mind.

He broke the kiss to gaze at her, the warmth of his hands on her shoulders as he slid the sleeves of her robe down her arms making her shiver. "Are you cold, darling?"

His voice was attentive. Tender. His eyes upon her felt like a caress. Every part of her was all too aware of him. Beneath the weight of that stare, her nipples hardened to puckered beads, stiffly poking the fine fabric of her night rail. Her breasts felt heavy and full, her entire body overcome by a simultaneous yearning and a sweet, heady sense of anticipation caused by his nearness.

"No," she forced herself to answer his question.

He cupped her breast, rubbing his thumb over her nipple in achingly slow, delicious strokes. The ache between her thighs intensified. She pressed them together to stave off the sensation, but it only served to heighten it. She was trapped in his gaze, cocooned in her own desire for him. Molten heat pooled in her core, making her wet.

"You look too damned innocent in this virginal night rail," he said, his voice low. Dark with sensual promise. He plucked at her nipple, caught it in a gentle pinch and tugged. "I am afraid I shall have no choice but to debauch you."

More wicked words from a wicked man. They should not affect her so. Her inner sense of caution warned her that allowing herself to wallow in the intensity of emotions and desire he stirred to life would only make it that much easier for him to break her heart. And not just break it, but smash it into useless little bits.

But she was in his thrall now. Caught in his liquid gaze, his hands upon her. Instead of moving away from him or attempting to quell the need rising like the waters of a flooded river, she stayed where she was. Arched her back, driving her breast into his palm.

He grasped her, making a velvety hum of appreciation. "You want this, sweeting."

It was not a question.

For they both knew he need not pose one.

Just as they both already knew the answer if he would.

"Yes," she said on a sigh.

## CHAPTER 11

Hattie's sweet body had given her away before her words could.

A surge of raw, potent lust hit him. Hardening his already burgeoning cockstand. Drawing his ballocks tight. Turning the blood in his veins to fire. There was something about taking all her virginal innocence and making it his that spurred him in a way no other desire he had ever experienced before had.

Her breast was a warm, tantalizing weight in his palm. He already knew her bosom was generous. All creamy curves tipped with hungry pink nipples to match her lush lips. But knowing she wanted him every bit as much as he wanted her —it was intoxicating.

He had to warn himself, remind himself to proceed with caution. To avoid tearing her modest night rail from her body like some ravening beast. To not simply stake his claim but to make her wild for him. Prolonging this bedding— bringing her pleasure, coaxing her body to life—would lead to a far greater reward than his mind could even comprehend. He was certain of it.

"Take it off," he told her.

She blinked. The passion coursing through her had given her lovely face a dreamy quality. She was relaxed, so very unlike the protesting, prim, proper Hattie she so often showed him and the rest of the world. He rather relished the prospect of being the only one who saw this Hattie.

The passionate lover.

"Your night rail," he elaborated when she seemed to freeze. "Take it off for me, darling. Please. I want to see you. *All* of you."

And he wanted the exquisite pleasure of watching her divest herself of that modest virgin's gown. To see it fall to the floor. To remove every barrier keeping him from his ultimate prize.

There were buttons on the high-necked affair. Her fingers went to them, plucking each from its moorings, one by one. He watched, need pulsing in his loins. He had never thought it possible to find the act of a woman undoing some buttons on spinster's weeds so damned delicious. Then, he was reasonably certain he would find Hattie disrobing erotic even if she were wearing a smelly old horse blanket.

One more button. Her eyes locked to his as her hands fisted the skirt of her gown. He held his breath, wondering if she would have the mettle...

In the next breath, she whipped it over her head, sending it sailing through the air. Of course she had the courage. What the devil had he been thinking? This was Hattie. *His* Hattie. And she had more daring in her little finger than most virginal misses had in their entire bodies.

He drank in the sight of her.

Gorgeous.

Pale curves, long legs, full hips, a waist that emphasized her generous breasts. Lord God, all at once, she was a miracle of womanly decadence. Her ankles were tapered, her calves perfection, her thighs pure beauty, and the mound at the apex...

Need slammed into him.

He could not even speak. Words were beyond him. Curses, prayers, anything—he was speechless. But the yearning for her was relentless. He broke. His hands were on her. Bare, silken skin kissed his palms like a benediction. Such unsullied perfection, kept hidden. Waiting for him. All for him.

He moved them to the bed. All he could think about was kissing her. Tasting every part of her body. He had fucked some of the finest courtesans in London. Women who knew how to intensify a man's need with clever ploys and tricks. Women who knew how to kiss and touch and tantalize. And yet, he had never wanted any of them in the way he wanted Hattie now.

"Ewan," she whispered, her eyes wide, lips parted. Her breath fanned over his mouth. Her hands had settled upon his shoulders, grasping for purchase.

His Christian name on her lips sounded strange and yet... he rather liked it. He liked everything about Hattie. Even her disapproval made him want to fuck her until she was mindless and breathless beneath him. Here was an unexpected development.

He had set out upon the course of marrying Miss Hattie Lethbridge for practical reasons, paying the debts he owed, both to the line and to his friend. But along the way, his need for her had surpassed every other motivation.

And it was his raging need for her that was driving him now.

"On the bed with you, pet," he urged.

She settled her rump upon the edge of the mattress, allowing him to guide her. He had the intense pleasure of framing her glorious hips in his hands until he had her where he wanted her.

"Perfect," he praised. And he meant her positioning as much as he meant her.

He stole another kiss from her beautiful lips. But before he allowed himself to linger for too long, he dragged his mouth downward. Back down that sleek throat. He took care to bite the sensitive nerve he had found before, relishing her breathy gasp and the tightening of her fingers on his shoulders.

"Ewan."

This time, his name emerged in a huskier tone. Part moan.

He vowed inwardly that he would have her screaming his name before this night was through. And it would be the most glorious sound he would ever hope to hear. God, yes.

He inhaled the sweet, innocent scent of her. Clean soap. Woman. Violets. *Good Lord*, when had violets ever been so damned carnal? He did not think he could ever smell their scent again without getting a stiff cock.

Monty played his mouth over her flesh, taking his time. The flutter of her pulse was strong, evidence of her desire along with the way she moved against him, bringing her bare breasts into contact with his chest. Her nipples burned him through the layer of his dressing gown, taunting him.

He had no choice but to work his way to them next. He sucked first one into his mouth, and then the other, bestowing equal attention on both. When he flicked his tongue over the hard bud before catching it in his teeth, she cried out. Her fingers went from his shoulders back to his hair, her nails raking his scalp.

The tender sting made his cock twitch.

*Yes. Oh, yes.* His Hattie was a wanton. He felt certain. And he would unlock her true nature one kiss, one lick, one touch at time. He caressed her thighs, urging them to part. Her initial resistance gave way when he sucked her nipple deep into his mouth once more.

Her legs opened. He stepped into them, and for one awe-inspiring moment, his aching cock was nestled against her mound. Separated by the barrier of his banyan alone. He gritted his teeth as he forced himself to go no further. Tonight was about teaching Hattie about desire. About making her want him as much as he wanted her. About taking her to the razor's edge and giving her a first true taste of passion.

He kissed the curve of her breast, murmuring his approval and appreciation. And then he withdrew just enough to sink to his knees on the plush carpet, her cunny was before him. Pink glistening flesh, blossoming like a flower, shielded by a satiny nest of dark curls. The scent of her, musky, sweet, earthen, reached him.

Need pounded through him.

"You cannot mean to..." Hattie was speaking. Protesting. Not bold enough to give voice to what he was about to do to her.

"Taste your cunny? Bring you pleasure? Lick you until you spend on my tongue?" he asked, being deliberately coarse, for part of the raging need inside him was founded in his complete claiming of her innocence in every way. "Yes, I absolutely can, my sweet. And I will. And you shall like it. I promise."

"But Ewan..."

All her protests died a swift death when he flicked his tongue over her pearl.

"Oh," she gasped.

*Oh, indeed.* The taste of her was decadent and rich, and he lapped her up as if she were the finest spirit, the most decadent dessert. Because she was all that and more. She was wet already, so perfect. He sucked the responsive bud of her sex as he had her nipples, gratified when she shifted instinctively on the bed, bringing her nearer.

But this was not enough. Still, he wanted more. He slid his hands under her bottom, filling his palms, and adjusted her angle as he teased her. Slow, steady licks alternated with fast pulses. He used his teeth to gently score the sensitive underside before running his tongue down her seam.

He could not resist penetrating her with his tongue. He dipped into her channel, humming with appreciation as her tight, wet heat greeted him. His cock throbbed with anticipation. God, he could not wait to sink deep inside her. This seduction was fast becoming a game of sensual torture. It was anyone's guess which of them would be first to succumb.

She was delicious, her dew coating his lips, his tongue. Her soft thighs cocooned his face. Her breathy gasps of appreciation spurred him on. He licked deeper, inhaling deeply of the musky scent of her excitement. She was moving against him now, her body undulating, and he knew she was getting close to release. He returned his attentions to her pearl, drawing her into his mouth. Ever so gently, he bit.

The husky cry of her spend echoed in the chamber as her body stiffened beneath him. She shuddered, her fingers once more in his hair, gripping with painful pleasure as she rode out the waves of pleasure. He waited until the last tremor radiated through her, doing everything he could to prolong the moment. Finally, he pressed a worshipful kiss to her mound, then stood.

She was like a dream, his wicked innocent perched on the bed, legs still open. Her hands ran down his chest, caressing. Her eyes were wide pools of emerald fire. He could still taste her on his tongue. He was as jaded a lover as could be when it came to bed sport, but Hattie was the most erotic sight he had ever beheld.

"Oh, Ewan," she said softly, sliding her hands inside his banyan to reach his bare skin, "that was…"

Her cheeks flared with a pretty pink as she struggled to finish her thought. As far as he was concerned, there were no words which could suffice.

"Yes. It was." He settled himself between her thighs once more, still standing, his cock hungry and hard and longing to be buried inside her.

*Slow, old chap*, he warned himself.

*Slow and steady.*

But then her nails raked over his nipple, and a fierce arrow of need shot to his ballocks. He groaned, his hands on her, devouring the smoothness of her warm skin, traveling the curve of her waist, lifting the curtain of her long, dark hair aside so he could caress up her back. His fingers found the strength of her spine. He did not think he could ever tire of touching her.

He kissed her neck, her ear.

"I want to see you, Ewan," she whispered.

*Hellfire.*

She was already pulling the twain ends of his dressing robe apart. He reached between them to help her, the silk falling from his body as he bit her earlobe. "You are glorious."

Adding action to his words, he cupped her breast, rubbed his thumb over the hard peak. She inhaled, tipping her head back as he kissed down her throat. She smelled so damn good here, and he thought he could spend all day worshiping the graceful column. Or the pronounced slash of her delicate collarbone. Or the elegant space where her neck and shoulder met.

*Slow*, he cautioned himself again. But it would not be easy. It was as if he had unleashed a sensual tigress. Hattie's hands were all over him, learning his chest, his back. She gripped his buttocks. Leaned forward and kissed his chest, directly over his stupidly thudding heart.

"You are more glorious," she declared, her voice low and sultry.

Her fingers dug into his arse. His hips canted forward. His cock nestled in her dew-slicked folds, and it required every bit of his sanity to keep him from driving home.

He kissed his way across her smooth, rounded shoulder, then gave it a bite. She filled him with a curious combination of ravening beast and tender lover. He wanted to possess her, to claim her, to fuck her until she screamed. But he also wanted to kiss her, to hold her close, to cherish her.

Rather than dwell upon it, he planted a slow path of kisses down her arm. She continued her exploration, touching up his back to his shoulders. The way she explored him took his breath. Almost brought him to his knees. For she caressed him with a reverence he had never known. She touched him as if she cared for him.

How could it be possible that a man who had bedded more lovers than he could even recall would be undone by a virgin? *Impossible*, said his pride. Yet, he could not deny the response her tenderness won. The need to be inside her bore down upon him with such force, he had to grind his molars to keep from spending then and there, on her thigh instead of inside his wife.

His wife.

*Ah, yes.* She was his, was she not?

Time to make that true in deed as well as word.

"Lie on the bed for me, pet," he told her, giving her a lingering caress before disengaging and taking a step back.

Her pupils were huge. The musk of her desire tinged the air. She knew what he was asking. The time had come to claim her. To consummate their union. Wordlessly, she slid onto the bed, doing as he commanded.

He was upon her in an instant, wedging his big body between her pale thighs. Spreading them. He lowered himself over her, stopping to kiss and suck the offerings of her pretty pink nipples. As he leveraged his weight on one arm, he gripped his cock in the other. He glanced over her folds once, then twice.

She sighed in contentment, moving against him, nestling him deeper. He rewarded them both by teasing her pearl with the tip of his shaft as his tongue flicked over her nipple. Then he kissed his way back to her throat. Her hands had settled upon his shoulders once more, holding him to her. Her small fingers were tense, biting into his muscles, her nails digging in.

She felt so damn good. So hot, so wet. She felt like home. Like forever.

But that was probably just the delirious fever of lust infecting his brain. He had not bedded anyone since the accident, since his decision to make Hattie his wife. Taking himself in hand to thoughts of her had not been enough. And now that he at long last had her precisely where he wanted her, he was thinking with his cock.

Yes, that was it.

That was all.

He had worked his way to her throat. And then he could not resist kissing her sweet, kiss-swollen lips. The kiss turned open-mouthed and demanding, their tongues slid against each other as she made soft sounds of need, her body writhing against his, seeking another release. Her uninhibited eagerness was the greatest aphrodisiac. He could still taste her, and he knew she must taste herself in the kiss also. He wanted her to. He wanted her wicked and helpless, ruled by desire.

Just as he was.

His ability to last was diminishing by the second. He

guided himself to her entrance, and the head of his cock was caressed by her heat. She was even wetter now, slick with need. And she was all his.

He broke the kiss. "Are you ready for me, darling?"

"Yes," she whispered.

He eased himself inside. She was tight, her channel gripping him, almost squeezing him out. "Breathe," he told her. "Relax."

Then he kissed her again. His fingers dipped into her sex, finding that exquisite center of her desire. He teased her gently as he thrust. The pleasure was intense, slamming into him with so much force, he almost forgot to breathe himself. The tension ebbed away from her body, and he felt her inner muscles relax. He moved again, seating himself even deeper.

There was the slight resistance, she tightened on him again, her body stiffening. A gasp from her lips. His name.

"Ewan. I…"

He would never know what she had been about to say next, because need was roaring through him. His body took control. He thrust. One long pump, and he was all the way inside her. So deep inside her. Her welcoming heat embraced him, and dear sweet God, he never wanted to leave her body.

He kissed her languorously. White-hot pleasure shimmered through him. His body was on fire. Need for her was more potent than anything he had ever consumed in an effort to render himself mindless. She was all he could feel, taste, see, hear, breathe. Everything. And though he claimed her body with his, she did the same with hers.

Pleasure owned him.

He lost control. It was impossible to stay still. He was moving within her now, long, deep thrusts. Measured at first, and then uncontrolled. Wild and frenzied. Again and again.

He tore his lips from hers, his breaths harsh and ragged.

Torn from him like his desperate command. "Come for me, pet. Come on my cock."

He circled her pearl with two fingers, increasing his pace and pressure, thrusting in and out of her. On a dazed cry, she gave him what he wanted, her complete surrender. Her body bowed from the bed, head rolling back into the mountain of pillows and the wild nest of her dark curls. Her cunny gripped him, dragging him deep.

As her spend rocked through her, the rein on his control snapped. He could not prolong this bliss a moment more. The violence of his own release took him by surprise. It was as if lightning cracked. Heat licked down his spine. His ballocks drew tight. His entire body seized with the feverish swell of his climax. He spilled himself inside her.

CHAPTER 12

Hattie sipped her tea. Alone, save for Sir Toby, who was curled upon her lap and happily purring away as he dozed. She wished she could summon even an inkling of the feline's easy contentment. Montrose's mother had left for the country in an effort, Hattie supposed, to give the newlyweds some time alone. The sudden nature of their nuptials meant no honeymoon had been planned.

As far as she knew, Montrose intended to remain in London. But then, there was so much of Montrose and his plans that remained a mystery. This morning was no different. She had woken in her rumpled bed. Also alone, save for the scent of him upon her sheets and the incendiary memory of his lovemaking.

Later that morning, she had broken her fast. Once more alone, save for Sir Toby, who ate his kippers with greedy relish on the floor at her side.

The ormolu clock on the mantel, with its golden eagle about to take flight perched atop, mocked her with each tick. It was just after two o'clock in the afternoon. She replaced her teacup upon its saucer with less care than she should have. Some of the liquid, now tepid, sloshed over the gilt-lipped rim.

Her initial disappointment at her husband's absence, following a night that had left her forever changed, was transforming with each passing minute into a different emotion entirely.

Anger.

Low, the Hamilton House butler, appeared at the threshold of the cheerful salon where she had decided to take her tea. He was not unfamiliar to her, as she and Montrose's sister, Catriona, were as close as sisters. But in spite of the previous occasions when she had come calling, and in spite of her new position as mistress of the house, he remained as stiff-backed and expressionless as a marble statue.

"How may I be of service to you, Your Grace?" he asked now as if she had not already called for him half a dozen times that morning.

"Has His Grace risen yet?" she asked, not even bothering to disguise her query this time.

Her tact was fast waning, much like her patience.

Last night, Ewan had made love to her so fiercely and passionately, she had fallen into a delicious, sated slumber with him at her side. Her heart had been bursting with love, her body humming with the newfound pleasures and hungers he had awoken within her. And then she had blinked her eyes open to early-morning gold slashing through the window dressings, her bed empty.

He had left her in the night.

"His Grace has yet to leave his chamber, Your Grace," Low informed her.

Once more, she made no effort to pretty her request. "Does His Grace often rise late, Low?"

"His Grace's schedule is at his discretion," the butler offered.

Oh, this fellow would be indomitable at cards. His countenance was carefully blank. The absurd urge to ruffle his feathers struck her, but she supposed that would not provide her with answers or an understanding of the man she had married. Nor would it solve any of her problems.

"I understand, Low." She scratched Sir Toby's soft head between his perky little ears, trying to calm herself. "What you are saying is that His Grace does not generally rise early."

He inclined his head. "I would not presume to say so, Your Grace. Would Sir Toby care for a snack? Monsieur Tremblay has set aside some livers for him."

Now, she understood the loyal retainer was attempting to distract her. But there truly was no means of forgetting the fact that her husband appeared to have been sleeping for far more hours than was ordinary. Or that he had left her alone last night. Or that it was clear he had not felt what they had shared last night as keenly as she had.

Had she expected any less? He had warned her, had he not? And she knew he was an experienced rakehell. Of course, the Duke of Debauchery would not find the act of making love with his wife transforming. What a simple, stupid woman she was. How foolish, how naïve, to have supposed for even an instant that he would have been as moved as she had been.

After all, it had been the first time she had ever made love. But for Montrose, it must have been a tired old chore by now. Bedding his wallflower wife surely paled in comparison to the pleasures he indulged in with experienced demi-mondaines.

"Your Grace?" Low prodded, frowning.

Pulling her from her vicious musings.

She stood, carrying Sir Toby in her arms. "That will be all, Low. Thank you. Sir Toby will be accompanying me. Please do convey my gratitude to Monsieur Trembley, and ask him to send them up in about an hour, if you please."

Low bowed. "Of course, Your Grace."

She swept out of the salon with Sir Toby, determined that her time of waiting and politely inquiring after her husband must come to an end. She was going to beard the lion in his den, as it were. Up the steps she went. Sir Toby protested on her march down the hall, wriggling and attempting to escape. Perhaps he could sense her ire.

Hattie made her way to her apartments, still feeling a bit as if she were trespassing in a stranger's home. Though her belongings had been settled in yesterday, neither the chamber nor Hamilton House felt like hers.

Nor did the master of the house, she thought grimly as she crossed the threshold, closing the door at her back lest Sir Toby attempt to wander. She did not trust the domestics enough yet to allow him free reign of the house. She settled him upon his bed and rubbed his head.

"There you are, my little cherub," she cooed. "Be a good lad."

Sir Toby watched her with his knowing gaze. One more scratch of his soft head, and she rose. Because Sir Toby was a cat, he had left his smaller bed in favor of making himself at home on hers before she had even made it halfway across the chamber.

But she had other matters to distract herself with now.

Namely, a husband who had seemingly disappeared.

She stopped at the door adjoining their chambers, wondering for a moment at the wisdom of invading his private space. She had only seen his chamber briefly the day before during her official tour of Hamilton House as the new Duchess of Montrose. Her impression had been that it was a starkly masculine space, filled with heavy, dark furniture.

There was no hope for it, she told herself. If she wanted

to see him at all today, she was going to have to venture over the unseen boundaries between them. Moreover, she could not shake the concern pricking at her mind, that sleeping so late was unusual. The servants did not seem surprised by his behavior, which meant it was likely a regular occurrence.

But why?

There had been no gin on his lips last night when he had kissed her. Indeed, the only taste on his mouth had been her, and the shocking, raw intimacy of the act still made her cheeks heat today when she thought of what he had done to her.

And how very much she had liked it.

*Do not think of wickedness now*, she chided herself. *You have a lion to beard.*

Firm in her decision, she opened the door. The first thing that struck her was the darkness within Montrose's personal realm. The window dressings had yet to be drawn back to admit the afternoon's sun. Or at least what remained of it, since a slow drizzle had begun to fall earlier that morning and had yet to relinquish its grasp.

The second thing she noticed was the silence, which told her that her husband was yet abed. Shoulders back, determination weighing her down, she crossed the threshold, breaching his lair. The previous day's abbreviated tour had not provided her much of an opportunity to familiarize herself with the layout of his chamber.

As she had no candle, she was forced to rely upon other senses as she slowly felt her way toward the windows. A thin slat of light was visible through a lone gap in the curtains, and she moved toward it.

And straight into a quite immovable piece of furniture.

Her knee connected with something wooden, sending pain shooting up her leg. She could not stifle her cry of pain.

She doubled over, rubbing the smarting area through the layers of her gown and petticoats.

Low masculine murmurings emerged from deeper within the chamber.

She recognized that voice, even if he was clearly still asleep, her clumsiness only partially having dragged him from the arms of Queen Mab. It was her husband's. *Ewan's*. Drat her foolish, traitorous body for the heat the mere sound of his voice and the thought of his name inspired in her.

She tamped it down. Thrust it aside. Cast it away.

Or at least, she tried. In the end, she had no choice but to inwardly seize her vexation with both hands and continue on toward the window. When she reached it at last, she drew back the thick curtains, allowing murky, gray light to billow into the room.

"There," she pronounced, deciding half the window dressings would do. All she required was enough illumination to locate her husband and to convince him it was time to wake.

At long last.

When she turned away from the window, however, she was wholly unprepared for the sight that greeted her. Ewan was sprawled in the bed, the bedclothes bunched around his lean waist, hooked over his hip. His chest was bare. And even in repose, fast asleep, he stole her breath.

He was beautiful. But so very still.

She moved toward him, drawn, as always in spite of her better intentions. She had meant to calmly wake him with a safe distance betwixt them. However, her feet were already moving. Taking her nearer. Ever closer to danger.

"Ewan," she called softly.

In sleep, he almost looked boyish. His face was relaxed, his beautiful mahogany hair swept away from his brow. There was none of the cagey, predatory rakehell about his countenance now. Instead, there was a surprising innocence. He looked almost sweet.

A surge of protectiveness beat to life in her breast. How she loved this man, even while she knew she should not. Although every part of her knew he would never love her. If she had harbored any silly notions he would change after their wedding, or even after the consummation of their marriage, he had dispelled them by his actions in the aftermath.

Strangely, she could not seem to summon up the necessary anger. He had stirred when she called his name, but his eyes remained closed. Now, he rubbed his chest slowly. Lazily. She watched, envying his hand as he made a low sound in his throat. His hand glided over the muscled bands of his abdomen, then lower, sliding beneath the sheet.

*Oh, dear Lord.*

He let out an appreciative moan.

She knew precisely what he was touching. As if she had been cast into flames, she jerked to life. "Ewan! It is time for you to wake and cease lolling about in bed."

There. She had even sounded stern. *Very much like a duchess*, she thought.

His eyes were closed. A disarming half grin crooked his lips. "Mmm. Hattie, love. Bring that sweet cunny over here and sit on my face, won't you? I want you to come on my tongue as you ride me. I'll lick you until you scream."

His words shocked her. Alarmed her. Shamed her.

*Intrigued* her.

Her cheeks burned. Her ears, too. She was certain this was not the proper way a husband ought to speak to his wife. But she was also certain the wickedness he was sleepily suggesting would be the sort she would enjoy, especially after last night.

*No*, she reminded herself sternly. You will not allow your

baser nature to lull you into forgetting he left your chamber and has been sleeping all day. Nor will you allow it to make you forget he warned you he will never love you.

She cleared her throat. Banished the sinful images he had brought to life. "Ewan. Your Grace. It is time to wake. It is nearly half past two."

It was possible she exaggerated about the time. Certainly, she did not think it could have taken her half an hour to find her way upstairs, settle Sir Toby in her chamber, and slam her knee into his writing desk. At the thought of her unfortunate collision, her knee ached anew.

His hand, much to her horror—and secret delight, it was true—began to move beneath the bedclothes. His eyes, however, remained closed.

"Ewan," she prodded.

"Or would you prefer to sit on my randy cock instead?"

*Dear. Sweet. Heavens.*

She was going to have to do something. To rouse him using some other means. She looked about for an alternative and discovered an ewer on the table alongside his bed nearest to her. In three strides, she could reach it. She grasped the handle and lifted it.

Tilted it.

Poured a splash of water directly upon his gorgeous, rakish head.

He sputtered and sat up, wiping water from his eyes. "Wainwroth, you whoreson! What do you think you are doing?"

Wainwroth was his unfortunate valet. And once more, Hattie's ears were burning because of her husband's vulgar tongue.

"It is not Wainwroth, Your Grace. It is your wife," she told him coolly, replacing the ewer upon the table.

His warm eyes opened, pinning her to where she stood as they sent a shock of awareness straight to her core.

Asleep, he had been precious. Awake, he was the picture of sinister masculine beauty. Though his dark hair was slicked over his head from the water she had poured upon him, it did nothing to detract from his dark looks. He melted her from the inside out.

But she must be made of sterner stuff.

"Hattie," he said warmly, her name alone the verbal equivalent of a seductive caress.

Blast him.

She dipped into a mocking curtsey. "You remember me. I suppose I must be grateful for small mercies."

He frowned at her, scrubbing a hand over his face to remove the lingering traces of moisture. "Of course, I remember you. I married you just yesterday, if you will but recall."

"I recall all too well." Feeling as if she were at a dreadful disadvantage with his naked chest on display before her and her stupid heart beating so painfully fast, she moved a few paces away from him. Distance, in this instance, was surely safer than proximity. "I am merely surprised you do. After all, you disappeared last night, and despite this being my first day here at Hamilton House as your duchess, you have not even deigned to rise from bed though it is nearly three o'clock."

"I thought you said it was half past two," he countered.

The conniving rakehell.

She glared at him. "When did you wake?"

"I believe it was when you crashed into the writing desk." He gave her an arrogant grin. "I am shocked to hear my lady wife utter such unbecoming obscenities."

All she had said was *bloody hell*, which of course she had learned from Torrie. Back when Torrie had been, well, himself. The reminder of her brother's memory loss sent a sharp arrow of sadness through her. Yet another reason why she must not trust the half-naked duke before her, in spite of her heart. And whether or not he was her husband.

"You said far worse," she was quick to remind him. Moreover, he had intentionally said those wicked things, knowing she would overhear.

"I confess, I enjoy watching a flush creep over your pretty skin, pet." His tone, like his countenance, was unrepentant.

He was enjoying this. Lying abed like some satyr. Her gaze wandered to the bedclothes, and she could not help but to wonder if he was entirely nude beneath them. Something told her the answer was yes. She cursed the longing that uncoiled in her belly, the wetness pooling between her thighs.

All the memories of the night before spilling over her like the raging rush of a waterfall. She was vexed with him, wary of him, charmed by him, suspicious of him. At once.

"Why did you leave me in the night?" she asked, and hated the neediness of her voice.

He extended his hand to her. "Come, darling. Join me."

She was sure she should not heed him. But her feet were moving. Taking her to him. Gingerly, she accepted his hand, cursing the sparks that skittered up her arm at the contact. Becoming his wife, lying with him, had not changed the attraction burning between them. If anything, it had fanned the flames.

He took her by surprise when he gave a sudden tug. She lost her balance and fell across his lap. Grinning down at her, he arranged her so she was on her back, gazing up at him.

"You tricked me," she accused without heat.

For she could not truly be upset to be near him, cradled in his big body. In his bed. The rumpled counterpane smelled of him. A lock of hair fell over his brow, and an unexpected tenderness burst open. She reached up, brushing it to the side.

He caught her hand and raised it to his lips, kissing her fingertips. "I hardly tricked you. I merely made you more comfortable. Settled you where you belong."

She did not want his silver-tongued charm to woo her. And yet, when he told her she belonged with him, in his arms, how could she resist? She traced the sullen curve of his upper lip with the pad of her forefinger. "You are aiming to distract me."

His lips quirked. "Is it working?"

Of course it was. The Duke of Montrose was the epitome of charm when he wished to be. In the past, she had not often been the recipient of that charm. Now, she could not help but to feel a keen prick of jealousy for every woman he had smiled at thus before her. And for every woman he would one day ply with his charms when he had tired of her.

For theirs was to be a standard society marriage, she reminded herself sternly. He had already warned her so. He would have his heir and then his freedom, as would she. But lying here in his bed, the heat of his body seeping into her skin, his mouth beneath her questing fingertips, freedom from him was the last thing she wanted.

"You cannot fool me," she told him softly. "You never have."

The smile fled his lips, and his jaw hardened, those changeable brown eyes darkening. "On the contrary, pet. I fool everyone, including you. You would do best to remember that."

For a moment, she spied the shadows he kept hidden from the world. His mask of seductive, devil-may-care scoundrel slipped. She wondered what secrets he kept. Wondered if she would ever slip past his walls to the true Ewan.

She was not going to allow him to warn her off, however. Until she bore him an heir, he was hers. Alone. She trailed her touch over his jaw, the prickle of his morning whiskers a delight to her senses.

"You do not frighten me, Ewan." She cupped his cheek, love for him beating with a life of its own in her heart.

How much easier their marriage would be to navigate if he did not own her heart so completely. But she could not change the way she felt. Her feelings were a part of her, even as she had done her best to keep them from overruling her.

"I should frighten you," he said. "I am far too much of a sinner for a glorious angel such as you. But like any rakehell, I am also selfish enough to make you mine anyway."

He had made her his, in word and deed yesterday. The knowledge hummed through her. How did he do this to her? Make her weak? Make her forget all her earlier ire and irritation? Strip from her every last defense she had against him?

"I do not think you are nearly as bad a man as you paint yourself to be." She paused, studying his face, part of her rejoicing that she could be here with him like this, in his bed, in his arms. That he was *hers* just as surely as she was his.

He remained unsmiling, and beneath her touch, his jaw clenched. "I am everything you have heard about me, all the rumors and the gossip, and worse, Hattie. I will not pretend I am anything other than who I am. This is the man you married, irredeemable sot who sleeps until the day is half done."

She did not like the manner in which he spoke about himself. "If I thought you irredeemable, I never would have agreed to wed you."

"You see?" His tone was wry. "Only an angel would think a devil like me redeemable."

She did not think he was a devil. Not at all. She thought

he was a man who hid his pain well. A man with secrets. Could she learn them? Did she dare?

She should not dare. She should guard her heart instead. Yet, he called to her now, more than ever. He had been inside her last night. They had been as close as man and woman could be.

"You do not look like a devil now, Ewan," she said, caressing his cheek.

"I feel like one with you in my arms, in my bed." His gaze dipped to her lips.

Beneath her, she felt the rigid evidence of his desire. "Ewan," she whispered. "It is the midst of the day."

"Who gives a damn?" he asked, and then his mouth was on hers.

His kiss was slow. Velvet and silk. He coaxed her to open, thrusting his fingers into her hair, holding her still for his ravishment. But he need not worry. She was not going anywhere. He held her helplessly in his thrall, as ever.

Her tongue met his. This kiss was not just a meeting of mouths. It was not just about seduction. It was a possession, thorough, scorching. He deepened it, kissing her as if he meant to consume. Kissed her until she was dizzy. Until passion once more beckoned. Until she was desperate for him to be inside her again.

Her core ached. She shifted her bottom, pressed her thighs together. The movement only served to wedge his hard length precisely where she wanted it. Such a pity bedclothes and her layers separated them. A deep groan hummed from his throat.

He broke the kiss, caught her lower lip in his teeth, then tugged. "What do you say to my initial offer, Hattie darling?"

It was difficult indeed to think whilst his mouth was so near. While he was doing such wicked things to her. While his cock was a stiff promise of sensual fulfillment beneath her. He kissed first one corner of her lips, then the other. What had he asked? She struggled to recall.

Ah yes, his offer.

He kissed the bow of her upper lip, traced the seam of her mouth with his tongue before dipping inside for another slow, thorough kiss.

What had it been?

*Oh, dear heavens.* He had asked her to sit on his face. The scandalous rakehell. The utter knave. If only the heat burning through her was outrage instead of curious hunger. As he kissed her, the buttons on the back of her gown were coming open. Sliding from their moorings.

More proof he was the devil he claimed to be, she supposed, intending to debauch her in the midst of the day when all of the servants would surely know what they were about. Thank heavens the dowager duchess was not currently in residence.

But before they could progress, the door to the chamber opened. Some part of Hattie's passion-fogged brain acknowledged the sound. The rest of her, however, could not be bothered to care.

Until a throat cleared.

Hattie jerked her mouth from Ewan's on a shocked gasp. Her eyes flew to the threshold, where his valet stood.

"Forgive me, Your Grace," he said, sounding unexpectedly ruffled by the sight that was greeting him. "I did not realize Your Graces were both within."

And, *oh*, what a sight it must be, the new duchess sprawled across the duke's lap. In *flagrante delicto*. Her buttons undone. Mouth swollen from kisses. She was sure she was missing a hairpin or two...

Ewan was first to recover. He offered the valet an easy smile, as though he were interrupted in just such a thing quite regularly. And perhaps he was, though she could not bear to contemplate it.

"No trouble, Wainwroth," he said cheerfully. "A tray would be just the thing, if you can manage it. Do knock first, however."

"I will see your customary repast brought. Tea and laudanum as well, Your Grace?" Wainwroth asked, averting his gaze from Hattie.

Out of respect, she supposed. Mortification made her cheeks suffuse with color. All the passion that had been clouding her judgment moments ago was dashed, as much by the unexpected presence of the servant in the chamber as by his mention of laudanum.

"The usual, yes," Ewan clipped. "That will be all, Wainwroth."

"Of course, Your Grace." On a bow, the valet made his hasty exit, leaving Hattie and her husband alone once more.

She turned to him, misgiving blossoming like an unwanted flower. "Why are you taking laudanum with your tea?"

His well-sculpted lips flattened. "My ankle pains me. The laudanum dulls the endless ache."

She thought upon his response. He did occasionally favor the ankle he had broken, it was true. But he had been eschewing his walking stick. He had also demonstrated many feats of dexterity over the past few weeks. His need for laudanum did not make sense.

"And yet you climbed a tree to get into my window," she pointed out. "You have not even been carrying your walking stick."

Her hands had migrated to his shoulders, and she felt them tense now.

"As I said, it pains me. Do cease your inquisition, Wife. I

already have one mother who is a deuced bore, and I most certainly do not require another."

His words stung.

The moment between them was effectively ruined. She scrambled from his lap and the bed, not liking the way he had changed so suddenly. It was as if a door had been slammed, and she was on one side, he on the other.

"Forgive me, Your Grace," she managed, attempting to gather the shreds of her dignity. "I would not dare to burden you. If you will excuse me, I am certain there are any number of household matters awaiting my attention."

That was a lie, for the staff had been dancing around her all morning. It was clear they considered the dowager the lady of the house, and even in Ewan's mother's absence, Hattie felt like an impostor. She felt as though she were playing at duchess. But no one could make her feel quite as low as her own husband just had.

"Hattie," he said, protest in his voice.

But she was not about to allow him to cozen her back into his lap. Nor would she be partaking in any more of his drugging kisses. He could not kiss her, make love to her, and then treat her as if she were a stranger for daring to ask him a simple question.

She curtseyed, unsmiling, doing her best to ward off a rush of tears pricking her eyes. It would not do to weep before him. And her emotions were foolish, she knew. Just as foolish as the rest of her was. He had warned her. For all her protestations, he was redeemable, here was evidence their union would not be an easy one.

Ewan had secrets and demons, but he had no intention of sharing them with her. That much was painfully, heart-wrenchingly clear.

## CHAPTER 13

Monty stared at the stacks of correspondence haphazardly strewn upon his desk and longed for a drink. Or some laudanum. He truly was getting itchy over it. The need was like an infection, curdling his blood. All because he had eschewed his morning ritual of a drop in his tea.

Because of Hattie.

His *wife*.

The memory of her questioning green eyes haunted him now, even more than the alluring promise of the laudanum he had foregone. She had wanted to know about the laudanum. Why he was taking it in his tea.

And he, heartless bastard that he was, had chased her away. They had been sharing a moment of exquisite passion. He had been jarred from sweet dreams of fucking his wife to the sound of said wife colliding with his writing desk.

Her muttered oath had made his already-hard cock even more rigid and ready for her. Teasing her had been too tempting to resist. There were words he might say under the guise of sleep which he would not have dared—debauched though he was—to utter to a lady.

He had been testing her, it was true. And she had passed. His Hattie was a wanton. She had been nettled by his morning—er, afternoon—torpor. He was not accustomed to having to answer to anyone. He was the Duke of bloody Montrose. The master of his household. He did as he pleased.

He told himself that was the reason for his curt words to Hattie earlier and not the intense desire to protect his laudanum consumption. And then he told himself he was a worthless, damned liar.

Everything he had said to her, every cutting word, had been a direct result of the need to continue on with his opium. The opium calmed him better than gin. It also brought him a more delicious level of oblivion. It enabled him to sleep through the night. Even better, Hattie could not smell it on his breath.

It had been her previous words to him concerning the spirits on his lips that had led him to decrease his reliance upon swizzle. He had no wish to die of barrel fever, after all. Especially now that he had undertaken the responsibility of a wife.

A decrease in gin, however, had seen an increase in laudanum. Particularly at night. After he had made love to Hattie, he had waited until she had fallen into a peaceful sleep. And then he had returned to his own chamber.

Just a drop, he had reassured himself. Only to help him sleep. If he was slumbering soundly, he had reasoned, he could not wake her with his nightmares. But one drop had turned into two, and finally oblivion had claimed him. As always, he had not wanted to wake this morning. Indeed, he had slept soundly, the sleep of the dead, until dawn. At which point, he had promptly taken himself in hand to thoughts of his beautiful wife, too sluggish to get out of his bed and find her in her chamber, before falling asleep once more.

Now, as he stared at all the epistles he had neglected over the last several months, he had to admit, Hattie was right. He ought to have read his damned letters. He had been neglecting far too much. Though he had entrusted the running of his holdings to his stewards, he was remiss not to involve himself directly. Not to take more care in the management of his estates. Not to take more care in the correspondence his own sister had sent him.

He was going to be an uncle, and he had not known. He still had no inkling as to when the happy event was to occur. He supposed he ought to have asked his mother, but talking to the woman inevitably ended in a harangue, and he had no wish to listen to her nattering.

He drummed his fingertips upon his desk. The blasted thing was covered in a fine sheen of dust because he had forbidden the housemaids from entering. His excuse was that his study was his private domain, the one place aside from his bedchamber where he could truly feel at home. In truth, it was where he preferred to drink. Often until he passed out.

He had spent many a night sprawled on his chair, only to wake with a thundering headache and a mouth that felt as if it had been packed with cotton batting.

*God's fichu*, what was the matter with him? Had he learned nothing from the night he had pulled himself from the wreckage of his phaeton? Hattie had been right to question him earlier. Right to wonder why he was yet abed at half past two in the afternoon.

On a sigh of disgust, he began with the nearest stack of correspondence, opening them, conducting a cursory search, sorting. Scottish estate matters on the left. His sister Cat on the right. In the middle, business matters.

He had hurt her with his stupid words earlier as well. The knowledge did not sit well with him. Instead of making love to her as he had been about to do, instead of kissing her sweet lips and undoing the rest of her buttons, he had chased her away. Sent her running from his chamber with the back of her bodice gaping open from his thwarted efforts.

What a cad. A worthless scoundrel. He had warned her, had he not, that he was the devil? Foolish chit refused to believe him. Called him redeemable. He had not done so yet. Did she truly think he could change? Nothing could remove the scars from his soul, the darkness from his heart. Nothing had ever squelched the nightmares that claimed him in the night.

Nothing except for the poison he poured down his gullet, that was.

And she thought she might change him? Not bloody possible. She would see, soon. Recognize his worthlessness.

But he ought to find her. Apologize. The rest of these letters could wait...

Just as the thought occurred to him, he unfolded a letter penned in a familiar, dreaded scrawl. Hands shaking, an icy sword of dread stabbing him in the gut, he read. The sight of the penmanship alone was enough to bring back the ghosts. To take him back to that dark day.

He read on, rage warring with pain. That old feeling of helplessness was back, but he would not allow it to win. Rising, he crumpled the letter. Arthur Parkross could go to the devil with a burdened soul as far as he was concerned.

Monty stalked across the chamber and tore the letter to shreds before tossing it into the fire. The pieces turned to ash in the flame as he watched, hands clenched impotently at his sides. And just like the letter, Parkross could burn in the eternal flames of hell.

Jaw clenched, hatred churning in his gut, he stalked from

the study and called for his carriage. What he needed right now was to escape and to slam his fists into something. Anything. Anyone. Gentleman Jackson's would do. And he needed a laudanum negus, which he knew he could procure at a seedy little East End hell with relative ease.

Violence.

Distraction.

Forgetting.

Stupor.

That was what he craved.

*You also crave your wife*, taunted an evil voice inside himself.

He banished the voice, donned his greatcoat and hat, and fled, much like his wife had run from his chamber mere hours before. The only difference between them was he did not know who he was running from more—himself or her. Hattie, however? She had been undeniably running from him.

And he could not blame her one whit.

\* \* \*

HATTIE WAS DOING her utmost to find a means of distraction. Following her solitary dinner, she had abandoned half a dozen books purloined from the library and now piled on the floor by the hearth chaise. None of them had proven amusing or intriguing enough to hold her interest.

She had bathed. It should have had a soothing effect upon her ragged nerves. Instead, the solitude had only proven an opportunity to further wallow in her own misery. Now, she was busying herself with studying every aspect of the duchess's chamber, from the green-papered walls to the equally verdant bed hangings and window dressings.

There was an abundance of gilt. One satinwood writing

desk. A table with a looking glass set upon it. A miniature statue of Ceres, the goddess of agriculture, stood on the mantel, watching her through sightless, marble eyes. Mocking her, she thought. For the only seed to be sown in Hamilton House was enmity.

Hers for Ewan, and his for hers. Already, she was regretting her hasty decision to agree to become his wife. In the span of a single day, everything she had feared had already come to fruition. She loved Ewan more than ever after she had given herself to him.

Her new husband, meanwhile, had returned to his old ways.

Heavens, what was she thinking? He had never even *left* his old ways. Yesterday, he had married her, bedded her, and then proceeded to sleep half the day away. The first drink he consumed when he woke was tea laced with laudanum. Hattie was not as naïve as Montrose would perhaps prefer to believe. She had heard stories of opium eaters, and she knew the ruin which inevitably came to their lives.

Her fear that he had become far too reliant upon laudanum had been confirmed by her dogged determination to interview some of his domestics. Though they were loyal retainers and feared for repercussions from their master should they be completely honest, she had been able to ferret out enough truth.

Hattie paced the length of her chamber for what must have been the hundredth time. Her back ached, her body throbbed in places she had not previously been aware existed, her feet hurt, and her heart was battered and bruised. Ewan had spent much of the day following their clash locked away in his study. When he had emerged, it had been to immediately leave in his carriage without even offering her an explanation as to where he was going or when he may return.

If ever.

Though she supposed she was being dramatic in such a thought. He had not given any indication he would abandon her. But then, he *was* the Duke of Debauchery. He had earned his moniker by years of misspent living. Endless mistresses and dissipation. Enough overindulgence to rival a despotic king. He was wild, untamable, reckless.

None of those traits were what had drawn her to him. Rather, it was all the parts of himself he did not often allow the world to see, the vulnerabilities hiding beneath his handsome, brash exterior. On the rare occasions when their paths had crossed, he had always been attentive. Unlike most gentlemen who did not bother to hear what she said, or only droned on about themselves and their estates, he had always *listened*. He had tried hard to win her laughter.

She thought about the moment she had fallen in love with him. It had been the Stanhope ball. She had been attempting to avoid the odious Sir George Bainbridge, who had been thrice her age and seeking a broodmare in the December of his life, when Montrose had rescued her by stealing her for a dance.

It had been years ago now, but she would never forget his mischievous smile. As if the two of them shared some great sally. Nor could she banish from her mind the tale he had regaled her with over lemonade, vividly describing the occasion upon which he had built himself a flying machine with the intent of leaping from the turrets of Castle Clare, one of the ducal estates in Scotland.

"Alas," he had told her then, grinning that beautiful rascal's smile he had, "on one of my trials, I was standing on the turrets when the wings, not fastened to me, were caught in a great gust of wind. They fell to the ground like my hopes and dreams, mangled to bits below. And that, my dear Miss Lethbridge, was the end of my attempts to fly."

It had been those rare glimpses of the real Montrose, and the shadows in his eyes, which had thieved her heart.

But it was the Montrose she had witnessed earlier today—remote, cool, uncaring, locking himself away, desperate to lose himself to oblivion—who could break her heart. How easily he could crush it beneath his heel, leave it in dust on the floor.

One day into their marriage, and she was already fearing the only course of action she had, the only means of self-preservation, was leaving him. Perhaps an annulment could be secured, given the newness of their union. She had understood, on an instinctive level, that her love for Montrose, coupled with the incessant pressing of his suit and his infallible charm, had rendered her vulnerable to him. But she had failed to realize, in her naïve and innocent hopes, that he would grow tired of her so easily. That it would only take one day, one heated discussion, to send him back into his old ways.

Somehow, she had believed, fool that she was, he would wait as he had promised. That he would not carouse until she had borne an heir. And somehow, she had placated herself that having Montrose some of the time—nine months, a year, perhaps two, however long it took to conceive a male heir—would be better than never having had him at all.

Tonight, she was no longer sure.

A soft rap at the door joining their chambers through their mutual dressing rooms disturbed her from her troubled musings. She froze, mid-stride, heart pounding. Surely it was not Montrose. She had not heard any sounds to suggest he had returned.

If she did not move, did not take a step...

The door opened with a click. Her husband stood on the threshold, clad in another of his silken banyans, this one a dark maroon to complement the mahogany of his hair. As always, he took her breath. Tonight, a new kind of awareness radiated through her, pooling in her center.

Drat her traitorous body, which did not know what her heart and mind already knew—that this man was akin to poison to her.

"Montrose," she said, careful to keep her voice cool.

She could not bear to let him see the tumult into which he had cast her for the last, seemingly endless hours.

"Hattie," he returned.

Instantly, she wondered if he was in his cups. Or if he had been with another woman. And then she hated herself for those doubts and fears. Even if history suggested they were not misplaced.

She drew herself up, attempting to be the indomitable duchess she wished she could be, the icy, cold pillar of strength. If only she could be as elegant and perfect as marble Ceres, incapable of being hurt, forever frozen in stone.

"You are home," she observed lamely.

"Yes." His gaze seemed to devour her then, dark and hungry, traveling the length of her body as if he could see through the modest night rail she wore.

Curse her weakness for him. She lit like a candle, from deep within, burning for him. Only for him. Always for him.

But she must not succumb. She tipped up her chin. "I am tired, Montrose. It has been a long day, and I am afraid I am suffering from a megrim as well. Was there something you wished to discuss?"

His jaw hardened.

It had been the wrong thing to say, she realized when, rather than driving him back into his lair, it propelled him forward. Into her domain. He was prowling toward her now, sensual menace in his air, his every step hewn into every sharp angle of his aristocratic face.

"As it happens, yes. There is something I wish to *discuss*,

Wife," he clipped, stopping just short of her. "It is your duty to provide me with an heir, and such a feat cannot be accomplished if you cling to your maidenly virtue and feign a headache."

He was near enough that she could see the obsidian of his pupils, wide, dilated discs. The scent of smoke reached her, telling her he had been somewhere libidinous. Likely in a gaming hell. Or worse, a brothel.

"I am tired," she repeated sternly.

She would not fall prey to his sensual onslaught as she had earlier that afternoon. Not after he had treated her so callously, as if her concerns were of no value, before abandoning her for the rest of the day. This time, her head would win over the rest of her.

*But he needs you*, taunted her heart.

*Do shut up*, she told the faithless organ. *He also needs drink and opium. I will be none of those sources of distraction.*

Moreover, there was the matter of where he had been.

And why he had gone.

"Too tired for your husband already, pet?" he asked, a sardonic twist to his lips.

"Do not call me that," she snapped, striding away from him.

More distance was what she needed. And determination. She could and would resist him. His devilish charm and beautiful face would do him no good tonight. He could spin her a thousand charming stories about flying machines and dance with her until the moon turned into the sun, and still, she would not give in.

She vowed it to herself. To her pride.

"Pet?" He followed her, chasing her down, like any hound bringing the fox to ground.

She reached the fireplace and stopped, the warmth of the

flames on her face. She stared into the grate, into the crackling orange licks of fire. "Do not act as if nothing has happened," she forced herself to say, her back to him. "You dismissed me earlier as if I were no better than a servant. And then you disappeared. If you think to share my bed tonight, you are sorely mistaken."

Hands settled upon her waist. A tall, lean masculine form stepped into her, molding to her from thigh to shoulder. The unmistakable ridge of his hard cock pressed against her bottom. She resisted the urge to move, to bring him nearer still.

Lips found her bare neck, just behind her right ear, and she regretted not having removed her pins just yet. Even as his mouth upon her skin sent a prickle of desire down her spine. Longing pooled in her belly. Between her legs, she was wet for him. Aching. She could not quell the spark of hope his touch lit within her. *Dear God*, how she loved him.

*Cursed body.*

*Stupid heart.*

He kissed her ear, his breath falling hotly upon her. "How mistaken am I, sweeting? It seems to me as if you want me just as much now as you ever have, if not more."

Again, the faint tinge of smoke, lingering atop his familiarly delicious scent, taunted her.

"Where were you?" she asked him.

Ewan found a particularly sensitive spot on her neck and nibbled there. "Engaging in gentlemanly sport."

*Sport.* Surely, he did not mean what she feared he alluded to.

She stiffened, and would have moved away from him had not his hands slid from her waist to her belly, trapping her against him in an iron hold. Still, she squirmed, tugged at his hands. "Release me."

"Calm, my wildcat." He dragged his lips over her skin in a

decadent caress she felt in her core. "The sport was boxing first, followed by some dice. Nothing more."

He made her feel like a wildcat, alternately ready to hiss and spit and claw, or just as easily purr. His words allayed the sharpest of her fears, but not all of them.

"You smell of smoke," she said, attempting to free herself once more.

The only thing she accomplished in her struggles was to wedge her bottom more firmly against his groin. There was no question of his desire. Although she was vexed with him, the knowledge he wanted her sent a rush of molten heat to her center. Her foolish body had no intention of heeding her mind, it would seem.

"Some of the chaps were smoking cigars." He nipped at her shoulder through the thin layer of her night rail covering it. "I promised to be faithful to you."

Until she bore him his heir.

After...

After, if he chose to carouse with a string of mistresses once more, she would be ruined. She did not know how she would bear it. Her heart could not possibly recover. If her love for him had already grown after just one day of marriage, she could not fathom how months or even years as his wife would impact her.

But she said none of those things, because he was kissing her. "You smell divine, Hattie darling. Like violets. Fresh as an early spring garden. I need you."

His raw rasp sent a bolt of desire through her. She did not want to read too much into those wicked words, and yet, she could not deny the warmth suffusing her. However, as much as she wanted him, too, he had to answer for his actions. If she was going to survive this union of theirs, she could not allow him to run roughshod over her.

Her hands settled over his where they remained splayed

on her stomach. Damn him, even his fingers were handsome. Strong, long, thick. They were capable of such strength, such tenderness, too. The touch of her skin upon his sent a new wave of awareness crashing over her.

"You owe me an apology, Ewan," she forced herself to say before she completely tossed herself, headlong, over the cliff of reckless longing.

His lips found the side of her neck, her pounding pulse. "I am sorry."

That was too easy.

Far too easy.

"Why are you sorry?" Her question ended on a gasp as he sucked on her bare throat.

"I am sorry I spent the day wallowing in my own misery rather than worshiping you as I should have done." He caught her earlobe in his teeth.

That was not precisely the apology she wanted. But it was a beginning. She found herself tipping her head back until it rested against his shoulder. She turned and collided with his searing gaze. For a heartbeat, she forgot what to say. Forgot what she wanted from him aside from his kiss and the sensual delights he could give her.

She reached up, burying her hand in his thick, dark hair. "I care about you, Ewan."

She had not meant to make the admission. Somehow, it had slipped from her lips when she had been staring into his eyes.

"You should not." He kissed the tip of her nose. "I am not worthy of your concern." He set his mouth upon hers then.

Warmth seared her. His lips were velvet seduction, toying with hers, playing over her as if he had all the time in the world. There was such tenderness in his kiss. As if he cared about her as well, and she thought if this were the last time she ever felt his mouth upon hers, she could die a happy woman. Because this meeting of mouths was about more than seduction; it was an apology in itself. An affirmation.

She wondered if he truly believed he was not worthy of her. He had said it often enough. It hurt her heart to think he held himself in such low regard. How she wished he would confide in her. Trust her.

There was so much of Ewan she needed to learn. So much he held apart from her.

He broke the kiss first, gazing down at her. "You are an angel, Hattie Montrose."

*Hattie Montrose.* It almost seemed impossible the name was hers now. That the man surrounding her with his strong body now was hers as well.

Even if there remained much he kept from her. A sudden profundity overcame her as she fell into the depths of his gaze once more. She was going to have to push him. Fight for him. If she was going to emerge from this marriage with her heart intact, she could not allow him to retreat from her as he had done earlier. Putting distance between them was his form of defense.

If he built a wall, she would have to tear it down.

"I am no angel," she told him. "I want you far too much."

So much it terrified her, in fact. So much it elated her, too.

*He will never love you*, whispered the voice of doubt within.

How she loathed that voice. How she feared it was right. But she must not think of that now. For now, she must live in the moment. And the moment was Ewan.

He kissed her again on a growl rather than answering her. Or perhaps the kiss *was* his answer, because this time, his tongue slid inside her mouth. He tasted of sweetness and spice. *Negus*, she thought dimly as she ran her tongue against his in response. It was not the first time she had tasted it on his lips, but she would not fret over it now, for wine seemed far less a concern than laudanum or gin. He had not appeared at all foxed tonight.

He seemed, instead, ablaze with intensity.

One of his hands slid lower. Over the curve of her belly, to the apex of her thighs. He cupped her there, through the fabric of her night rail. Desire radiated outward. Her hips jerked into his touch, seeking more. And he gave her more, his thumb somehow finding the most sensitive part of her and stroking.

But it was not enough. She did not want any barriers between them, because she knew how delicious it was to have his bare skin upon her. His tongue. All her good intentions fled. She was aching for him, longing in a new way. She understood her hunger. Knew what the empty ache was deep within, an ache which only he could fill.

She wanted to erase the awfulness of the day, too. To start anew.

He caught a fistful of her night rail as he kissed her, dragging it upward. Cool night air caressed her ankles first, then her calves, all the way to her thighs. Anchoring the hem at her waist with one hand, he wasted no time in delving between her legs with the other. Wicked fingers stroked her.

She cried out, hips moving, seeking more. The sparks ignited. She was engulfed in flame. No matter which direction she moved, there was Ewan. Behind her, his cock was a hard promise of pleasure. Before her, his knowing fingers were unlocking her surrender like a key that had been made for her alone.

He kissed her harder, his fingers increasing their pace upon her center. She clung to him, falling into his body, knees weak with need. How easily he had stripped her of determination. But he was the man she had loved for so long. And he had awakened her body.

His fingers dipped lower, circling her channel. Another noise emerged from her, foreign and almost animal. Perhaps she was the wildcat he had declared her after all. He bit her lower lip enough that the sting surprised her. A current of white-hot need simmered through her. After the sting came delight.

A finger slid inside her.

Deep.

Her knees did buckle then, and she would have collapsed to a heap upon the floor had he not held her to him with the arm banded about her waist. His stiff rod prodded her bottom as he leveraged her, keeping her standing. Her lips still clung to his when he inserted a second finger.

In and out, he moved them in unison. Just when she feared she would go mad with wanting, he curved his fingers and reached a new place inside her. A place of shock and spark and desperate thrill. When his thumb nestled between her folds, working her bud once more while he drove into her again and again, she lost herself.

The bliss rained over her like an explosion of fireworks at Vauxhall—searing, brilliant, powerful. Her entire body shuddered with the violence of her release. And still, he continued to kiss her, his wicked fingers playing over her sensitive flesh as the last ripples of ecstasy washed through her.

He withdrew from her and turned her around to face him at last. She was unsteady, dizzied. Her palms flattened on his chest, seeking purchase, and her head tipped back. She drank in the sight of him, like a dark god towering over her.

Dear heavens, the way he looked at her...as if she were the most ravishing creature he had ever beheld. As if she had astounded him.

"My God, Hattie," he growled. "You are more sensual than I could have even imagined. What a treasure you have been hiding all this time."

She did not know what to say to his praise. Her cheeks went hot. "You…I…we…"

She faltered. Words were beyond her. Her heart was pounding, and the sweet aftershocks of her climax were still throbbing through her. Ewan's proximity—being in his arms, a bed just behind them—did not help matters.

"Precisely." He kissed her swiftly, quickly, before raising his head once more. Holding her gaze, he raised his fingers, glistening with her essence, to his mouth, and sucked. "Sweet, so sweet."

Oh, how wicked he was. Wicked and wanton and holding her heart in his beautiful hands.

She slid her right palm over his chest, stopping above his heart. The steady thumps pounded beneath her, the vibrant evidence of his life source. "Ewan," she said softly. "I need you."

It frightened her just how much truth hid in those four simple words.

CHAPTER 14

She needed him.

*God's fichu, he* needed *her* more. Far more than she could comprehend. Far more than he understood. Far more than he dared say.

What a miracle she was, Hattie Lethbridge. Nay, Hattie Montrose now. And somehow, she was all his. He had her in his arms and naked on her back before he could even think.

He still had on his damned banyan. The silk was smooth as a whisper on his flesh, but not nearly as soft and delicious as Hattie's bare skin against his would be. He wanted her curves, her pale cream burning into his sinner's body. He wanted her goodness to obliterate all the badness in him, all the ugliness that had come before her, to erase the memory of any other mouth but hers, any other touch.

God, he had treated her like a cad, abandoning her the day after they wed to pound out his demons in his unsuspecting sparring partner's face. And then he had drowned himself in the calming succor of a laudanum negus at a smoke-filled gaming hell filled with culls and laden with the stench of sex, bad intentions, and sour ale.

All to come home to this angel who responded to him so sweetly. Who gave herself to him without question. Who wanted to believe him redeemable. He did not deserve her. Never would. Could not do enough to earn her in his bed, at his side.

How had he lived all this time without her? It seemed impossible after one day, the notion of a life without Hattie as his wife.

He kissed her ravenously. Like a beast. Without regard for tenderness or for skill. He kissed her with all the intensity brimming within him. With all the desperate hunger. He was not himself tonight. There was something about her raw surrender, allowing him to bring her to release, the spicy taste of her on his lips, that made him wild.

He tore at his banyan. The silk may have ripped in his eagerness to shuck it. He knew not. All he did know was it was gone. He was naked, poised between her spread legs. He ached with the need to drive inside her. To lose himself in her tight heat.

But yesterday had been her introduction to lovemaking. He must not forget. There was the possibility she was yet sore, and though he was insatiable when it came to her, he would not hurt her. He would sooner draw his own blood than inflict pain upon Hattie.

She was too good. Too pure. Too damned intoxicating. Everything was Hattie. Violets. Raven hair. His fingers were busy plucking more hairpins, freeing the long, thick tendrils of her mane. He kissed her as if he would die if he broke his lips from hers, if the seal ended.

Here was a new sort of mindlessness: in her arms, in her bed. Her body under his, giving and welcoming. Her hands moving over him in worshipful caresses. Her fingertips traced his shoulders, his back, found his buttocks and gripped him hard.

The last had him rocking into her, his ready cock glancing over her wet folds. Her dew on him only served to increase his ridiculous hunger. How she held him in her thrall. He was possessed by her. Obsessed with her. The hours he had spent away from her now seemed the greatest travesty.

The folly of a coward. A man running from his past, hiding from the demons within. But no matter how fast he ran, or how much he imbibed in an effort to free himself of the ghosts, they always followed. He could not outrun himself.

Not even the relief he had found in the opium he had consumed compared to what he felt as he feasted upon Hattie. But he promised himself he would not be a rutting animal. He would tease her. Tempt her. Prepare her for the savagery of his claiming. For surely, it would be savage when it came. There was no other way.

She brought out the darkest desires in him, and he meant to feed them all.

If he could not free himself of the demons, he could at least lose himself in her. In this all-consuming, voracious craving he had to be one with her. To take her in every way he possibly could and then begin again.

The thought of fucking her everywhere, of making her his beautiful sybarite, made his ballocks tighten and his prick so hard, he had to grit his teeth to keep from spending. He knew he had to pace himself. To go slow. He wanted to be deep inside her when he spilled.

At last, he dragged his mouth from hers. Down her throat, he went, kissing, licking, biting. He explored the roundness of her bare shoulder, enjoying her sharp inhalation and kittenish mewl when he nipped her there. He found her puckered nipples, hard little jewels begging for his attention. He sucked on one as he braced himself with an arm and reached between them.

He dragged the tip of his cock up and down her seam. She was soaked. A cry tore from her. Intent upon his prize, he flicked his tongue over her nipple again and again. She was writhing now, murmuring sweet nothings.

"Ewan, mmm."

He bit her other nipple, then sucked away the sting.

"Oh," she said.

He kissed down her belly. Licked into her navel. Her hips shot upward.

"Please."

The way she embraced her sensuality made him even more desperate for her. The contrast of the prim, disapproving wallflower and the decadent vixen beneath him was delicious. He would have never known. Never could have guessed. But now that he knew what a sensual woman she was, he could not get enough.

Never.

"Tell me what you want," he said, glancing up at her.

Her emerald eyes were heavy-lidded, lips swollen with his kisses, parted. Her cheeks flushed. Her breasts jutted like offerings, tipped with the most luscious pink nipples he had ever sucked. She looked like a sacrifice. Like a goddess. She looked like his.

She tasted that way, too. He licked the jut of her hip bone, getting nearer to what he wanted most, her sweet cunny. He wanted to make her spend again on his tongue before he slid inside her.

But she had not answered him yet. Which meant his sweet goddess needed some more encouragement. Grinning, he applied himself to his task.

\* \* \*

Hattie was awash in sensation. Floating on a cloud of delicious pleasure. In Ewan's capable hands, losing herself, forgetting all her worries, was easy. He was kissing his way down her body now, nearing her most intimate place. He was sinfully close to the part of her that he had already left humming with pleasure.

But, oh, the sight of his gorgeous mouth grinning that wicked rakehell's grin, kissing her hip...

"Ewan," she said his name, a simple sigh of longing. She knew what she wanted, but she did not dare ask for it.

The deed was far too wicked, even if it was one of the most pleasurable acts she had ever known.

He kissed her inner thigh, his big hands on her hips, caressing. One of his hands guided her legs farther apart, opening her to him. And then she felt the burn of his gaze. He was looking at her, as if he committed her to memory. As if he found her beautiful.

As if he were entranced.

But still, he did not give her what she wanted. He kissed the tender inside of her other thigh, then higher. All the while, his hands caressed. He neared the hollow between her mound and her thigh.

She inhaled, then held her breath. Watched as he remained where he was, in such aching proximity to the part of her that hungered for him the most.

"Please, Ewan," she begged at last, desperate for him to do something. *Anything.* Desperate for his mouth, his tongue. For the same sensual torture he had visited upon her the night before.

"Tell me what you want, darling," he said again, blowing on her sex. "I am yours to command."

What a heady proclamation. She would have reveled in it had not the warmth of his breath upon her core left her breathless. Mindless. She jerked toward him, hips lifting off the bed, seeking. He retreated incrementally, keeping himself just out of her reach.

He was going to make her ask for it, she realized. He wanted to hear her give voice to the wickedness. A proper lady would be outraged. Indeed, she likely ought to be. But all she felt was hungrier for him. It was that hunger, visceral, real, unlike anything she had ever before experienced, that prompted her to find the words she needed to say.

Her fingers sifted through his thick, lustrous hair. He was so beloved to her. Every moment only led her deeper down the path of desire, strengthened the love she had been harboring for all these years.

"I want your mouth," she managed to say. "On me."

"With pleasure," he growled, and then his head dipped between her legs.

His tongue found the bud of her sex, teasing her with light, leisurely strokes. She moaned, her fingers tightening in his hair. Last night, everything had been new. She had been nervous. Shy. Tonight, she had the advantage of experience to make her alive to every sensation.

She did not want to miss a single second. The scent of him in the air, mingling with her. The sight of his gorgeous face between her thighs. The slick glide of his knowing tongue over her. The rasp of his teeth. He made a deep sound of pleasure as he licked her, as if he savored her, as if he could not get enough.

"So delicious, darling," he murmured, kissing the flesh he had just tormented. "You taste sweeter than honey."

And then, his tongue was upon her again. Faster. Harder. The pleasure he had already given her meant she was teetering on the edge. Bliss was a wave crashing over her, a torrent all at once, threatening to drown. Her hips bucked. He caught her in his teeth and tugged.

Everything inside her tightened. She was ready. Desperate. He sank a finger inside her sheath and nibbled at her again. That was all it took. She was lost. A spasm rocked through her. She thought she gasped. Maybe she screamed. She was incoherent. Her body was a slave to the pleasure he gave her.

It did not matter. Nothing mattered but Ewan.

He rose over her suddenly, and in one thrust, he was inside her. Deep. He was hot, hard, stretching her. Her body was still not accustomed to such an invasion, to the size of him. She tightened on him instinctively, and a wave of shudders rocked through her as another spend seemed to possess her.

He braced himself on one arm and cupped her cheek with his other hand, remaining still within her. "Relax for me, pet."

He kissed her then, and she welcomed his kiss, his mouth. His tongue tangled with hers, bringing with it the musky flavor of her own sex. She clutched at his shoulders, kissed him back with the frenzied need driving her. Desperation mingled with desire. She bit his lower lip, moved against him to bring him deeper. Her nipples grazed his chest.

He groaned into the kiss and began to move at last.

"My wildcat," he murmured, his tone laden with approval. "You like it when I fuck you, don't you Hattie?"

There was that vulgar word again. How she loved it in his dark voice. How she loved him inside her, the delicious weight of his big body pinning her to the bed.

"Yes," she gasped as he increased his pace, sinking inside her only to almost withdraw entirely, again and again.

"Say it," he commanded. "Say it, and I'll fuck you harder."

Did she want that? Yes, she did. She was splintering. She wanted anything he would do to her. Everything he would do. She was breaking into a thousand shards of light. Her body was his to claim, his to control. The pleasure was all she could think, all she could feel. She was so wet, the slippery sound of him sliding in and out of her channel echoing through the chamber.

He withdrew and held still, staring down at her, his countenance harsh, the tendons in his neck raised in testament to the restraint he exercised. "Tell me, pet."

"I love when you fuck me, Ewan," she said, breathless.

The rest of the words, even awash in the mad throes of ecstasy, she kept to herself.

*I love you, Ewan.*

As if he had heard those words, too, he wrapped her legs around his waist and slammed into her, driving deep. Intense pleasure overtook her. His mouth was on hers again, and this time, the rhythm was more punishing, yet more delicious. She tightened on him, her release abrupt and fierce. She cried out into his kiss, digging her nails into his shoulders as she came undone.

He moved faster, his strokes shorter. His body tensed against hers, and then he broke the kiss, burying his face in her neck. A hot rush filled her.

She had never loved him more.

CHAPTER 15

Monty woke with his arm around a deliciously feminine waist and his hard cock nestled against the cleft of a luscious arse.

The scent of violets and lovemaking were heavy in the air.

*Beautiful way to greet the dawn*, he thought, nestling his face in the cloud of silken hair spilling all over the pillow. He had stopped spending the night in his lovers' beds some years ago when the violence of his nightmares had rendered sleeping with another unwise. But as dawn light crept through the window dressings, bathing the chamber in seductive shadows and the promise of another round of bedding his wife, he found himself wishing he could begin each day just like this.

*Hattie.*

Sweet, wonderful, glorious, prim, wallflower Hattie. He had used her quite roughly last night. He had been crazed with lust for her, and he had not treated her with the proper care a husband no doubt ought to devote to a gently bred lady. But she had not seemed to mind. If anything, she had been as desperate and mindless for their joining as he had been.

He had treated her poorly. He kissed her shoulder now, determined to make amends. Determined to do better. To try to lock away the demons for her. Because she deserved the best he could give her.

His hand slid up to cup her breast. Her nipple was already a hard bead nestled in his palm, her skin soft, silken warmth. He wondered if her cunny was wet. He wanted her with a ferocity that shook him, for she was the first woman he had ever bedded whose allure had not diminished after he'd had her beneath him.

Instead, he desired her more with each passing moment.

She was an obsession, infecting his blood. All he wanted was to be inside her. To lay abed with her all day. To spill inside her until he had not a drop left to give.

His hand left her breast, gliding down the satiny curves of her belly, before finding her silken curls. She was hot. His fingers sought the answer to his question. Soaked. *Dear God*, she was so wet.

"Good morning," she murmured, her voice throaty with sleep and desire.

"Minx," he said lightly, kissing her ear. "How long have you been awake?"

"For a few minutes, no more." She turned her head toward him, adorably sleep-rumpled. Her green eyes were half-open, lined with thick, dark lashes. "You stayed."

"Yes," he acknowledged, keeping his voice light.

It would not do for her to know the enormity of the step he had taken, just how much of his guard he had abandoned in the wake of their lovemaking. His fingers were still happily drenched and warm between her thighs. He stroked her sex now, trying to distract her from further conversation.

"Thank you," she murmured as calmly as if he were not petting her sweet cunny at that very moment.

He wanted to tell her he had not stayed for her but for himself. Because he was a selfish bastard who had wanted to wake with her within arm's reach. But that was not entirely true. How surprising to realize he was not quite the bastard he had supposed himself to be.

He had spent the night in her chamber because he had been replete in a way he could not recall ever having felt before. Because Hattie…comforted him. Strange as it was. He had been lulled to sleep by her calm, even breaths in the night, by the scent of violet, by her body aligned to his.

Instead of lying, he kept his silence, distracting himself by taking a moment to admire her face. Everything about her was impossibly lovely to him. It was as if he was seeing her—truly—for the first time. From her high cheekbones to her softly rounded chin, her perfect, almost elfin nose, to her mouth. *By God*, her mouth was made for kissing. So lush, so full. Lips any courtesan would envy. Lips a man could not help but imagine sliding around his cock before she took him down her throat.

The mere thought made his prick twitch. But that was no way to introduce her to the pleasures to be had in their marital bed. There was time, plenty of it, to lead her down the path of debauchery.

He could not resist closing the distance between them, sealing their mouths. He kissed her with all the gratitude singing in his soul. With all the hunger burning inside him.

But then he remembered his determination to make amends. As much as he wanted nothing more than to fuck her all morning, all afternoon, and all night, too, he needed to attempt to ameliorate his sins against her. He pulled back, ended the kiss, and withdrew his fingers from the paradise between her thighs.

Oh, what an effort it took to lie there alongside her and roll her toward him rather than pouncing upon her. They faced each other now. Knowing he would be lost if his rampaging cock came into contact with any portion of her anatomy, he kept their bodies at a safe distance, settling his hand upon her waist to anchor her where she was.

A slight frown marred her otherwise flawless brow. "What is troubling you, Ewan?"

Had he given himself away so well in failing to ravish her like the lustful beast he was? And where to begin? He had never before possessed a wife. Nor a meaningful relationship with any woman he cared about.

The thought was sobering, for along with it came a shocking realization, he cared about Hattie. She was not just a feminine body to slake his passions. She was not just the woman he had married. She was something far, far more.

He swallowed against a rush of unwanted emotion and forced himself to speak. "Yesterday, I was a bastard to you. I am sorry, Hattie. You deserved better treatment."

She blinked, surprise softening her countenance. "You already apologized last night, Ewan. I have accepted. Our marriage is in its infancy, and I would not begin it in enmity."

*The good Lord's chemise*, she was such an angel. Practical as ever, his Hattie. How had he somehow been blessed with the fortune of taking her as his wife? There had been a time when matrimony was anathema to him, when there had been no inducement he could have fathomed, which would have seen him caught in the parson's mousetrap. But something about marriage with Hattie—hell, something about everything with Hattie—felt so damned right.

He reminded himself he owed her more than the apology he had given, when he had been too hell-bent upon seduction.

"I am sorry I was harsh with you," he elaborated, hating

himself more than he ordinarily did. "I am also sorry I left. I ought to have dined with you."

*Damnation*, what was he saying? He did not want her to expect him to spend every evening with her like a loyal puppy at his master's heels. Surely this newfound obsession with her, while unique, would not last forever. It was a matter of course that he would eventually tire of the novelty of having a wife to bed. His demons would come crowding in once more, and he would seek oblivion again in the usual fashions.

Drink.

Women.

Opium.

*You did not leave the opium behind*, reminded that insidious voice. Indeed, it was only a matter of time before he poured laudanum-laced tea down his throat.

Hattie was staring at him, unspeaking. Unsmiling. It was as if she was trying to see inside him, to read his thoughts.

"Why do you take laudanum in your tea, Ewan?" she asked. "Why did you wish to hide it from me?"

*Fuck.*

"My ankle still pains me," he lied, and hated himself for it. "I am a prideful man. I…did not want you to think me weak."

But the truth was, his ankle was not his greatest pain, nor his primary ailment. And the more disgusting, humiliating truth was that the laudanum helped him to forget. It was more effective than gin or whisky. More effective than the oblivion between some wench's legs.

More effective than Hattie? He could not yet say for certain.

"Your ankle," she repeated, searching his gaze.

She was right to doubt him. Of course she was. Because he was lying to her. Lying to everyone around him. Just as he always had.

"The sawbones did not set the bone properly, I fear," he continued, adding another dark mark against his soul.

In truth, his ankle occasionally throbbed. But even this sporadic ailment was not the reason he was an opium eater. The true reason was one he would never reveal to another person, for as long as he possessed a heart beating in his chest.

He saw her inwardly weighing her choices. Did she believe him, or did she further press her case? He held her gaze, unflinching, knowing it was what he must do for her sake as well as his. He would never tell her the truth. Not about this.

"It is particularly painful in the morning," he added, hoping she would let the matter rest at that.

He had already had a word with Wainwroth about his laudanum tea and Her Grace. The mistake would not be repeated.

The furrow between her brows lessened, but still remained. "Do you take it every day?"

*Tell her the truth.*

He knew what would happen if he did.

"No," he told her. "Only when it is necessary."

She compressed her lush lips, and then her hands were on his face, so gentle, so tender, he could have wept at the beauty of it. At the beauty of her. Her thumbs traced the ridges of his cheekbones, her brilliant, green eyes boring into him, as if she could see through him if she only looked hard enough. Her caresses were like a brand on his skin, warming him to his toes. His still-hard cock jerked back to unruly attention. Although he had just had her last night, he wanted her again.

And he would have her, he knew.

Finally, she spoke. "I would never think you weak, Ewan." Her hands slid from his face, traveling to his shoulders, his chest. One of her hands gripped his biceps. "You are strong. So very strong."

There was physical strength and there was a man's inner strength, and the two were not related. He could have told her as much. Within, he was a coward who could not face what had happened to him. The muscles he honed in gentlemanly sporting pursuits had nothing to do with the man he was on the inside.

But that was the Monty he hid from the world. The man he would do anything to hide.

"Thank you, pet," he told her, kissing the tip of her nose once more. "I am trying to be a better man for you. Beginning today."

That, at least, was true. He should have tried yesterday. And mayhap he had, but he had also failed, unutterably. He had ample reason to try to be the husband Hattie deserved.

Not that he could ever attain such a vaunted standing. For it was undeniable that he would never, ever deserve her. Just as it was undeniable that he would have her anyway. She was his. And he meant to keep her.

Monty decided the time for talking was over. Distracting her would be easy. Manipulation was one of his many talents, especially when it came to the women in his bed. He caught her hand, slid it lower, down his abdomen. Guided her fingers around his rigid cock.

Her eyes flared, her lips parting. "Th-thank you, Ewan."

She was breathless. He released her hand, and she kept her fingers as they were. A telling and promising sign.

A slow grin stretched his lips as heat radiated from where her slender fingers grasped him. He was on fire for her. Ready and so hard, he ached. "Why are you thanking me, darling? Are you thanking me for my—"

"Hush," she interrupted, her grip tightening on him as she

chastised him. "Do not say anything else that is wicked, I beg you. I was thanking you for your words, and you know it. For wanting to be a better man for me. I... I want to be the same for you. I want to be a good wife. I want to make you happy. To please you."

*Beelzebub's earbobs*, there was no earthly means by which Hattie could possibly be a better woman. He was certain of it. Especially when she stroked him, from root to tip. The movement was untutored and hesitant, but it tore a growl from his throat and had his hips moving toward her just the same.

"You already make me happy," he told her with ease. This, at least, was not a lie. Nothing in his life had ever made him happier.

He would not ruin this, he vowed to himself. Hattie was the sun in the bleakness of his days. Before, he had been seeking distraction and oblivion everywhere and with everyone he could. It had taken the kisses and the innocent passions of a dark-haired siren to make him realize he had been looking in all the wrong places.

"Will you show me what to do?" she asked, her voice hesitant. So soft he could scarcely hear her above the pounding of his heart.

*Bloody everlasting hell.*

*This woman.*

She had stilled in her strokes, her thumb rubbing over his cockhead. The air fled his lungs. Moisture had seeped from the tip, and she slicked it over him. He nearly spent in her hand.

Gritting his teeth, he sank his fingers into the lush curtain of her hair, cupping her head, drawing her mouth toward his. "More of what you are doing, darling."

Though he itched to touch her intimately once more,

there was something incredibly seductive about giving her all the control. About allowing her to lead them in their lovemaking. His Hattie was bold, curious, and sensual. Beautifully fearless.

"I want to give you pleasure, Ewan," she said against his lips.

"You do, my darling. Bloody hell, how you do," he returned.

Their lips moved as one. The kiss was deep and decadent. Their tongues tangled. The musk of their lovemaking the previous night was redolent on the bedclothes. It only made him want her more. The seriousness of their conversation fell away. So, too, any thoughts of his past. His world had shrunk to the size of this bedchamber.

He had a brief, mad moment of wondering if the two of them could remain here forever, making love and calling for trays of food, never allowing reality to intrude. He thought he could live within these four walls with her always. He thought he could give up gin, opium, other women, anything at all for her.

But that was hardly realistic thinking. He had obligations, as did she. At some point, they would need to leave this chamber. Not now, however. Not even today. They were on their honeymoon, were they not? And whilst they had not traveled to the country since his country seat was the last place he wished to visit, and since their nuptials had been rather sudden, it stood to reason that they could remain at Hamilton House for at least the next sennight.

Perhaps fortnight.

Her hand had resumed its tentative exploration, and he groaned into their kiss, his hips thrusting of their own volition. He yearned to sink inside her. His ballocks drew taut as she moved her hand up and down his shaft with greater confidence. She was going to make him spill with her hand alone.

*Good God*, when was the last time he had spent in a woman's hand? He could not recall. It had been years. And he was not about to do it now. On his third day of marriage. What was happening to him?

He was turning into a milksop.

Their kiss deepened. He found her waist and hauled her atop him, rolling to his back. He was not going to lose himself anywhere other than in his wife's sweet cunny. But if she wanted to learn, who was he to deny her?

Her hips opened for his, her sex nestled against his rod.

She broke the kiss before he did, sitting up with a gasp as she found herself suddenly atop him. Her hair was a decadent curtain falling all around them. Her breasts were lush and full, her nipples hard. Her hands flew to his chest as she regained her balance from this new position.

"Ewan, what are you doing?" she asked, her voice low and husky.

She was not displeased but surprised. What great pleasure he would take in introducing her to the pleasures to be found between a man and woman. Just as long as he was the only man with whom she indulged in such pleasures.

But he would not think of that now, for they were promised to each other until she gave him an heir. Which meant he had a duty to bed her as many times as possible until she was increasing. And making love to his wife would not be a hardship. Not at all.

"I am showing you how to give me pleasure," he told her, his hands on her waist. Her skin was so soft. So luxurious. Her hair fanned over the backs of his hands in a delicious whisper of sensation.

Her curious cat's eyes searched his, so bright, so vibrant even in the dim light of the morning. Just when he thought he had learned all the hues hiding within their depths, he spied another color. Like all the rest of her, the beauty of his wife's eyes was a source of amazement to him.

"Oh," she said. "How can I...how will this work?"

He would show her. With great pleasure.

"Lift yourself, pet," he said. "Get onto your knees."

She obeyed, rising to her knees, hovering over him in the golden dawn light. "Like this, Ewan?"

"Yes, darling." He released her waist with both hands then.

From this angle, he could see the flushed, pretty lips of her cunny, glistening and ready beneath the shield of silken curls. He wanted to haul her to him, to settle her over his face, and to lap up all her juices until she came, just as he had teased her the day before. But such indulgence would have to wait.

He had all the time in the world to devour her. To teach her the heights of passion. To seduce her and make her body sing with the pleasure only he could bring her.

He gripped his cock with one hand and her waist with the other, guiding her down upon him. Wetness and warmth greeted him, along with a grip so tight, he almost spilled immediately. But he ground his jaw and forced himself to maintain his control. He wanted this moment to last. Wanted to bring them both to a delicious crescendo before spending inside her.

He drove upward while grinding her down upon them, until he was deep, so deep. They sighed as one when he was sheathed in her cunny.

"God, Hattie." The words were torn from him. Moan, plea, benediction. His hips having a mind of their own. They surged. Driving himself deeper still. The angle was incredible. And she was so damned slick.

Elysium. She was perfect. So perfect. Far more than he had ever hoped to have in every way.

Hattie's hands were upon his chest once more, seeking purchase. Her expression was one of amazement. She looked like a woman overcome by desire. She looked wild and ravishing. He wanted her to fuck him to oblivion, to take control.

"How shall I..." Her question trailed off as she moved, lifting herself until he almost slid free of her body. "Oh."

Yes, oh. But not enough.

He gripped her waist and guided her back down upon him. Her breasts bounced. The sight was so unbearably erotic, he could not resist taking the peak of one into his mouth. She rewarded him with a moan and a fresh rush of dew bathing his cock. He sucked harder, gripping her waist with one hand and guiding her.

She undulated her hips on a gasp, and then instinct took over. She moved over him, taking him deep, then lifting, only to bring him deep again. The rhythm she began was maddening. His heart pounded furiously as the early signs of his impending release took over.

He caught her nipple between his teeth and tugged. She cried out, arching her back, tilting her head back until her dark hair brushed over his thighs, gliding whisper-soft over his tightened ballocks. It was the single most sensual moment he had ever shared with a woman.

A furious rush of need to possess her claimed him then. He surged upward, hips thrusting from the bed, and she took him deep. They both turned frantic. They moved as one, chasing ecstasy, faster, higher, harder. He reached between their joined bodies, unerringly finding her engorged pearl. He stroked her there, hard and desperate.

She came on a choked cry, her cunny clenching on him with such sudden power he lost the ability to withhold his seed. Her fingers were in his hair, grasping, holding his head to her breast as if he were hers to command.

Because he *was* hers to command.

If he had wondered before, he had his answer now. He spilled into her, losing himself, losing control. And it was good, so damned good.

So damned good, it hurt.

So damned good, it terrified him.

## CHAPTER 16

The day had been good. So good, in fact, it terrified her.

Trying to distract herself from such inconvenient fears and emotions, Hattie strolled along a wall of books in the Hamilton House library following dinner. They had spent the morning making love before getting dressed separately. Aside from their brief parting, they had spent every minute of the day together. Her husband was not just a charming, flirtatious rake.

He also possessed a wicked sense of humor, glimpses of which she had only seen on rare occasions in the past. She had discovered he could make her laugh until she cried as they spent their breakfast inventing more nonsensical oaths.

Satan's handkerchief, the devil's petticoats, and ruffian's slippers were some favorites.

But that was not all. He kissed her as if she were the most glorious woman in the world. He looked at her as if he could not wait another moment to have her in his arms. And when he held her…

Any defenses she had once mustered against him had

been effectively banished. One day of his skillful seduction, his ardent attention, and she was as helplessly in his thrall as she had ever been. More so, of course. She loved him too much.

"If you wish to make any changes to the library, you must do so, of course, darling," he said, his low voice far nearer than she had supposed.

Her nipples were already hard, merely from being in the same room with him. Cursing herself, she turned around, only to find herself lost in those sumptuous brown eyes. How was she ever going to survive being married to this man?

His gaze was lazy, appreciative.

For an indeterminate span of time, she forgot what he had even said to her.

*Ah, yes. Books. Library. Changes...*

"Perhaps we could add some more poetry," she suggested, though she had scarcely taken in all the titles she had passed by. Her thoughts had been far too preoccupied with him.

"Anything you want is yours." He reached out and swept a stray tendril of hair from her face.

She resisted the urge to nuzzle his hand as if she were a cat. His touch had fast become an obsession for her. She could not get enough of it.

"Anything?" she asked teasingly.

In truth, she knew the one thing she wanted more than anything—his heart—could not be so easily attained, if at all. But she had no wish to ruin the tenderness of the moment with such heaviness.

He drew her into his arms, then lowered his forehead to rest against hers. "Anything."

The gesture was so tender, so loving. She inhaled deeply of the scent of him, her arms going around his waist as if it were the most natural thing. Because for her, it was. She had loved him for so long. Today seemed as if it had been ripped from her dreams.

"What if I want something that cannot be bought?" she dared to ask.

Oh, she was not fool enough that she would ask for his heart, or that she even believed a mere day of accord between them was enough to suggest he had feelings for her aside from the obvious physical connection they shared. But at some point during the course of the day, she had realized she was going to fight for him. The notion of them going their separate ways after she bore him an heir grew increasingly unpalatable.

If they could spend their time together, laughing, talking, and making love now, why should it not always be so? Why did this paradise ever need to come to an end? Because he had decreed it so? Because he was too afraid to follow his heart? Because he was doomed to be an inconstant lover?

Surely, she could scale any wall he attempted to build between them. Surely there was hope for their marriage, for their future. It was that belief which propelled her forward now. Headlong into bliss or misery—that much would be determined over time.

He raised his head and stroked her cheek with the backs of his fingers. "And what is it you want that cannot be bought, pet?"

*Your love.*

No, she could not say that. Did not dare.

"What I want more than anything is to know more about you," she said instead.

He stiffened in her arms, and she wondered if she had somehow misspoken.

"What a deadly, boring subject, darling," he drawled at last into the silence that had descended.

At least he had not withdrawn from her. His arms were still firmly around her.

"I do not find you boring at all, Ewan," she told him seriously.

She did not. She wanted to get to know the enigmatic man she had married. Not the Duke of Debauchery. Not the wicked rake. Not the devil-may-care friend of her older brother. The true man hiding behind the mask he wore for society. She wanted to know the reason for the shadows in his eyes. Why he had so oft steeped himself in drink. What he was running from. What secrets he hid.

Earning his trust would take time, she knew. And effort. But she was determined, persistent. She had time and love on her side, and she was not afraid to use either to her advantage.

"There is not much to tell, pet." His jaw was a sharp, ridged line, so taut, she fancied she could cut her fingers upon it if she dared to touch him there.

She cupped his face. His flesh was soft and warm and giving. So very human. The sole roughness on him was the prickle of his dark whiskers. "Whatever there is, I want you to tell it. We are husband and wife now, and I scarcely know anything about you."

Aside from all the rumors.

Aside from what she had witnessed herself.

"On the contrary, darling, I think you know everything you need to know about me." He gave her a slow, wicked grin, and pressed a kiss into her palm.

In true Ewan fashion, his tongue slid out to graze her skin, sending sparks of fire up her arm. They danced through her and settled low in her belly. Lower still, between her thighs. But she was not going to allow him to distract her with lovemaking just yet, despite the desire he awoke.

She was smiling in spite of herself. He truly was charming

when he chose to be. "Do not tell me this is another form of palmistry?" she asked, referencing the day he had asked her to marry him, and she had finally said yes.

It seemed like a lifetime ago already, but in truth, it had not been long ago at all.

"It is indeed," he said against her palm, his grin deepening. He traced a path on her palm with his tongue. "This line says you will allow your husband to settle you on the chair by the hearth, lift your skirts, and lick your pretty cunny until you spend all over his greedy tongue."

*Oh, wicked, wicked man.* He said the most vulgar things, and they never failed to fill her with heat and desire.

"Where is the line that says my husband is a sinful scoundrel?" she demanded, resisting the frisson of need rolling through her.

This was serious. He could distract her with lovemaking later. Tonight, she wanted to learn more about him.

He licked another path, his stare intense upon hers. "I could not find that line, but this one says you love his big cock sliding deep inside you."

Of course she did, the knave. And he knew it. But that was all beside the point.

Her cheeks went hot. "Ewan, stop this game. I truly want to know about you."

He kissed her wrist. "Very well, pet. I will tell you my boring life history. In return, you must tell me yours."

There was a bargain she could manage. "Of course."

He nibbled on her inner wrist. "And you must promise to let me have my wicked way with you when our conversation is done."

Another bargain she could easily manage.

She smiled. "I would not have it any other way."

"Wicked darling." He kissed the top of her hand, then laced their fingers together and tugged her across the chamber, to a seating area. "Come. Let us have done with it."

He settled in a chair, and when she would have seated herself at his side, he hauled her into his lap. The position was indecent, and she loved it.

She loved *him*.

*Oh, stupid heart.*

She shifted, trying to situate herself as gracefully as she could, and felt the unmistakable ridge of his cock beneath her. Her gaze shot to his, and he was watching her with a heavy-lidded, hungry gaze that told her she would need to begin this discussion soon, before he devoured her.

"You are truly the Duke of Debauchery," she said.

Instantly, she regretted mentioning the sobriquet he had earned in far more nefarious manners. Manners which did not involve her.

The grin fled from his lips. "Yes, I am, and you would do well to recall it, Hattie darling."

She searched his gaze and tenderly brushed a rakish forelock from his brow before settling her hand over his heart as he had once done to her. "But you have a heart, though you try your best to pretend you have none. Here it is, beating beneath my fingertips."

"A black one to be sure," he quipped. "Hardened, jaded. Nothing more than a husk of what a heart truly ought to be."

"Why?" She had to know.

His expression changed, hardened. "I have seen far too much. Do not ask questions you do not truly want the answers to, pet."

But she did want the answers. Only, it would seem he was unwilling to give them to her. Fair enough. She could not expect him to reveal all to her on the third day of their marriage. She had time aplenty to discover more. Instead, she would proceed slowly. With great caution.

"What were you like when you were a lad?" she asked.

"Troublesome. My father despaired I would ever make a proper duke, and he was right." Ewan gave her a wry half smile then. "I was fond of playing all sorts of horrid jokes upon him. Adding paste to his inkwell, pouring sawdust in his shoes, that sort of boyish nonsense."

She could envision a small, adorable Ewan, playing tricks upon the duke. For a brief, spellbinding moment, she imagined what their child would look like, should they be so blessed.

"You have always been troublesome," she said, smiling and stroking his hair. The freedom to touch him was such a delicious luxury. How beloved he was to her. How precious.

His lips quirked into a full smile. "I invented troublesome, darling."

Somehow, she found troublesome far more alluring than staid and proper.

"Tell me more," she urged him. "Did you ever play any tricks upon Her Grace?"

"But of course." He winked. "I would tangle her necklaces together, hide her earbobs. Put pepper in her pearl powder, a frog in her chamber pot. And neither was poor Cat safe from me. She was terrified of spiders, so naturally whenever I discovered one, I hid it in her bed."

"Oh, you wretched boy," she said, laughing. "Tell me more."

He shook his head. "It is your turn. I want to hear about you. What was sweet little Hattie like? Just as angelic as you are now, I have no doubt."

"I was forever reading a book, much to my mother's disgust," she recalled. "I thought Torrie was the finest brother in the world. I followed him everywhere whenever he was home. He doted over me quite sweetly as I recall it now."

The reminder filled her with sadness.

She wished she had not offered the recollection, for once more, her husband tensed beneath her.

"Christ, Torrie." Ewan's eyes slid closed, his expression tightening with pain that could not be feigned. "I wish to God I had never agreed to race him that night. That I had not been so deep in my cups I failed to realize neither of us should have been driving a damn thing…"

There was no denying the agony in her husband's voice. Nor the regret.

"You never meant for either of you to get hurt," she said, still combing her fingers through the thick strands of his hair. "I know that, Ewan. I have always known that."

"But you resented me for what happened," he guessed.

Correctly. She had been furious with him when she had first discovered his involvement in her brother's nearly fatal accident. But she had known, all along, that in his heart, the Duke of Montrose was a good man, in spite of his predilection for sin and scandal. He had loved Torrie like a brother, and he would have never intentionally wanted to see him so gravely injured. In time, her anger had waned, washed away by the relief that her brother had recovered—at least physically, if not mentally—and her own foolish love of Ewan.

The way she felt for him, even in the depths of her anger, had never changed.

"I resented losing the brother I knew and loved." She kept her voice gentle, soothing, as she explained. She had no wish to ruin the intimacy of this moment, so unlike the intimacies they shared with their bodies and every bit as cherished and important. "I was angry with the both of you for having been so reckless with your lives. Because I care for you both, so much."

He stilled. "You care for me?"

How could he believe otherwise? Her heart ached at the hesitance in his tone, almost as if he could not believe she would possess tender feelings for him. Or worse, that he was not worthy.

She did not dare confess the truth. Not yet.

She smiled instead, lovingly stroking his hair. "Of course, I do, Ewan. If I did not care, I never could have married you."

If she had been expecting a similar declaration from him, however, one was not forthcoming.

Instead, he caught her hand, brought it to his lips for another kiss. "You honor me, darling. I do not deserve you."

Of course he did. He deserved so much more. He deserved love. She wondered if any of the women he had known before her had ever loved him. Had ever even professed to care. From his surprise at her words, she would wager they had not.

Foolish creatures, not knowing what they had.

She would do better, she vowed. She would show him he was worthy of love, show him his heart could be won.

She pressed a finger to his lips. "Hush. I will hear no more of that. You must know by now I hold you in very high esteem, Ewan."

"Because you have the mettle and generosity of an angel," he said against her finger before kissing the fleshy pad. "But trust me in this, if in nothing else, I do not deserve you. I am not worthy of your esteem. I am not a worthy husband for you. But I promise to spend each day doing my damnedest to try."

She longed to ask him about the agreement they had reached, wherein they would live separate lives after she bore him his heir. But she knew it was too soon. There would be time to change his mind.

"And I will try my best to be a worthy wife for you," she promised.

She had never imagined she would be a duchess, least of all Montrose's duchess. Strange how what had once seemed impossible was now commonplace. Part of her was afraid it was too good to be true. That this handsome rake avowing he would do his utmost to be a good husband to her would change his mind. Return to his roving, reckless ways.

"You do not need to try, Hattie darling." He dipped his head, pressed his lips to hers for a quick, hard kiss before retreating again. "You are elegant, beautiful, and I want you so much, I cannot think properly."

If he was attempting to distract her from further conversation, he was succeeding.

His cock was rigid as ever, straining against her bottom. This time, she moved first, slamming her lips on his. His tongue swept into her mouth. One of his hands slid from her waist to cup her breast. She could not quell the desire burning inside her for him as their kiss deepened, growing carnal. Voracious.

His other hand slid beneath her skirt, trailing a searing caress from her ankle, up her calf, to her knee. He explored the hollow there, before moving higher, up her inner thigh. She was not straddling him, but she suddenly wished she were, for she could undo the fall of his breeches and take him inside her.

Kissing him while his hand slowly crept toward her center was such sweet torture. They had not made love since that morning in her bed, and she was keenly aware of all the hours her body had spent longing for his. All through the rest of the morning, during their luncheon, all afternoon. Dinner had been spectacularly tempting, a feast of senses in every way as Ewan's chef had sought to dazzle them with his undeniable talent. Sitting across from Ewan with the footmen in attendance, no means of putting an end to the ache deep within her, had been the greatest temptation of all.

But now, he was beneath her, surrounding her with his warmth, his lips firm and knowing on hers. She loved the way he kissed her. The way he touched her. His fingers dipped into her folds, finding her pearl with unerring certainty. One stroke and she was arching into his hand, gasping into his mouth.

"Ewan," she said against his lips, half protest, half plea. "We must not here in the library. Anyone could come upon us."

"No one will enter," he promised her, dragging his lips down her throat. "I was clear in my orders."

Her cheeks went hot. "If you told the servants not to disturb us, surely they will suspect..."

"I do not pay them to suspect. I pay them to do their jobs," he growled, kissing the tops of her breasts.

He sank a finger inside her. She no longer fretted over the servants or what they must think of her. All she could feel was the intensity of the pleasure he gave, radiating through her body. One of his hands had traveled to the tapes at the back of her gown. He undid them with ease, her bodice gaping to accommodate his hungry mouth. He made short work of her chemise and stays.

In a blink, or so it seemed, she was half-naked, lying across her husband's lap while he worked a second finger into her sheath. Days ago, she could not have fathomed such an intimacy, not with any man and certainly not with Ewan. How quickly that had changed. Even as she rejoiced in this newfound freedom and sensuality, in the passion he had unleashed and the desire he had awakened, part of her feared he would grow bored.

That he would tire of her, just as he had all the other lovers he had known.

That when his heir was born, he would walk away, return to his life of hedonism, forget all about her.

But then, he dragged her nipple into his mouth, and it was as if he had pulled a knot tight within her. He curved his fingers, sliding in and out of her in slow, sure motions that had her clenching on him and crying out her release before she could even manage another coherent thought.

He flicked his tongue over her nipple, before blowing on it, gazing up at her as he withdrew his fingers and settled the skirt of her gown back into place. His gaze alone was enough to turn her insides to pudding. She was doused in flame. A proper wallflower no more. Her debauchery was complete, and he had managed it in a matter of days.

Such was the power of the Duke of Montrose.

If only he did not own her heart as thoroughly as he owned her body.

"My turn for questions, Hattie darling." His lips quirked into a tiny, self-assured grin. "What do you want?"

What she wanted was horridly complex and painfully simple all at once. She wanted to be a true wife. To chase away the shadows in his eyes. To cure him of all the demons of his past. To love him. She wanted him to love her in return. To raise half a dozen babes with his chocolate eyes and eccentric sense of humor. She wanted to believe him when he told her he did not rely upon laudanum each day. The best of him—that was what she wanted to believe. All of him—*that* was what she wanted.

But she could say none of those things now.

All she could do was hold his gaze and tell him the one word that was also the truth. "You."

In every way.

"You have me," he told her before his lips were upon hers once more.

Their lips clung. This kiss was not just about desire, but something more. A promise, not just of the passion of the next moment, but of something far more profound.

Suddenly, her world was moving in a whole new way. She felt as if she were falling and flying at once. She clutched at him, and it took her two of his powerful strides to realize he had risen with her in his arms, and holding her, was carrying her across the library as if she weighed nothing more than a bird.

She weighed a great deal more than a bird, and she knew it.

"Ewan," she protested. "Your ankle..."

"Can go to the devil," he finished for her, not even hesitating. "Nothing feels more perfect than you in my arms, Hattie. I would gladly suffer any pain just to hold you thus."

"How gallant of you," she said and meant it. "But I would never want you to hurt because of me. I want to be the one who takes away all your pain."

"You see?" He glanced down at her as he continued walking. "You are an angel, Hattie Montrose. And you were waiting for this devil to claim you."

She hated the way he spoke of himself. The way he viewed himself, the irredeemable Duke of Debauchery, a man who was somehow her inferior when in fact the opposite was true. She loved him because of his imperfections, not in spite of them. One day she would make him see himself the way she did. She would cut down all the weeds in his garden, allow the flowers to flourish and blossom.

"I am no angel," she reminded him. "Only look at me now."

Her breasts were free of her gown and stays, her nipples hard and dark from the attention he had paid them and the desire humming through her. Her gown was a crumpled mess, and her hair, it was certain, resembled an abandoned bird's nest, coils worked free of her simple braid by her husband's wandering fingers.

"Oh, I am looking, sweet." There was no mistaking the admiration in his voice. "I cannot fathom it took me this long to find what was before me all along, but I am deuced glad I came to my senses."

She was still the same woman she had always been—too tall, too carved, hair too dark, lips too wide, too quiet, and bookish. But she no longer felt like the wallflower hiding behind potted palms, eavesdropping upon two wretched ladies mocking her. Instead, she felt impossibly beautiful, incredibly powerful. She felt as if she held this gorgeous man in her thrall the same way he held her in his.

Hattie was most certainly not grateful for the accident. She still mourned the brother she knew and loved. But she was grateful for this unexpected chance at happiness. For it was here—Ewan was here—and she meant to seize them both.

He lowered her to her feet at the opposite end of the library, where the fire crackled merrily in the hearth and a plush rug greeted her. She rose on her toes, for as tall as she was, he was taller still, and settled her hands on his broad shoulders.

"I am deuced glad, too," she told him.

His lips twitched with suppressed mirth. "Oh, dear, I do believe my debauchery is catching. Listen to you, speaking with such a vulgar tongue. Whatever shall we do with you, Duchess?"

"Whatever it is," she told him, holding his gaze without flinching, "I hope it is wicked."

"Always, my darling Hattie." He kissed her. "Always."

His lips claimed hers then, and as they kissed, their hands roamed over each other's bodies. There was no grace or finesse in this prelude to lovemaking. There was only raw, unfettered hunger. His jacket fell to the floor. So, too, her gown. She freed the buttons of his waistcoat from their moorings, and he shrugged it away. Slippers and shoes and stockings were removed in haste. Her stays and petticoats were followed by his shirt and breeches.

Last to go was her chemise. They fell to the floor, desperate for each other. She was on her back, and he was astride her, his cock nudging her entrance. The luxurious wool of the carpet was a decadent abrasion on the skin of her back and buttocks. Her every sense was alight and alive.

He teased her pearl and then slid inside her with one swift thrust. She was instantly filled, her body awash with pleasure so intense she cried out. Heavens, perhaps it was a scream for the way her voice echoed through the cavernous, vaulted ceilings of the library.

If the servants had wondered before, there would be no doubt now, she thought, but then he withdrew, only to sink deep inside her once more, and this time his mouth feathered over hers to catch her cry. And nothing mattered. Nothing but Ewan. Their rhythm was sweet. Fast. She felt as if a lifetime had passed since the last time they had made love.

The way he moved within her, the way he touched her, the tenderness in his every movement, all burrowed inside her heart. She found his back, raked her nails down the strong plane. Their tongues battled. He tasted of the sweetness of their dinner wine, of sin, of himself.

Of love.

His clever fingers on her pearl made her spend on one of his deep thrusts. He dragged his mouth from hers and pumped into her. Three short strokes, and there was a rush of warmth inside her that made her subsiding shudders of bliss renew. She clung to him, her face pressed to his neck.

How she wished she could keep this moment forever, Ewan almost a part of her, his body joined with hers, his lips on her throat, their hearts pounding as one.

CHAPTER 17

"My correspondence, if you please, Low," Monty requested. "Along with tea."

*Satan's cravat*, how he hated knowing what he was going to do with the tea. But he kept his expression carefully bland. Fought down the guilt which had been eating him in small, vicious bites for the last fortnight.

"Of course, Your Grace," said the butler, bowing before disappearing from Monty's study.

He was a liar. A disgusting, pathetic weakling. Monty knew it. Christ, Low probably knew it. The staff had eyes and ears everywhere. And whilst he trusted his valet implicitly, he had no doubt that footmen he had sent to apothecaries in search of additional laudanum had gossiped. The entire bloody house was on tenterhooks, and he felt it more than anyone. They all knew it was just a matter of time until the Duke of Debauchery crashed another phaeton, punched another footman, pissed on the rug, or broke the nose off an ancestral bust. They all knew, Monty most of all, that this Elysium would never last.

Because the joy was too great. The happiness too dangerously real. It was akin to the bliss that stole through his veins, that sweet serpent of opium, whenever he consumed laudanum in his tea. In his wine. However, he could have it without his wife realizing what he was about.

*Ah, Hattie.* His sweet, beautiful, trusting, sensual gift of a wife. They had been married for just over fourteen days, and each day was like a waterfall of miracles upon the last. She was not just an angel. She was a goddess.

Each night, he fell asleep in her bed, and every morning, he woke to her in his arms. They were well-matched in passion, wits, and humor. They spent their time alternately laughing, fucking like mad, and debating important subjects.

Subjects Monty had not even bothered to contemplate in years. Such as poetry. The good Lord's chemise, when she read him poetry in her glorious, dulcet voice, it never failed to give him an erection, even if the tone of the poem was mournful. Even if it was a valediction. They fed each other tarts from their fingers, breakfasted on hothouse pineapples and strawberries, stayed up too late, slept until dawn, woke only to make love, and then fell back asleep once more.

He had never been so taken with a woman. Never. The way he felt for Hattie…it was terrifying. Terrifying and beautiful and intoxicating, just like she was. Not even the return of his mother to Hamilton House had served to dampen his mood. It was damned odd. Concerning, too, this obsession he had with his new duchess.

Obsession? *Hell*, who was he trying to fool? He was besotted. His every waking thought centered around Hattie. It was ludicrous. Shameful. Unbelievable. He ought to try to put some distance between them, he knew. Go to his club.

Except, he had no wish to. No desire to do anything other than live his life as Hattie's husband. As the Duke of Montrose. *By God*, he was a man of responsibility once more. In her eyes, he was a far better man than he truly was. And somehow, he had come to believe himself capable of becoming that man his duchess believed in. To that end, he had worked his way through all the tired stacks of his correspondence in their entirety, and he had begun reviewing his correspondence on a regular schedule.

Schedules and Monty, the Duke of Debauchery were anathema.

But schedules and Ewan, the dependable husband Hattie had come to know, melded.

As for him? He remained hopelessly mired, trapped between the man he was trying to become and the man he had once been.

Low returned then, and the relentlessly loyal retainer saw to it that all Monty's newest epistles were laid before him. The tea tray was brought as well. He dismissed the servants and prepared a cup. He told himself he could eschew his customary drop of laudanum this morning, but his trembling hand called him a liar.

Monty opened a drawer in his desk where he kept a bottle of laudanum for just such a purpose. One drop to get him through the next few hours. What was the harm? He added a drop, stirred his tea, and then took a sip, the ill feeling inside him at his shameful secret—one of many—dissipating as the opium began to do its job. A few more sips, and a comfortable glow had settled within him.

He hated this part of himself, his need for a cure which could never truly heal. But he forced aside all guilt as he began working through his letters. Even this mundane, ordinary task provided an excellent means of distraction. But lying just beneath the surface of his every movement hid one thought. One thought which troubled him, which nettled his conscience, forbidding him from striking away the guilt.

His wife.

Hattie was changing him.

She was changing *everything*.

What to do with that knowledge? Monty did not have the proper answer, so he sipped some more tea and worked his way through the letters as the pleasant hum of laudanum overtook him. More platitudes from various acquaintances. Deliriously contented words from Cat, who had found more joy in her marriage than Monty could ever hope to find himself.

*Truly?* asked an insidious voice within. *Not even with Hattie?*

The truth was, he felt certain he *could* find joy with her. But his conscience knew he would have to be honest with her. He would have to, at the very least, admit he had been eating opium each day. That he relied upon it as he had once relied upon gin. That all her fanciful notions of him were grand delusions.

That he was still the Duke of Debauchery, thoroughly irredeemable, and only worthy of her disdain rather than her trust.

On a heavy sigh, he reached the next letter in his stack. He recognized the pinched slant of the penmanship instantly, his heart going cold. He already knew without having to look that the letter had come from Arthur Parkross.

Damn the evil bastard to the fiery pits of Hades where he belonged. This was the second letter in a month's time. After so many years of silence, such a visceral reminder of his past felt like a physical attack.

Clenching his jaw, Monty forced himself to read. The words flitted to him in bits and pieces.

> *It is imperative that I meet with you at once...*
> *A matter of grave import...*
> *I am in desperate need...*

All about himself, as usual. That was all the vile cesspit of a human being had ever cared about.

Monty slammed his fist on the desk with so much force, his teacup rattled in its saucer. Seeing it, the symbol of all his weakness, the evidence of the way the sins of his past haunted him still, he took up the teacup and hurled it across the room. It hit the wall in an explosion of fine porcelain, raining to the carpet. He stared at the stain spreading down the wallcovering.

Then he threw open his drawer, extracted the laudanum, and threw it, too.

The bottle hit with a satisfying smash.

To hell with opium to dull his pain. To hell with Arthur Parkross.

Monty crumpled the letter, stood, strode across the study, and tossed it into the fire just as he had the last. The time had come to change. He was consigning the past to the ashes where it belonged, and he was going to rise.

Rise like the bloody phoenix.

\* \* \*

SOMETHING WAS WRONG WITH EWAN.

Hattie observed him in troubled silence as the dessert courses were laid before them at dinner. His skin was pale, almost gray. His countenance was stern and harsh, almost as if all the life had been extracted from him. All through their meal, he had been withdrawn. No longer filled with sensual smiles and easy teasing.

She waited until the servants departed, leaving them to enjoy their *gateau à la Madeleine*, to give voice to her concerns. "Is something amiss, Ewan? You have scarcely eaten anything all evening, and you are so terribly quiet."

He extracted a handkerchief from his coat and dabbed at

his brow. "I am perfectly well, sweet. Thank you for your concern."

She did not believe his reassurance. Instinct told her he was prevaricating to placate her. In the light of the chandelier, she took note that he was sweating, when the room was not overly warm. He dabbed at his forehead, his hand shaking.

"Are you feverish?" she pressed.

If he was coming down with an illness, that would certainly explain the sudden changes in him.

"It is excessively hot in this cursed chamber," he said. "Do you not find it so?"

Worry for him grew. "No, I do not. Ewan, are you certain you are well? You do not look like yourself."

"Do I not?" At last, his sensual lips quirked into a grim smile. The shadows in his eyes seemed remarkably pronounced tonight. Indeed, his entire countenance seemed as if it were cast in them as well.

But perhaps that was just fanciful thinking on her part.

"No," she said softly, struggling to understand this sudden change in him. "You do not."

How she wished his mother had not chosen to attend a musicale tonight. Perhaps the dowager duchess could have spoken to her fears. Or allayed them. Then again, Hattie had not failed to note the tension simmering between her husband and his mother.

"Perhaps I look like a stranger to you this evening," he mused, lifting his wine to his lips and taking a healthy draught of it. His hand shook, sending a splash of claret to his cravat. An ominous red stain blossomed, ruining the elegance of his intricately tied neckcloth. "Did you ever think it is because I am a stranger, Hattie darling? Did you ever think you do not know me at all?"

She frowned, trying to make sense of his questions. It was as if he spoke in riddles.

"Of course, I know you, Ewan," she countered, the lush cake on her plate remaining untouched. She had not the stomach to eat another bite. Not when her husband was acting so unlike himself. "I have known you for years."

"Have you?" He gulped down the rest of his wine. "I think not."

"I have certainly grown more acquainted with you over the last fortnight," she agreed, trepidation lending her voice an edge. She could not shake the suspicion he was hinting at something. Trying to tell her something.

What? A confession?

Had he done something he regretted?

Her aching heart gave a pang at the thought, but it was instantly chased away by guilt. How dare she think the worst of him when he had given her no reason to suspect he had been disloyal?

Still, the worry was there. Burning like a flame.

"The last fortnight has been the best I have ever known," he told her solemnly.

And she was more confused than ever. She had felt the same—that aside from the miserable first day of their union, she had spent her tenure as his wife in utter bliss. Utter, unexpected happiness. A sea of sensual pleasures. He had taught her so much. Had awakened her in so many ways. And her love for him had grown exponentially.

Perhaps that was why his abrupt shift worried her so much now. Because it was a sign that her greatest fear—that he would grow tired of her and move to the next woman's bed—could come to fruition.

"It has been the same for me." Her eyes searched his, seeking answers and finding none. "Will you not have a bite of your cake?"

"I do not want cake." He pushed the plate away from him.

Again, she noted a tremor in his hand. This time, it was punctuated by a shudder running through him.

Her instinct was not wrong, she was sure of it. "Ewan, please. Do I need to have someone fetch the doctor for you?"

"Do not look so troubled, pet." He gave her the ghost of a smile. "No sawbones can cure what ails me."

She did not understand. Apprehension lanced her anew. "Will you not confide in me? I cannot help but to fear something is wrong."

"Everything is wrong, sweet Hattie." The look he gave her was piercing in its intensity. "Everything but you. I am afraid I have not the stomach for food this evening. Nor do I have the fortitude for my husbandly duties. I will not be coming to you tonight."

His words could not have shocked her more. He had come to her each night, staying in her bed until morning. Often, they woke in the morning and made love all over again. Surely this was a sign that something was far more wrong than he was suggesting.

"Have I done something wrong?" she asked, struggling to make sense of what was happening.

She felt as if she had been rudely awakened from a glorious dream, only to discover the world she had been inhabiting was not real.

"Aside from marrying me?" he shook his head, another shudder coursing through him. "Nothing, my angel."

At his last shudder, she rose from her chair, determined to close the distance between them. He was ill, and it was growing more painfully apparent by the moment. Stubborn man. Did he think to hide a weakness from her? Was he ashamed? Or was he so ill that he did not realize something was wrong with him?

Whatever the reason, it hardly mattered, for when she

reached him, she discovered he was radiating heat. She pressed a hand to his brow. "Ewan, you are feverish."

"I have never felt better," he drawled.

His skin was damp. She smoothed his forelock into place, then took his hands in hers. "Come, darling. We must get you to bed. You need to rest so you can get well."

He allowed her to pull him to his feet, but when he looked down at her, it was as if he was looking straight through her. "I will never be well, darling. More's the pity."

He went even paler as she tugged him away from the table.

"Christ, Hattie, stop moving me," he rasped, sounding as if he were about to be sick.

She stilled, worry compounding. What in heaven's name could be wrong with him? None of the servants were ill, and they had scarcely left Hamilton House in the last fortnight. It made no sense. Still, she knew he could not remain here in the dining room in such a condition. He needed to get to his bedchamber, and she needed to send for his physician.

"You must come, Ewan," she told him gently. "You need rest. Let me take care of you."

"All you have been doing is trying to heal me ever since we wed," he muttered. "It cannot be done."

"Yes," she countered firmly. "It can. And it will. All you have to do is allow it. All you have to do is let me in."

She sensed his inner struggle, watched as he vacillated before her.

At long last, the struggle seemed to drain from him before her eyes.

"Very well, Hattie mine. I will allow you to try."

She should have known a swift rush of relief at his words and his surrender both. But all she felt as she led him to his chamber was the rising tide of apprehension ready to drown her.

## CHAPTER 18

Monty was cold, colder than he had ever been. He huddled beneath bedclothes soaked with his own sweat, teeth chattering as another violent surge of nausea clenched his gut.

*Beelzebub's earbobs*, how many more times would he need to cast up his accounts? Surely there was nothing left to vomit. Surely this would all soon subside. He had never, in all his life, been so miserable. At least, not in his adult life.

There had been a time…

A paroxysm overcame him. *Nay*, he would not think of that time now. His misery was great enough. He wondered how much longer this wretched sickness would last.

He had heard, of course, about the sickness that invariably affected opium eaters when they abruptly ceased indulging. He was no stranger to vice. He had not expected it to be so incapacitating, however. Nor had he imagined it would be prolonged, over the course of days.

It had taken him a full day of going without laudanum for the signs to begin to show. He had foolishly persuaded himself, in the interim, that his consumption of laudanum had not been great enough to render such an ill-effect. Much like the tales of drunkards suddenly quitting swill and becoming violently sick, for he had never suffered such an ailment, he had supposed himself inured.

But by dinner last night, he had known something was desperately wrong. He had suffered through the courses in a valiant attempt to keep his wife from discovering his shame. Though she had been insistent she call for his doctor, he had somehow convinced her to wait.

Through the darkness of the night, when the nightmares had come to claim him, she had rescued him from their vile clutches when she appeared with her candle, illuminating the shadows, bathing his fevered brow with a cool cloth. She had been present for his endless retching. Through it all, she had soothed him with her sweet voice and her gentle caresses.

Blearily, he glanced around the chamber, finding himself alone.

He did not want her to be here, so it was just as well Hattie had finally heeded him and gone. He had no wish for her to see him brought so low, and all by his own recklessness. There was another prick for his guilty conscience.

She still believed his malady was caused by something innocent, when in fact he had created it himself.

He should have told her. Should have explained. But he could not bear to see the inevitable disgust in her eyes. Or to be faced with the questions she would ask. *Why* was not a query he was prepared to answer. The reasons he sought oblivion were not reasons he would impart to anyone.

Ever.

His gut clenched.

Where was the damned chamber pot? Blindly, his hand fumbled through the covers surrounding him. At last, he found it, blessedly emptied. He supposed she was responsible for seeing to it that the servants kept him as comfortable as possible as well. Of course she was. His angel was brave and strong and true, refusing to do anything other than see to his every care.

If she only knew the truth.

The truth of who and what he was.

He doubled over the chamber pot then, his stomach heaving. Nothing emerged from his stomach, but the sickness was not through with him. His gut clenched again. Three more dry heaves, and he collapsed back against the mound of pillows Hattie had arranged for him some time in the night. The ethereal scent of violets tinged the air, blending with the sharp tang of sweat.

He shivered again and bundled the covers around himself.

Perhaps this was how he would meet his end.

It was fitting, he had to admit, for a scoundrel like him.

His eyes fluttered closed once more as another shudder claimed him. An indeterminate span of time passed. He may have drifted to sleep for a few blessed moments of peace. But when his eyes opened once more, it was to his wife's beautiful, worried face hovering over him.

She stroked his hair gently. "I have sent for the doctor, Ewan. You should not be this ill."

Bloody stubborn wench. He had told her he had no wish to be poked and prodded by a damned sawbones. He already knew what was wrong with him. And unless the bastard was going to pour some laudanum down his throat, there was no remedy for his ailment.

"No doctor," he growled.

"You must be seen to," she countered, still stroking his hair.

He loved the way she touched him. Even as lost as he was now, washed up on the rocky shoals of despair, almost drowned, he wanted more of her sweet caresses. More of

Hattie. More of his angel. She had been sent here to save him, to pluck him from the darkness, to bring him into the light. He shivered again, wishing he could escape the damned bedclothes and take her in his arms as he so desperately longed to do.

"No doctor," repeated, but his voice was not firm. Rather, it was a thin, pathetic quiver.

"Hush," she told him, kissing his brow. "Try to rest, my love."

He shuddered again, feeling weak. Broken. Useless.

He had enough strength to reach from beneath the counterpane and grasp her hand. Their fingers entwined, hers giving him hope.

He fell back into delirium to the sound of two precious words.

*My love.*

* * *

SHE SHOULD HAVE IGNORED her husband's wishes and sent for his physician last night as she had wanted, Hattie told herself as she paced the hall outside Ewan's chamber. But she had listened to him. He had been so adamant then, so certain all would be well by morning. He had made her promise not to send for Dr. Young, and she reluctantly had.

But over the course of the evening, his condition had gone from poor to grave. He had been shouting, suffering violent nightmares. Fevers continued to wrack him. And then the retching had begun.

Fear infected her now as she waited for the physician to emerge from the duke's apartments. Her chest ached, and it felt as if it were constricting. Breathing hurt. Ewan was so very ill. He had been retching all morning, but there was nothing left for him to bring up.

"Do try to calm down, Hattie dearest," entreated Ewan's mother, breaking into the tumult of her thoughts. "It does you no good to fret. Dr. Young is an esteemed physician, and Montrose is in excellent care."

She wished she could be as blasé. All she knew was a sick sea of dread. "How can you not worry? He seemed so very ill."

"If he is ill, it is likely caused by an ailment of his own making," the dowager observed acidly. "I have known Montrose all his life, if you will recall. He has ever been reckless, with no shortage of foibles."

What a bloodless manner of thinking about one's own son.

"Do you not care at all?" she snapped, irritated with the dowager for her seeming lack of compassion.

"Of course I care." Ewan's mother sighed heavily. "But your marriage to him is so very new, my dear. You scarcely know him. In time, you will understand precisely why I do not excite myself over my son's ways. One grows tired of looking after the mischief he makes for himself. He will never change."

There it was again, the suggestion she did not know her husband, much like the warnings Ewan himself continually issued to her. What was it that her husband and his mother knew, which she did not?

The door opened before she could ask, and the physician emerged, looking grim.

Hattie rushed forward, somehow managing to speak past the fear choking her throat. "How is His Grace, Dr. Young?"

"He is as well as can be expected in such a circumstance," the doctor said. He was scarcely older than Ewan himself, tall and lean with a hawk-like nose and thinning blond hair.

"How much longer will he be this ill?" she asked next,

praying his answer would be what she wanted to hear, that Ewan would be on the mend soon.

"Naturally, in matters such as this, the duration of the illness is dependent upon the patient." Dr. Young paused, frowning at her. "How much laudanum has His Grace been consuming, and how long has he been consuming it?"

"Laudanum?" she repeated, confused. "I am afraid I do not understand what that has to do with his illness..."

Her words trailed off as she thought of Ewan's valet, wondering if he would be taking laudanum in his tea. She recalled her conversation with him following that incident. He had claimed to take laudanum to abate the pain in his ankle.

*Do you take it every day?* she had asked him.

*No*, he had told her, *only when it is necessary.*

"Forgive me, Your Grace," Dr. Young said, sympathy tingeing his voice now. "This is a sensitive matter indeed. The illness His Grace is suffering is what happens when someone has been consuming laudanum in quantities beyond the ordinary, and on a regular schedule. He was not particularly forthcoming with the specifics of his consumption, and I was hopeful you might be familiar with it."

She struggled to comprehend the information the doctor had just imparted. "That is impossible, Dr. Young. His Grace only takes laudanum occasionally for the pain in the ankle he injured recently in a phaeton accident."

"Ah, I see," said Dr. Young quietly, his countenance grimmer than it had been before.

"What do you see?" Desperation was mingling with despair within her now, accompanying the already queasy sense of dread. "Just what is it you are suggesting, Doctor?"

"As is common in such circumstances, His Grace has been hiding his laudanum dependence from you," the doctor said quietly. "The violence of his reaction suggests His Grace was using the laudanum in greater quantities for a prolonged period of time. He has admitted to me that he abruptly stopped taking drops of it two days ago, which explains the reaction he is currently suffering."

If what Dr. Young was telling her was correct, Ewan had lied to her. Like the jagged shards of a broken porcelain vase being glued back together, the truth was gradually taking shape in her mind. So much of what had happened made sense. Ewan claimed to need the laudanum for his ankle, and yet he had climbed a tree to reach her. He had danced with her. Carried her in his arms. This was what he had been referring to when he had warned her she did not know him.

When he had told her he was irredeemable.

This was also the reason why she had no longer smelled spirits on his person.

He had traded one vice for another, and his dependence upon this one had been far greater than the last. This time, he had been struck low when he attempted to stop it.

"I can see I have shocked you with this news, Your Grace," Dr. Young told her gently. "Once again, I am sorry. All I can do is reassure you that His Grace's illness will pass. This is the body's ordinary reaction to the cessation of opium consumption in large and regular quantities. The best you can do for him now is make him comfortable. Attend to him, give him broth when he is able to take it."

She was awash in a confused swirl of emotion. Anger at Ewan for keeping such a secret from her, continued worry over his illness, confusion over why he had been consuming so much laudanum in secret.

"Thank you, Dr. Young," she managed to say.

The dowager placed a hand on Hattie's arm, reminding her for the first time that she had an audience. When the physician had emerged from Ewan's chamber, all her thoughts had turned to him.

"I warned you, my dear," Ewan's mother said. "In time, you will simply come to expect this behavior from him. Montrose has been this way far too long for him to change, I fear."

Hattie did not believe that, and his mother's calm acceptance of what was clearly a deeper problem irked her. Hattie shrugged away from the dowager's touch.

"Everyone is capable of changing," she said coolly. "Perhaps you would be kind enough to see Dr. Young below while I attend to His Grace?"

She was effectively asking the dowager to keep from Ewan's sickbed. The dowager stiffened at her dismissal, but inclined her head. "Of course, Your Grace. Dr. Young, if you will follow me?"

Hattie was being horridly rude, but she did not care. All she did care about now was her husband. About seeing to his comfort, nursing him back to health, and uncovering the truth. She offered a hasty curtsey to both of them before turning back to his chamber.

She knew where she belonged, and it was by his side.

## CHAPTER 19

Monty woke to dawn painting his chamber golden, and Hattie curled up alongside him, sleeping. After days of suffering, he finally felt a bit like himself. And how bloody welcome that sensation was, as if a crushing weight had been removed from his chest.

Not more welcome than the woman at his side, however.

His angelic wife had been here in his sickroom, tending him without fail. They had not spoken of the true reason for his illness. Not yet. But he had taken one look at her pinched expression when she had reentered his chamber following Dr. Young's visit, and he had known, even in the depths of his misery, that she *knew*. He also knew she was waiting to discuss the subject with him until after he was well again.

And whilst he still felt as if the devil had danced a country reel all over his body, today was the first day since he had stopped taking laudanum that he was not heaving or otherwise bilious, not ridden with fever. He felt strangely lucid.

The world looked sharper.

Hattie looked softer.

More beautiful. Her tresses were plaited in a simple braid,

but even in the early light, it was lustrous and rich. Her lips were parted as she breathed evenly. Her hands were clasped beneath her cheek, completing her angelic aura, for it looked as if she had fallen asleep in prayer.

Praying for what, he wondered? His soul? His survival? Her own ability to forgive him?

Part of him was thankful for her ceaseless devotion to him. Part of him hated she had seen him so low, that she knew one of his darkest secrets, and feared she had only been present at his side out of duty rather than desire.

Memories returned to him then, of the vilest depths of his opium sickness. He had reached a horrid point where he had been desperate for more. He had begged her for it. Railed when she refused him. *Dear God*, had he thrown an ewer of water across the chamber? He distinctly remembered the sound of smashing crockery and knew he had.

He closed his eyes and inhaled against a sharp wave of shame slicing through him. When he opened them again, she was still there, at his side, hauntingly beautiful. So good, she made his chest ache. If she wanted to leave him after this, he could not blame her. He would fight for her, of course. He would follow her, beg her to come back to him.

As if sensing the maelstrom of his thoughts, or mayhap more likely sensing his gaze pinned upon her, Hattie stirred, the dark lashes fanning her cheeks stirring. Suddenly, he found himself drowning in a sea of brilliant green.

"Good morning," he told her softly, uncertain of himself for the first time.

Ordinarily, all he had to do was be wicked, and ladies fell into his bed. With Hattie, he had but to charm or tease, to kiss her into agreement. Vulgar words made her flush but also made her want him. The clever persuasion of his hands, lips, and tongue had always held him in good stead.

What a strange feeling it was not knowing where he

stood with her. Knowing she had witnessed the monster hiding beneath his beautiful mask. He was horridly aware of the fact that he had not bathed in days, and he must smell wretched. That she knew he had lied to her. That she knew he was weak.

"Good morning, Ewan," she returned, lifting herself to a sitting position, much to his regret.

She looked as if she were a fairy about to fly away.

He barely restrained the urge to capture her wrist, keep her here. For he had no right. Not after the way he had deceived her, and the way she had selflessly tended him all the same.

"You have been taking care of me," he observed, his voice hoarse and dry. It cracked as he spoke, much to his chagrin.

The most sought-after rakehell in London could not even utter a proper sentence. He had been more defenseless than a child, taken with fever and hunched over a chamber pot. The good Lord's chemise, he and Hattie had been wed under three weeks' time. She ought to have run as if Cerberus nipped at her heels.

She patted her braid, smoothing stray wisps into place, and straightened her plain, serviceable gown. It was not even a proper night rail, and she had spent the night in it as if she were a charwoman rather than a duchess.

"How are you feeling this morning?" she asked instead of addressing his statement. "You look…"

She trailed off as her bright gaze assessed him, wakefulness gradually replacing the soft slumber which had eased her mien.

"As if I have been dragged behind a carriage from London to Bath?" he asked, attempting a sally.

In truth, this was no laughing matter. He was not smiling, and nor was she.

They stared at each other in tense silence.

She was the first to break it, speaking at last. "I do think you would have been a corpse upon your arrival, had you been dragged that far."

"I feel something like one." He passed a weary hand over his face, as if he could so easily scrub away the horrors of the past few days. As if he could erase all he had done, all she had seen.

If only it were that simple.

That effortless.

Life never was, was it?

She pressed a hand to his brow, and here was his true test of recovery. His cock twitched to life. Awareness pulsed through him.

"You do not feel feverish," she said.

He could have argued the opposite. He felt feverish, but it was a reaction once more of her nearness, as it should be, rather than his abandonment of the laudanum crutch which had seen him through each day for the last few months.

"Hattie," he began, knowing he must apologize. Attempt to explain. "I am sorry about…everything."

"Everything?" She frowned, her gaze searching his. "What do you mean by that, Ewan?"

He was making a muck of this. As he oft did when it came to her. But that was integral to what made Hattie so damn special, so different from all the rest, was it not? He could not be self-assured with her. She mattered far too much to him. With others, he had not cared. They had been easily replaced by another, more enthusiastic version of the last.

There was only one Hattie.

She was rare and good and true.

How strange it seemed to have such mental clarity. He felt as if he had been viewing his life through a smudged window pane, and it had been suddenly cleaned. He could see everything, everyone, in such startling detail. The numbness that had ever been his companion had fled, and in its place was a rich, surprising capacity to feel.

But she was still awaiting his response, her countenance growing more drawn by the moment as he muddled through the complexities of his emotions and realizations.

"I am sorry about keeping the laudanum a secret from you," he forced himself to say, and this admission was not difficult for him to make. "I am sorry I was drowning myself in it, using it to forget, using it to remove myself from all my worries and cares. The truth is that while my ankle does cause me pain sporadically after the accident, I was taking drops of laudanum every day. I was lying to you each day."

And he felt sick about it. He felt disgusted with himself as he thought about it now. He had spent all the precious days of their marriage in a fog of laudanum and pleasure. Although everything between them had been real and true on his end, he wished he had not spent every moment of their marriage pouring laudanum down his worthless gullet with his tea and negus.

"Why, Ewan?" she asked, that question he had been dreading. "Why would you grow so dependent upon it? Why did you deceive me?"

He could not give her the answer, the true answer. Not in full. He would have to lie to her again. Because if he told her the horrible truth, he would lose her forever. She would never look at him the same. And losing Hattie, well, he could not fathom it. Losing her was not even a consideration. It was an unbearable prospect.

He cared for her far too much.

Perhaps that was something the laudanum had been dulling him to as well—the way he felt for this incredible, resilient, compassionate, giving woman he had married. But there were bounds to compassion, he knew. There were limits to understanding. He would not test or break them now. Not when he needed her so.

"I was desperate after the accident," he told her, and that much, at least, was true. "I was in great pain. I felt myself responsible for what happened to Torrie. That night was... my God, Hattie, I love him as if he were my brother. Afterward, all I could think about was how if I had declined to race him, he would not have been lying at death's door. Later, when he recovered but could not recall anything past waking up at Torrington House, it was as if a part of me had died. I... I relied upon the laudanum because it helped the pain. All of the pains within me. Only, in the end, it became the pain. It *caused* the pain."

*There.* He had revealed all of himself he possibly could to her. If lying by omission was a sin, he was guilty, and he would gladly go to hell for it rather than tell her about the other source of pain in his life. The one buried deep within his past.

For a long time, she sat alongside him, searching his gaze, a frown marring the creamy perfection of her forehead. He could not help but to feel as if she were testing him. Attempting to look inside him, to see to his heart, to determine whether or not he was being honest with her.

He was. About everything he said. It was merely what he had not said, which he would necessarily have to carry on. It was a burden he would bear.

"I am sorry, too, Ewan," she said, shocking him to his core.

"You are sorry?" It was unbelievable. She was unbelievable. And he did not deserve her, just as he had always known. "You have nothing to be sorry for, Hattie darling."

"I blamed you as well." She paused, seeming to gather her thoughts, tears shimmering in her expressive eyes. "I told you that you were responsible for what happened to Torrie. I wanted to believe it, too, because blaming you was far easier than blaming him. It gave me a reason to be angry with you, to guard my heart against you."

"I was to blame," he countered. "If we had not gotten into our cups, and if we had not decided to race, your brother would still have his memory."

"He chose his actions, Ewan. Just as you chose yours. I cannot blame you for his any more than I can blame him for yours." She stopped once more, reaching for one of his hands, linking their fingers. "We are all of us responsible for our own decisions, are we not? And we must live with them."

He felt such shame in the face of her forgiveness. But he squeezed her fingers just the same, as if he were a drowning man adrift at sea, and she were his only means of saving himself. Because it was the truth. He needed this woman.

*His* woman.

"I am damned sorry for most of my decisions," he told her with feeling. "Nearly all of them. I am sorry for lying to you. Sorry for what happened to Torrie. Sorry you had to see me this way. Sorry you had to tend to me whilst I was out of my head."

"I did not have to tend to you, Ewan," she returned, her gaze steady upon his. "I *wanted* to. I told you before, I care about you. Do you regret marrying me? Was that…was what we have shared because of the laudanum?"

"God, no." His fingers tightened on hers. "Never. Marrying you is the only good thing I have ever done in my entire misbegotten life. And nothing—no part of it—was because of the opium. I am sorry you even need to question it, but please know I am honored to have you as my wife."

He still did not deserve her. He never would.

"Do you mean it?" she asked, her expression so tense, so stricken, she reminded him of a wild bird, poised for flight at the slightest provocation.

"Of course I do." He raised her hand to his lips, kissed it with all the reverence he could manage in his weakened state. "I need you, Hattie."

She was silent for far too long.

But at long last, she cupped his face with her free hand, the trepidation melting from her lovely face. All he saw in its place was an exquisite, unfettered caring, so raw and real, it robbed him of his breath. "Good. Because I need you, too."

CHAPTER 20

The day was surprisingly warm and bright. Autumn would soon give way to winter, but they were enjoying a rare shift in temperatures that made gray London seem as if verdant spring had unexpectedly settled in.

"Are you soon finished?" Hattie asked her husband, feeling foolish indeed in her satin and lace evening gown when it was only afternoon, and she was alone with him in the small square garden of Hamilton House. The roses had already withered on their trellises, but the Sweet William were yet in full, brilliant bloom. She sat on a stone bench with statues of Ceres and Proserpina standing silent sentinel.

A lone bird sang overhead somewhere, its trill clear and full-bodied.

"Yes." The smile Ewan gave her was shy. Boyish.

It sent an arrow that landed directly in her heart. She had never seen him look so young, or so unguarded. Over the course of the last sennight, he had fully recovered from the opium sickness, which had lain him so low. He was still the same man she had married, but there was an undeniable difference to him now—he seemed as if years had been peeled away from him, as if a weight had been removed from his shoulders.

He seemed, in a word, *free*.

"I feel horridly silly," she protested, "and my bottom is growing quite weary of this seat."

"I shall be more than happy to kiss away any aches," he said, his grin deepening. "And there is no need to feel silly. You look ridiculously beautiful. Like a faerie queen come to preside over us mere mortals, if only for an hour."

She frowned down at the gown she wore, for it was the same Pomona green satin and jonquil robe affair she had donned the night she had been hiding behind the potted palms. When those two awful creatures had been snickering over her choice of dress and the notion the Duke of Montrose might ever be interested in a plain old wallflower such as herself.

"That wretched Lady Ella and Lady Lucy had quite a bit to say about this gown," she reminded him primly, wondering at his request.

"Those vapid harpies were envious," he told her, lifting his pastel crayon in its holder aloft as he stood before his easel. "People often attack that which makes them jealous. It is a sad commentary on themselves more than anything else. I find you enchanting in this gown. Of course, I find you equally enchanting out of it."

Warmth flared in her cheeks and elsewhere, too, between her thighs. She pressed them together in an effort to stave off a rush of longing. "I thought you wished to draw me, not seduce me."

In the wake of his illness, Ewan had confided in her that he had once had a passion for sketching. That passion had been steadily replaced over the years by all manner of vice and debauchery. She had been surprised at how readily he had agreed with her suggestion that he resume the art once more. And shocked when he had suggested she pose as his first subject.

His searing gaze traveled over her now, igniting a fire deep within. "It is a matter of course that I always want to seduce you, pet. But for now, I shall settle for sketching you. Do sit still, or I shall never have a hope of finishing any time soon."

He had chosen the backdrop for sketching her and the gown. The poor dowager had seemed quite perplexed by the sight of Hattie in an evening gown and Ewan with his case of pastel crayons under one arm and his easel beneath the other. After commenting that Ewan had not sketched in years, she took herself off in search of the day's social calls. The strain between mother and son was still evident. Hattie wondered at it, but she had yet to broach the topic with her husband.

Small steps.

One at a time.

They had already progressed quite a bit from where they had once been, and she must not grow too impatient with him, she knew. He had changed so much. The man he was becoming did not resemble the dissipated Duke of Debauchery he had once been in the least, aside from his omnipresent good looks and charm. Even that had enhanced. He looked healthier now in a way he had not before—his complexion was brighter, his lean form fuller.

But still, her bottom was aching, and she was growing weary of remaining still. "I think I have been sitting here for two hours," she groused.

His lips twitched as he leaned over the easel and made some bold strokes. "Has anyone ever told you that you make a very impatient subject, Hattie darling?"

Part of her impatience stemmed from not only the hard stone of the bench beneath her, but also the necessary evil of remaining still whilst his eyes roamed all over her. Each look was as seductive as a caress.

She was growing most uncomfortable in an entirely different manner. "You are the first to be so bold."

"I find I enjoy being bold with you." He glanced up, giving her a small, knowing smirk.

Yes, he did, the wicked man.

And she loved every moment of it.

She loved *him* even more.

But she had not said the words aloud just yet. She was not certain she dared. Certainly, Ewan had not offered proclamations of tender feelings to her either. Still, their lovemaking was another way in which things between them had changed. There was a poignant reverence to each encounter now. He touched her differently, with such gratitude in addition to desire.

"And I like when you are bold," she forced herself to say, irritated with herself at how husky her voice emerged.

He selected a different pastel crayon from his case and placed it inside the metal holder before returning to his task. "Do you know, I cannot find the proper shade for your eyes? The color of them is so unique that I have had to blend no less than three different pigments."

More warmth unfurled within her. "They are only green, and not even a proper green, but a rather muddy one."

He continued working strokes over the paper, his concentration evident in the stern set of his jaw. "Nonsense. They are the most beautiful eyes I have ever beheld. A rare combination of Prussian blue, yellow ochre, and a hint of burnt sienna."

Her heart gave a pang. Just when she thought she could not possibly love him more…

"No one has ever paid such notice to my eyes before," she

said, fidgeting with the fall of her gown. Trying to tell herself his attentions did not mean more.

He was an artist with his tools, attempting to capture a likeness. She must not fancy he had feelings for her beyond desire and the common concern any gentleman would have for his wife just because she loved him so much it hurt.

"Then no gentleman has ever been worthy of capturing you," he said softly, his gaze flitting back to her.

A new frisson of awareness slid through her. The air between them seemed to change, growing more heated. The silly bird, wherever she was, sang from above with greater enthusiasm.

"I never wanted to be captured until you," she found herself revealing before she could think better of the admission.

It was true, and once spoken, could not be recalled.

"Hattie." His voice was low, velvet to her senses. Beloved.

She thought she could happily listen to her name uttered in his decadent baritone every day for the rest of her life. With each day that passed, the notion of them living separate lives one day grew more and more impossible for her to fathom. She could only hope he felt the same.

"Yes?" she asked hesitantly, watching as he set down his pastel crayon and stepped away from the easel.

"If I do not have my cock inside you in the next five minutes, I am going to die," he growled, striding toward her.

She shot off the bench as if it were made of flame rather than cold marble and went willingly into his arms. His familiar scent hit her, along with desire, and love so powerful she trembled as she locked her hands behind his neck.

"That is just as well," she told him. "Because if I do not have your cock within me in the next five minutes, I shall turn into flames."

"*God's fichu*, I love it when you say filthy things with that angelic mouth of yours." He kissed her slowly, swiftly. "Then it stands to reason we must save each other, mustn't we?"

"Oh, yes," she agreed, breathless, lips still tingling from the bliss of his mouth upon hers.

Before she knew what he was about, he bent and swept her off her feet, holding her in his arms. She was weightless, cradled against his chest, and it made her giddy.

"I have just the plan, sweet." But instead of returning to the house as she had supposed he would do, he strode deeper into the small garden.

"Ewan," she protested on a squeak. "Surely you do not mean to… Anyone could see us here…"

"That is part of the fun," he told her. "The thrill of getting caught. Knowing that at any moment someone could peer out a window and catch a glimpse of what we are doing."

His words shocked her. To her amazement, they also stirred the fires of her desire. Between her legs, she was not just aching, but throbbing. Desperate for him.

"That is indecent," she said anyway as he carried her deeper down the gravel path to the center of the garden, where more Sweet William blossomed in large urns and a sundial revealed the time of day.

Though they were surrounded by hedges, they would remain clearly visible to anyone who ventured to the windows overlooking the garden. She wondered, before she could stifle the thought, if this was something he had done before. Unbidden, the bitter words of his mother returned to her, chiding, bringing with them an unwanted pinprick of doubt. *He will never change.*

The dowager was wrong. Ewan had changed. He was no longer the wild and wicked rakehell he had once been. He had promised to be faithful to her.

*Until he gets an heir on you.*

Ewan set her on her feet, and she wished the thought to

the devil. Doubt had no place in their marriage. Nor did fear or misgiving. He was being honest with her now. There were no more secrets between them, and she had to trust in that. To trust in him.

"Two minutes have already passed," she teased him, growing bolder.

One of his hands sank into her hair, cupping her head, while the other clamped on her waist, hauling her into him. "Fuck, I want you."

"Then have me." Her hands were still linked behind his neck, and their closeness meant her breasts were crushed deliciously against him. She pulled his head down to hers.

Their lips sealed. There was no languor in this kiss. Only desperate, raw hunger. She opened to his questing tongue as the kiss deepened. He made a low sound of approval that made her ache. They kissed as if they would cease to exist if they stopped. Kissed as if they never wanted to part.

It was a forever kiss.

Her initial embarrassment fled in the face of his feral passion. The need to pleasure him rose within her, and it would not be denied. Breaking away from him at last, she sank to her knees on the gravel, not caring if she ruined her gown, not giving a fig that the sharp rocks dug into her sensitive skin through her layers. She had tended to him in this manner before, and she wanted to give him a release now. She wanted to sin with him. To give in to desire. To give him everything.

"Hattie, darling, no," he protested. "The path is too hard."

"Yes." She undid the fall of his breeches and his cock sprang forth, giving lie to his denial.

He wanted this every bit as much as she did.

She grasped his thick, smooth shaft. This part of him, like all the rest, was beautifully formed. A drop seeped from the tip, and she could not resist catching it on her tongue, relishing the taste of him.

He groaned, his fingers tightening in her hair. "You do not need to do this, pet."

"I want to," she said, and then she took him in her mouth. As much of him as she could.

His hips jerked, his cock surging to the back of her throat.

"Hell," he rasped. "Your pretty mouth is so hot and wet."

Yes, it was. And he was hot and hard and delicious. She hummed her approval as she moved, taking him deep before dragging her lips along his length, and then sucking him once more. She kept one hand on the root of him, and with the other, she gently massaged his heavy sac. Once, he had flooded her mouth with his seed, and the remembrance of the power to make him spend spurred her onward.

"Enough," he gritted, disengaging from her. "I want my cock inside your sweet cunny when I spill."

She wanted it, too. She allowed him to pull her to her feet. He surprised her by turning her around and leading her to a nearby statue of Mars. He placed her hands upon the marble deity's muscled calves.

"Stay just like this," he instructed her. "Do not move."

He kissed her nape, caressed her waist, and then she heard the crunch of gravel behind her.

"Ewan," it was her turn to protest. She glanced over her shoulder to find him kneeling behind her.

"Turn around, darling," he ordered. "If you cannot behave yourself, I will not give you what you want."

*Oh.* She swallowed and turned forward, shivering with anticipation as she felt his hands on her ankles. His touch made her mad for him. He grasped one firmly, guiding them apart. And then he caressed higher, up her calves, past her knees, all the way to her thighs.

His tongue flicked over her without warning, and she

could not contain her cry. It echoed in the garden, reverberating against the walls. As he licked her center, his fingers parted her, and he found her pearl with unerring ease. She was so ready for his touch, she almost spent then and there.

But he was not finished with her yet. He began a maddening rhythm, sinking inside her with his tongue and rubbing torturous circles over the bud of her sex. White-hot sensation bolted up her spine. She held on to Mars, the cold marble a delicious contrast of sensation to the warmth of Ewan's fingers and tongue between her legs.

Her heart was pounding, breath emerging in gasps. He moaned as if he were consuming the most delicious dessert, the vibration of his pleased voice setting off little tremors within her, the prelude to something wild and furious.

"You taste so sweet," he murmured, giving her a long, slow lick that made her knees buckle.

He caught her with his free hand, keeping her from sinking into a pool of quivering lust at the base of the statue, and she tightened her grasp on the war god. All around her the day was bright, the colors more vibrant, the pleasure inside her more frenzied than it had ever been before. It was as if the small garden had been bathed in gold, as if she had.

The splendor building inside her could not be controlled. His tongue sank deep, and he increased the pressure on her pearl. She lost herself. In a radiant haze, she spent, a burst of pleasure quaking through her with almost violent force. Her heart was galloping, her breath ragged.

He stood behind her, lifting her skirts. In one hard thrust, he entered her. Deep, so deep. She instinctively pressed her bottom toward him, seeking more even as the ripples of her release continued. He began a maddening rhythm.

"God, you are so wet," he said, nipping at her neck and he drove in and out of her.

She was speechless, her body moving against his as if they were one, seeking more of the pleasure he promised.

"I want you to come again, darling." He kissed her ear. "Come on my cock. I want to feel you."

*Dear heavens.* His words were wicked. So very vulgar.

She liked them. And she was on the precipice once more, about to fall headlong into the abyss.

"Do you think anyone is watching us, pet?" he asked as he thrust harder, deeper.

She thought of all the windows around them. With him inside her, she no longer found the prospect mortifying. Instead, she found it oddly thrilling.

She made a sound, half cry, half whimper, as she neared her peak.

His fingers grazed over her swollen bud once more. It was the nudge she needed. She reached her pinnacle in a dazzling fury of bliss. Her body clenched on him, tightening, and in two more thrusts, the hot release of his seed flooded her.

He collapsed against her, breathing as heavily as she was, their bodies still joined. They remained that way, pressed together for an indeterminate span of time, as reality slowly intruded upon their idyll in the form of fat droplets falling from the sky.

It was raining, Hattie realized.

The dazzling gold of the day had vanished behind a cloud, and once more, London was enrobed in gray. Ewan kissed the side of her throat, then withdrew from her and flipped down her skirts.

She turned around to the sight of him tucking himself back in his breeches.

The sky opened in truth then, unleashing a sudden deluge.

"Damn it all," he cursed, holding out his hand to her.

"Come, sweet. We must get you inside before you catch a chill."

How sweet of him to worry over her, she thought, allowing him to lead her back down the path. By the time they reached the easel where he had been working on her portrait, the likeness he had devoted hours to had turned into nothing more than a smear of wet colors.

"Oh Ewan, your beautiful drawing!" she exclaimed. "It is ruined."

"It was a pale comparison to you anyway," he said. "I can always make another, especially if your sitting for me ends in such spectacular fashion."

She was sure she was flushing furiously beneath all the rain. They gathered everything as best as they could and rushed back inside, dripping all over the rugs and laughing at the messes they had made.

"Next time," her husband told her with his rakehell's grin, "I am going to draw you naked in your chamber. No chance of rain there."

She wrapped her arms around him and kissed him again, thinking she had never been happier.

## CHAPTER 21

"The Honorable Mr. Arthur Parkross is calling, Your Grace," Low announced.

Seven words.

That was all.

And Monty's life imploded.

If there was ever a time when he had needed a substance to fortify himself—a glass of gin, a drop of laudanum, it was now. Of all days, a perfectly happy Wednesday at the end of November was the day when the monster from his past chose to reemerge at last.

He supposed he ought to have anticipated such a move by the manipulative bastard. His uncle's notes had continued to arrive, growing more desperate and threatening in tone, and Monty had continued to ignore them. He could refuse to see him now, but that would only prolong the agony, the wait.

His face felt as if it would crack if he moved it. He swallowed in a mouth that had gone suddenly dry. That old, sick dread unfurled within him.

"Send him in," he managed to say at last.

Low bowed.

It was all quite ordinary.

Except for the fact that his world as he knew it—the carefully crafted paradise he had won with Hattie—was about to burn down to nothing but ash.

He attempted to prepare himself. Struggled to maintain his calm. But by the time Arthur Parkross stood at the threshold to his study, he leapt to his feet, hands balled into fists. He was dimly aware of sending his butler away, waiting for the door to close.

His heart pounded harder. "I would bow," he said, "but I have no intention of pretending I hold you in any sort of regard."

Parkross bowed to him. He was dressed elegantly, an older version of the monster who haunted Monty's dreams. His dark hair was silver now over his balding pate. He appeared thinner. There were sharp lines of age marring his forehead. The hand gripping the filigree head of his walking stick shook ever so slightly.

"I will show you the respect you deny me," said his uncle, his tone mocking.

"What the hell are you doing here?" Monty snapped, part of him breaking inside.

Here was the man who had tormented him when he had been a lad. The man who had hurt him. Who had misused him. The man who was family. A man who should have been trustworthy and honorable. The need to do him violence teemed, ugly and festering inside him.

"You did not answer my letters," his uncle said. "I had no choice but to seek the lion in his den."

"If I were a lion, I would have already ripped off your ugly head and made you my dinner," he said coldly. "I made it clear that I want nothing to do with you. Ever again. You are dead to me."

His uncle's smile was forced. "Ah, but here I am, still very much alive. And desperately in need of funds."

Money.

Of course.

"I would sooner die by my own hand than give you a fucking farthing," he spat.

"Do not be hasty," Parkross said calmly. "I understand you are married now."

His uncle's allusion to Hattie made Monty's blood go cold. "You are never to speak to her. She will never know you."

"Do you think you control me, Montrose?" his uncle asked. "I can assure you that you do not. I can seek out Her Grace at any time I choose. How do you think she would feel if she knew about what you have done?"

His gut curdled. "It is not what I have done, but what was done to me."

Again, the sick bastard smiled. "That is not how I remember it, my boy."

"Do not call me that," he bit out.

"What happened was an aberration," his uncle said soothingly. "A sin. But no one ever need know."

"As long as you get your funds," he guessed, feeling as if he would retch.

"Precisely." Parkross's smile faded. "I am in need of ten thousand pounds. The creditors are darkening my door. I will give you three days to make your decision. If you do not provide me with the funds I require, I will regrettably be left with no choice other than to inform Her Grace of her husband's shocking depravities."

"You will not go near her, you brazen whoreson," he said, but even as he bellowed the order, he knew there was no way he could enforce it.

If Parkross chose to seek out Hattie and tell her about

what he had happened so long ago, there would be no stopping him. Desperation lanced through him, followed by despair. His entire body felt as if it had seized up, as if he were one of the marble statues in the garden, cold and dead.

"The choice is yours," his uncle said calmly. "I need the ten thousand pounds, and I need it desperately. Desperation will drive a man to do things he would otherwise not."

"And what was it that drove you to hurt an innocent boy, one who was your own flesh and blood? Was that desperation, Parkross, or was it the pure evil festering inside you, you spineless maggot?"

"I was weak then, but I have repented my sins." His uncle started forward, as if to menace him.

But Monty was not the defenseless lad he had once been. He was taller than Parkross, far stronger, and age, all these years later, was a boon to Monty instead of a curse. His uncle was elderly. Likely ailing. He would have no hope of defeating Monty in a bout of fisticuffs. Indeed, the drubbing he could give him would likely end him.

Monty moved forward, warning in every angle of his body, ready to defend himself if he must. His uncle shrank back, apparently realizing the error in his judgment. It was a moot point. He could not murder Parkross, regardless of how tempting putting the sick bastard out of his misery was.

"I am not giving you ten thousand pounds," he seethed instead. "I do not give a damn if you spend the rest of your miserable existence on the streets. Stay the hell away from my wife, and stay away from me."

"You think I am bluffing," Parkross guessed, his countenance serious. Grim. "I assure you I am not. If I lose everything, there will be no reason for me to keep my silence. I will not stop at Her Grace, either. I will go to the gossips with it. All the land will know what you are. You will be ruined. Shamed. Is that what you want, Montrose?"

Of course it was not what he wanted.

He had not buried his memories, attempted to dull the pain by any means necessary, so that his bastard of an uncle would unleash the demons of his past upon the world. And especially not upon Hattie.

His sweet, angelic Hattie, who had always deserved better. If she knew the truth...

Nay, he could not bear to think it.

He needed time to think. To formulate a plan.

The desperation in his uncle's gaze and voice could not be feigned.

"Get out," he ordered hoarsely. "Get out of my house and do not ever dare to return, or I will beat you to within an inch of your wretched life."

"You know where to find me," Parkross said. "Three days, my boy."

He had no intention of seeking his uncle out.

"The next time I see you, it will be in hell," he vowed, hating the tremor in his voice.

Hating the reminder that, deep inside, he was still the same, scared lad whose uncle had defiled him.

\* \* \*

As had become her daily habit, Hattie sought out Ewan in his study. Ordinarily, he did not receive callers in the later afternoon, for it was when the two of them reconvened after their day's activities and shared tea. Often, he sketched her while they chatted. Or she read poems to him while he rested his head in her lap, and she strummed her fingers through his hair, as if he were a musical instrument only she could play.

What a fanciful notion, she thought, smiling to herself as she made her way down the hall, following her familiar path. But it pleased her. Their connection was growing deeper with each passing day, and she could not be more content.

She was about to knock on his study door when it flew open and an older gentleman bearing a walking stick emerged. She drew up short, taken aback.

"Forgive me, sir," she apologized, dipping into a curtsey.

Her gaze instantly flew to her husband, who stood at the stranger's back, a vicious scowl on his face. It was clear to her that whomever this man was, he was a most unwanted guest.

The man bowed. "Your Grace, I presume? I am Arthur Parkross, Montrose's uncle."

*Uncle?* She had not even known Ewan had one. Neither he nor the dowager had made mention of such a person. The enmity emanating from her husband was almost palpable, but polite manners dictated she treat the man as an honored guest.

"I am pleased to make your acquaintance, Mr. Parkross," she offered, casting a questioning gaze in Ewan's direction.

"Mr. Parkross was just leaving, my dear," Ewan told her, his voice rigid as his bearing.

"Yes, forgive me for the haste with which I must pay my call," said Mr. Parkross. "I look forward to seeing you again, Your Grace. Montrose."

With another bow, he took his leave.

Hattie watched him go, confusion over her husband's reaction swirling through her, along with misgiving. Something was wrong, though she could not determine just what it was with such a cursory meeting. She had never before seen Ewan so icy cold, so rigid.

"I did not realize you had an uncle," she began hesitantly when they were alone once more. "You never mentioned him."

Ewan's gaze was so dark, it was almost black. He looked

different—as if he teemed with fury. "I do not have an uncle. That excuse for a man is not my family."

The biting ice in his voice shocked her. "You have a quarrel with him, then?"

"No quarrel." He passed a hand over his tense jaw. "I hate him, and that is all. He is not welcome here, and he knows it."

"Do you want to talk about it, Ewan?"

He shrugged away from her touch for the first time since they had wed. "No. I do not."

Hattie tried to suppress the hurt that welled up within her at his curtness, telling herself the anger and coldness was not truly directed at her, even if she was bearing the brunt of it. "Of course. Forgive me."

Ewan looked away from her, raking his fingers through his hair. "What do you want, Hattie?"

She flinched at the sharpness of his question. The sensual lover and caring husband she had come to know over the course of their marriage was nowhere to be found in the stranger before her. The little fears she carried, lingering with the doubts, rose to the surface at once. How many times had she worried he would grow bored of being a husband? That he would miss his life of debauchery and endless women and revelries?

That she would not be enough to hold him, in the end?

She swallowed down a knot of trepidation. "Are we not going to take tea together today?"

His gaze jerked back to her, his expression still taut with anger. "Not today, I am afraid. I have many matters to attend to, and little time to play the milksop."

*Play the milksop?*

She frowned as the misgiving deepened, trying to understand the sudden change which had come over him. "Have I done something wrong, Ewan? Have I displeased you in some way?"

He exhaled on a sigh. "I think we have been spending far too much time in each other's company. It is not natural for a husband and wife to be so oft together."

Hattie could not shake the suspicion his abrupt sea change had been caused by the meeting with his uncle, but if he was not willing to confide in her, what more could she do? She did not want to push him.

"I will leave you to your *many matters*, then," she said quietly, still unable to quell the hurt his brusque manner caused. "Perhaps I will pay a visit to Lady Searle."

"Yes," he agreed, sounding distracted. "Why do you not do that, madam?"

Ewan had never spoken to her so formally. The absence of endearment was glaring. Troubling. He was already turning away from her, going back to his study.

She caught his coat sleeve, staying him, knowing she had to try one more time. For his sake as much as for her own. She hated seeing him like this. Hated the distance he was forcing between them. "Ewan, wait. Are you certain you do not want to talk about whatever happened with Mr. Parkross just now?"

He looked back at her. "Quite certain. Give my regards to Lady Searle, if you please."

With that, he shrugged free of her touch, strode back into his study, and slammed the door behind him. Hattie remained where she was, staring at the door, feeling suddenly, unutterably, alone.

CHAPTER 22

*M*onty had never been so sick in all his life. Not even those horrible days he had spent casting up his accounts and shuddering beneath the wrath of fevers as he weaned his body from opium could compare. He had reached a bitter realization as he watched Hattie speaking to Parkross.

The juxtaposition had not been lost upon him, everything that was good in his life standing before the root of all the darkness. He could not allow the evil to touch her.

He knew what he needed to do.

There was only one way to send Hattie away from him forever. To make certain he could never hurt her again, nor sully her with the sordid demons of his past. He was not worthy of an angel like her, and he never had been. All along, he had known it. And he was damned glad he had savored her whilst he had the chance.

Because now, he was going to set her free as best as he could. Hattie was stubborn, determined to always see the good in him. If she knew the truth, her disgust would be violent. Crushing. Of that, he had no doubt. No, he would spare her the horror of learning what her husband was.

When he had cleared away all his spirits and laudanum following his illness, he had hidden away a bottle of gin. Just one. He retrieved it now, pulling it from a drawer. Hand shaking, he opened the bottle, held it to his lips, and took a deep, burning draught.

Fire shot down his gullet.

Along with shame.

Self-hatred.

He closed his eyes and took another sip, then another and another. On a hoarse cry, he slammed the bottle back down upon his desk. The motion was so forceful, the liquor sloshed out of the bottle, raining upon the back of his hand. Another sound emerged from him, and he realized to his horror that his cheeks were wet, his vision blurred.

Tears.

He was crying, *by God*. And it was the first time he had cried since those long-ago nights. Since the first time...

"Fuck," he bit out, pounding his fist into the desk. All these years, and he was still the same weak lad who had allowed Arthur Parkross to abuse him.

He snatched up the gin once more, held it to his lips, and drank.

He drank away the pain of knowing he was about to lose the only woman he had ever cared for. The only woman he would ever want. He drank away the loathing. Drank away the shame. Drank away the disgust at knowing he was breaking every promise he had made to Hattie, to himself.

And then, when he could bear no more, he rang for his butler.

Low appeared at the threshold. "Your Grace?"

"Send word to Madame Marcheaux that I require the presence of two of her freshest lovelies," he said, his gut curdling at the request as much as the thought of what he must do.

Touching another woman made him want to retch.

Hurting Hattie...

"Madame Marcheaux, Your Grace?" Low asked, a frown creasing the loyal retainer's brow. It was the only sign of his disapproval.

"Yes," Monty said before he could change his mind. Before his courage flagged. "And be quick about it, if you please."

The butler inclined his head. "As Your Grace wishes."

With a bow, he was gone, looking as grim as any ghost.

Monty's eyes slid closed after the servant was gone. Bile rose in his throat. Perhaps he did not have to do this. Perhaps there was some other way. Any other way.

*No.*

He knew the answer as surely as he knew his own name. He could not bear Hattie's disgust. Or worse, her pity. If she learned the horrible truth of what had happened in his youth, it would be the end of him. He would drive her away the only way he knew how. And in so doing, he would be granting her the biggest favor he could possibly give her, freedom.

He would spare her the curse of ultimately hating him one day, should the truth ever arise.

Even if doing so felt as if he were tearing his beating heart from his own chest.

More gin was what he needed. Fortification. He needed oblivion to subdue his rational mind. To no longer think or feel.

He raised the bottle to his lips, took another sip. But how bitter it tasted on his tongue. His stomach was a sea of sick. He swallowed the gin, thought of hurting Hattie, and his stomach lurched.

*God's fichu*, he was going to be ill.

He scarcely made it to the chamber pot he had long since kept in his study for just such a purpose before violently casting up his accounts.

* * *

THE HOUR WAS LATE, approaching dinner, by the time Hattie returned to Hamilton House after paying a call to the Marchioness of Searle. But after a reassuring talk with her new friend, Hattie was ready to seek out Ewan once more. Her determination was renewed. She would not allow him to drive a wedge between them because he did not want to discuss troubling matters.

*Make him speak to you*, Lady Searle had advised. *Do not allow him to hide away.*

Hattie was heeding her advice. She handed off her hat, gloves, and pelisse.

"Where is His Grace, Low?" she asked the butler, deciding she would not waste another moment in seeking Ewan out.

One way or another, she would discover what was troubling her husband. Lady Searle had a tremendously happy marriage with her husband, for theirs was a love match. Although it had not begun as such, Lady Searle had confided. Which gave Hattie hope.

Perhaps one day, Ewan would return her affections. Or perhaps her heart was foolish to hope.

"His Grace is in his study, Your Grace," Low informed her.

"Very good, thank you." She set off down the hall, her thoughts already traveling to what she would say.

"I would not recommend entering His Grace's study just now, Your Grace," Low said, following in her wake. There was an edge to his tone that was not ordinarily present.

She paused and turned to the servant. His countenance was not as stoic, as bereft of emotion as it usually was, either. Something was wrong. Worry knotted in her belly. Fear made her cold. There was only one reason for the butler to suggest she avoid her husband's study. To look and sound so disturbed.

Was Ewan drinking gin again? Or consuming laudanum? Had that been the reason for his coldness earlier?

The moment the suspicions hit her, she hated herself for them. How dare she think the worst of him when he had worked so hard, when he had suffered to rid himself of his vices? He had come so far. And they had come so far together. Of course, he would not jeopardize what they shared by getting into his cups or eating opium again.

Of course he would not.

Guilt made her cheeks go hot.

"I need to speak with His Grace," she told the butler. "Is he having a private meeting?"

She could not otherwise fathom the butler's resistance to her calling upon her own husband in his private domain.

"Yes," the butler said. "His Grace is otherwise occupied with a matter of import. May I take the liberty of having a bath drawn for Your Grace? Sir Toby has yet to enjoy his midday repast. Shall I inquire with Monsieur Tremblay as to what treats may await him?"

Hattie was about to answer when a distinctly feminine titter echoed through the silence.

Everything within her froze. And the dread she had been holding at bay for the entirety of her union to Montrose surged forward like a deluge. Drowning her. She held herself still, listening, praying she had misheard, that her imagination had somehow conjured the sound of her greatest fear.

More sounds reached her. Laughter. Moaning.

She felt sick.

Low's expression shifted. There was no denying the pity in his gaze. "Shall I have the bath drawn, Your Grace?"

He asked the question as if they had not just heard the evidence of her husband's adultery. As if the reason Low was attempting to keep her from Ewan's study was not painfully obvious.

"No bath," she managed past numb lips.

She turned toward the sound, knowing at once that she must verify the source. That she must see for herself. Knowing, too, the sight would be the end of her. Her heart would be forever broken. She could not bear…

Her feet were moving. Dragging her toward the abyss. The study door loomed. More sounds assaulted her, but she scarcely heard them over the pounding of her heart.

Low was calling after her, his tone pleading.

"Your Grace, do not, I beg of you…"

But nothing would stop her from finding out the truth. *Oh, Ewan, how could you?* They had found such happiness together. Though he had never said the words to her, she had been so certain he at least cared for her. That his feelings for her were every bit growing. Moreover, he had vowed to remain faithful until she gave him an heir.

She had trusted him with her heart. Trusted his word.

*You promised me, Ewan.*

She reached the door. More low, keening moans split the air. She opened it with such force that it crashed into the wall within. But she did not care about the damage to the plaster. Nor she did care about the spectacle she was causing.

All she cared about was the sight greeting her.

Ewan was seated at his imposing study desk. Two women she had never seen before were seated upon it, their gowns pooled at their waists. Half-naked. They were both golden-haired, both undeniably beautiful. Everything Hattie was not.

There was a horrible moment of silence as she stood on

the threshold, taking in the scene before her. Ewan's gaze met hers from the space between the strumpets seated upon his desk. His expression was cold. Emotionless.

It was as if she were facing a stranger.

"Ewan." His name left her, strangled, part curse, part question.

"Whatever it is you require, I am afraid it must wait. I am currently occupied," he said coldly.

Those words hit her like a physical blow.

The women's gazes were upon her, their expressions undeniably curious. They looked as if they were enjoying this spectacle.

"Quite occupied," said the one on the right.

Ewan's hand was on the woman's bare spine, gliding up and down.

But his eyes had never strayed from Hattie.

How she hated that woman, hated that she knew her husband's touch. Hated her husband for what he was doing. For what he was destroying, not just her love for him but everything they had shared together. Had it all been a lie?

"Go," he ordered her.

Still, she stood there like a fool, begging him with her eyes to stop this madness. To move away. She noted he was fully clothed, his cravat perfectly knotted. Not a hair was mussed out of place. Surely he had not been debauching these wretched females. She thought she could even forgive him this. If he stopped now…

"Ewan, please," she begged.

"Kiss," he said.

Like vassals obeying the order of their king, the women on his desk embraced each other, their lips coming together. A husky moan curdled the air.

"No," Hattie cried out.

It was as if she lost control of herself. As if her mind had completely broken away from the rest of her, like a runaway horse.

His gaze still pinned to her, Ewan slid his hands up each woman's bare back, sinking his fingers into the skeins of their unbound hair.

"Go," he said again, cruelly. Coldly.

And this time, she heeded him. She spun away, a sob choking her, pain lancing her heart, and fled. She ran. Ran from Hamilton House, past a grim Low. Ran from the Duke of Montrose, her shattered heart, and all his broken promises.

\* \* \*

TWO SETS of feminine hands were all over him, caressing his chest, his abdomen, but Monty was scarcely aware of them. He was too fixated upon Hattie. Upon the horror and the hurt in her gaze, the paleness of her face.

He felt hollow. Ill. He felt as if all the light had suddenly been extinguished from his world. Because she was the light. She was the light in his darkness. His angel. His *love*. And he... He had just destroyed her. He had seen it in her eyes.

*It is better this way*, he reminded himself. *What Parkross has to say cannot hurt her if she already loathes you. You are giving her the best chance to survive this scandal.*

This was the only means to maintain Hattie would not suffer unduly because of him, aside from giving in to Parkross's demands for the ten thousand pounds. But that he would not do. He would not pay his tormentor. Arthur Parkross would never again have power over him. When the hands moved over the fall of his breeches, he caught them. Two wrists in a manacle grip.

"No," he bit out, shocking even himself with the suppressed violence in his voice.

The lightskirts Madame Marcheaux had sent him stared in astonishment, halted in their attempts at seduction.

The idea of any woman other than Hattie touching him was repugnant. She was all he wanted. All he would ever want. But he would have to settle for wanting her from afar now. He ought to have known the past would come back to haunt him, that the paradise he had with her had never been meant to last long. His glimpse into bliss had been gone in a flash.

"Your Grace," objected one of the women—he did not know their names, and he could scarcely tell them apart for they were both golden-haired. The opposite of Hattie. Had they told him their names? He could not recall. He had been so bloody sick over what he must do.

"Show us your big, hard rod," said the second. "I want to be able to say the Duke of Debauchery's cock has been in my mouth. After I'm done sucking you, Henrietta will have her turn and get you all stiff again. Isn't that right, love?"

"Oh, yes," cooed the other. Henrietta, it would seem.

The name Henrietta was far too close to the name Harriet. To Hattie. His heart felt as if it were about to shatter into a thousand ugly shards.

"Hush," he snapped, swatting at their hands, which had resumed their attempts to seduce.

Had such a thing ever made him randy?

*Beelzebub's earbobs*, he could not recall how or why.

"Do not be coy," said one of them, for he was already confused which was Henrietta and which was not. He had scarcely even looked at their faces.

"We have heard all about you and your insatiable appetites," added her friend.

How much longer did he have to remain in here? He wanted there to be no doubt in Hattie's mind that his betrayal of their vows was true, and to fully convince her, he could not emerge from the study with two unsatisfied lightskirts grumbling behind him. He had to wait until he was certain she was gone.

"I will give you each two hundred pounds if you will cease nattering," he snapped, moving away from them. "And for God's sake, clothe yourselves."

They blinked at him, disbelief evident on both their faces. Once, he would have been incredulous at his own actions. The old Monty would have sought solace in their bodies, used them in the name of his attempts to forget. He would have quaffed enough gin to carry him away to oblivion.

But he was not that man any longer.

He was the man whose heart was owned by Hattie Montrose. She had shown him what love meant every day, forgiving him, trusting him, caring for him when he was ill. And that man understood all the gin, opium, and willing cunny in the land would never give him the solace he sought.

"Do you want to take us while we are wearing our gowns?" asked the first, her voice tentative. "If you would prefer it that way, Your Grace, we will be happy to comply. You can have Henrietta first, and I will lick—"

"Silence," he cut in, interrupting her before she could finish her vulgar offer. "Three hundred pounds. Each. You speak of this to no one. I am not tupping either of you. I love my wife."

Saying that precious word aloud—the admission—how wrong it seemed before these two women whose vocation it was to feign and imitate the true emotion. Fucking was not love. Nor was it a panacea any more than laudanum and blue ruin were.

*Love* was—damn it, there were tears blurring his vision once more. Sending Hattie away like this, pretending to betray her, it was akin to cutting off one of his limbs. He was losing the very best part of himself. But he loved her so damned much he knew it was a necessity. He would do anything, *anything*, to protect her.

"You don't want to tup us?" asked the one he thought was Henrietta then.

"No." He blinked furiously.

"Are you crying, Your Grace?" the other queried.

"Henrietta," chided her friend.

*Satan's banyan*, he had been wrong about who was Henrietta. Unless they were both named Henrietta?

"I do not want to tup you," he confirmed, dragging a handkerchief from his pocket and dabbing surreptitiously at his eyes. "And I am crying. Yes, I am damned well crying. I just chased away the only woman I will ever love. I hurt her."

And hurting her was killing him.

He spun away from his confused audience and rang for Low, who appeared promptly at the door, his expression carefully blank.

"Has the duchess left?" he asked.

"She has," confirmed his butler, a tiny note of disapproval creeping into his voice. He took care to avert his gaze from the Henriettas, who were in the process of tucking their bosoms back into their gowns.

Low had certainly seen far worse in his tenure as Monty's butler, however.

"Thank you," he told Low, taking pity on him. "That will be all."

Low bowed and was gone.

Monty strode back to his desk, extracting some notes, and giving them to the Henriettas. "Here you are. Do not, I beg of you, give this to your abbess. You deserve better in this life than what you have chosen for yourselves. Believe me, for no one has learned that bitter lesson better than I."

They each accepted the notes with solemn care, their

gowns restored to proper order. "Thank you, Your Grace," they said in unison.

Lord knew what had driven them to their current path—desperation, hunger, ruination, lack of work in their villages? Shame on him for never wondering before with any of the women with whom he had taken his pleasure.

"My carriage will see you to wherever you desire," he told them. "My felicitations, ladies."

Looking bemused, they left, clutching their small fortunes. He hoped to hell neither one of them returned to the brothel from whence they had come. When his study door closed on their retreating backs, the true enormity of what he had done came falling down upon him, nearly crushing him beneath the weight.

He had lost Hattie.

Without ever telling her he loved her.

He had pushed her away in the cruelest way he knew how.

And he had never hated himself more.

He tossed his handkerchief into the fire, and then he went on a mindless rampage, hurling pictures from the walls, smashing the bottle of gin to bits, sweeping the entire surface of his desk clean. He kicked his chair. He slammed his fist into the wall until he had managed to destroy the wallcovering and the plaster and had bloodied up his knuckles quite badly.

Cursing himself, he sank to the floor, his back to the wall. His arse thumped on the carpet as he surveyed the destruction, symbolic of the charred ruins which had so suddenly become his life. It seemed a dream that just this morning, he had risen with Hattie in his arms. That he had rolled her onto her back and made love to her as the sun rose over London with the indefatigable promise of another day.

Suddenly, a purr and then a tentative meow interrupted

the deafening silence which had descended. In disbelief, he turned to find a fat, white feline sauntering toward him.

*Sir Toby.*

Somehow, she had left behind her cat, who had taken to stealing into his study for lengthy afternoon dozes. *God's fichu*, she would have been in a hurry to leave him if she would abandon her precious Sir Toby. The cat must have been hiding in his study for a nap and gotten caught in the fray.

He and the feline had reached a pax of sorts, recently. The feline adored him. Monty was still hesitant. But the cat was all he had left of Hattie at the moment, and he was damned well going to take comfort.

"Come on then," he told Sir Toby, who paused and watched him hesitantly after all the commotion Monty had just caused. He patted his lap. "Up. I shan't hurt you."

No, he would only hurt the woman he loved.

But that was why hurting her was a necessity. Pushing her away, forcing her to leave him, was the better option. Far preferable to making her stay after Parkross made good on his threats. She would never be able to hold her head high in polite society again. As it was, the scandal would taint her because she was his wife, separated or no.

However, if the full details were made known as his uncle threatened to do, Monty hoped Hattie would have a chance to obtain an exceedingly rare divorce, thanks to his sins. He would not argue they had not been committed during their union. No, he would allow her to make whatever accusations she must.

Sir Toby, perhaps sensing a creature in great need, at last crawled into Monty's lap. He stroked the cat's luxurious fur, grateful for the solace, and steeled himself in preparation for what he must do next.

CHAPTER 23

Her brother pressed a glass containing an amber-colored liquid into her hand.

Through the tears blurring her vision, Hattie frowned at Torrie. "What is it?"

"Brandy," he said grimly. "Drink."

She was seated in the salon where she had so oft done her needlework before she had married Ewan. When she had suddenly arrived at Torrington House, devastated and in tears after fleeing the undeniable evidence of her husband's infidelity, she had been dismayed to learn her mother was not at home. Only her brother was.

Her brother who did not remember her.

She had stood in the entryway, crying, feeling utterly alone, when Torrie had come to her, sweeping her into a comforting embrace. For a moment, it had been as if she had her brother back. He smelled the same, he felt the same.

Until he had called her Harriet.

She lifted the glass to her lips, taking a tentative sip of the brandy. It tingled on her tongue, and she did not care for the flavor, but she swallowed it, wincing as it singed a path down her throat.

"It will help to calm you," Torrie told her. "Drink more."

She did as he ordered, but the despair was still a heavy weight upon her chest, threatening to crush her. She would need far more than brandy to calm herself. To survive this agony.

"Another," her brother said. "Hattie, I have not seen you this distressed since your fat old cat died."

She swallowed a third sip of brandy and froze. "Torrie?"

He frowned, looking as perplexed by what he had just said as she was. "I…I remember Miss Pudding. She was black and white. She always hissed at Father…"

Hope rose within her. "Yes, Torrie. She was. She also once brought that headless mouse to Mother. Do you remember?"

"During tea." He blinked. "I do. Mother screeched. She demanded you keep Miss Pudding in the nursery from then on. You have always liked cats and mischief, haven't you, Hattie?"

Thank God some of his memories were returning at last! Despite the sadness drowning her, she smiled, tears of bittersweet relief pricking her eyes. "Yes, I have."

"And you have always loved Monty."

His observation shocked her, for even before her brother had lost his memory, she had not known he suspected. There was no sense in denying it now. She bowed her head, stared into the glistening brandy in her glass. "Yes."

"He is the reason for your tears now, is he not?" Torrie prodded.

"He…" She struggled to give voice to what he had done. To make sense of it. Indeed, she could not, for it made no sense. This morning, they had been happy.

"Has he hurt you? Has he raised a hand?" her brother asked.

She shook her head. "No, he would not. His uncle paid him a call today, and he was suddenly a stranger. Rather the same way you were after your accident. He looked at me as if he did not know me."

Hattie could not bear to put into words the rest of what Ewan had done. The half-naked women on his desk, his hands on them...*dear God*. She closed her eyes against another rush of desolation.

His betrayal was more than she could bear.

If he had been untrue from the moment they had wed, it would have been easier than his defection after so many weeks of shared bliss.

"His uncle," Torrie repeated then, his tone contemplative. "Parkross."

"Yes." She forced her eyes open, glancing up to her brother, searching his face. "Do you know him? Can you recall?"

It seemed too much to ask, that her brother's fragmented memory could provide her the information she sought. She was still trying to understand what had happened, she realized. Still trying to make sense of Ewan's actions.

"I recall something." Torrie's face was a study in concentration. He raked his fingers through his hair. "Monty told me something. I know he did."

With shaking hands, she deposited her brandy glass on the table at her side, for she could not bear to consume another drop. "Have your memories been returning to you?"

"Slowly," he admitted. "In dreamlike pieces. At first, I thought that was what they were—nothing more than slumber's delusions. But more and more, they return."

"That is wonderful, Torrie," she said, relieved for him. "I want my brother back."

"I am changed." His countenance was somber. "I will never be the Torrie I once was."

She knew the feeling, for she, too, had changed. And neither would she ever be the same Hattie she had been when she had left Torrington House as Miss Hattie Lethbridge. She returned as a duchess with a broken heart.

Unless...

Hope, ever foolish, would not loosen its hold upon her.

"You do not have to be the Torrie you once were," she told her brother. "The most important thing is for you to remember your family, your friends."

"The doctor says I may never remember everything." Torrie scrubbed at his jaw, frustration evident in his voice, his bearing. "But I must try. Tell me what else Monty has done. I do not believe you would have arrived here as a watering pot merely because he treated you coldly after Parkross paid him a call."

"He told me he wishes to be free to pursue the life he once led," she embellished, avoiding confessing all.

She was sure what she had witnessed earlier had been the return of the Duke of Debauchery. Damn him to perdition. She wanted Ewan back. But how could she fight for him when he was, even now, with those two horrible women, touching them, kissing them, making love to them as he had to her...

A shudder wracked through her.

"Then he should not have damned well married you," Torrie bit out. "I am sorry, Hattie, that I encouraged you to make this match. If Monty is a faithless bastard, your misery is on my head. I did not think he would ill treat you."

"I did not think he would either," she said, her misery threatening to overwhelm her. "Torrie, would you mind if I were to stay here for a few days, at least until I determine what I am to do next?"

"Of course not." Torrie frowned. "This will always be your home. The doors are always open. I..."

His words trailed off, his expression shifting.

"What is it, Torrie?" She searched his gaze. "Have you remembered something else?"

"Monty's uncle," her brother said suddenly, frowning. "I remember Monty telling me he was sick. That he was the sort of man who preyed upon lads. We were in our cups. He swore me to secrecy. I remember it now—we were at the Duke's Bastard, in a private room, drinking gin."

"Preyed upon lads," she repeated, struggling to comprehend. "What does that mean, Torrie?"

Torrie's expression was stark. "There are some vile villains, Hattie, who misuse children."

Shock made her mouth go dry. She had not even known such a horrible thing existed. Hattie felt as if all the breath had been stolen from her. As if she had been punched in the stomach. Dear God, if what Torrie recalled was true, Ewan's hatred of his uncle made terrible sense.

Everything made awful sense.

The visit from his uncle. How withdrawn Ewan had seemed. His suggestion she pay a call on Lady Searle. He had plotted the entire bawdy scene with such care, knowing she would take one look and flee. He had *wanted* her to run. Because he had been chasing her away.

And she had left him. She had done exactly what he had known she would do, and she had believed the worst of him. How easy he had made it, arranging for some lightskirts in his study. She thought back to his expression. To the dullness in his eyes. He had not kissed either of the women. He had merely acted the part of marionette.

"Hattie?" her brother's worried voice broke through her wild thoughts.

"I need to go back to Hamilton House," she said. "Now."

Torrie nodded. "I will see the carriage is brought for you.

But if he hurts you any more than he already has, he will answer to me."

It was good to have her brother back. At least, in this small measure. She could only hope that in time, more of his memories would restore themselves to him.

Impulsively, she embraced him again, then pressed a kiss to his cheek. "Thank you, Torrie. For everything."

* * *

MONTY WAS STILL SITTING with Sir Toby in his lap.

He could not see the ormolu clock on the mantel, and neither did he have his pocket watch at the ready. He had no inkling how much time had passed since the Henriettas had departed. Since Hattie had left him.

His arse had fallen asleep.

The effects of the gin had faded.

His heart hurt.

He was broken. More broken than the shards of the gin bottle he had smashed earlier. More broken than he had ever been. Without Hattie, he was a barren night sky without the sun to rise in the morning and chase away the emptiness of the dark. Without her, there was no laughter, no sweet kisses, no poetry, no fingers running through his hair, no soft body curled against his, no sweet scent of violets.

Without Hattie, there was nothing.

Without her, *he* was nothing.

The door to his study opened. The damned butler had been checking upon him in steady increments ever since he had left his study in rubble.

"Go to the devil, Low," he said hoarsely.

He had no wish for company now.

"I am not Low." The sweet, melodic voice of his wife reached him.

For a delirious moment, he was convinced he must have imagined it. His head jerked toward the door. There she stood on the threshold, surveying the damage he had done. His stupid heart surged at her presence, but he tamped down any hope. She was probably here for the goddamn cat.

With a half purr, half meow for his mistress, Sir Toby rose, stretched, and left Monty's lap. He sauntered toward a nearby chair and leapt into it, settling himself for another nap. Or perhaps all the better to preside over Monty's misery.

"Why are you here?" he asked Hattie, forcing himself to keep his tone cool. To not allow her to see the rush of pure joy he felt at her return. To hide the love, burning for her, consuming him from the inside out.

She glided into the study, closing the door behind her. At least, that was what it seemed to him. She was otherworldly perfection, her jonquil gown complementing her black hair in stark contrast, the return of the light.

It was only when she neared him and sank to her knees before him, skirts pooling around her, that he took note of the puffiness about her eyes, the pink tip of her nose. Hattie had been crying.

Because of him.

And even if he knew it was for the best to push her away, he ached to take her in his arms. To beg her forgiveness. To tell her how much she meant to him.

"Where are your friends?" she asked him, studying him with a calmness that unnerved him.

It took him a moment to realize she referred to the Henriettas. He had already forgotten them.

"I finished with them," he lied. "Have you come back for the cat? Here he is, perfectly hale. I never cared for the creature anyway."

"I came back for both of you." She leaned forward, cupping his face in her hands. "I love you, Ewan."

Agony seared him. He wanted to jerk away from her, and yet it was the sweetest gift, her warm, tender touch. But an even greater gift was her words, her love for him. He had never dreamed she might come to care for him so deeply, when all he had done was burden her with his sins.

And there were far more than the ones she knew about.

"You do not love me," he bit out. "You cannot love me. You do not know my past, the wickedness. If you did, you would be disgusted. You would run from me, as fast and as far as you could go."

"I do know, Ewan," she said, those eyes he had never quite been able to capture properly on paper burning into his. "The only running I am doing is to you. To your arms. You are home to me. You are where I belong."

Foolish, beautiful, angelic woman. She did not know what she was saying.

"The truth is far worse than anything you can imagine." He took a deep, shuddering breath, knowing he must forge onward. He had not wanted to, Lord knew, but she had a right to understand. She had come back for him, despite thinking he had betrayed her, and professed her love. "The man you saw today, Arthur Parkross…he…God, Hattie."

"I know, Ewan," she said, tears shining in her eyes. "I know. Torrie's memory is returning slowly. He recalled you telling him about your uncle."

Horror seized his chest, rendering him incapable of taking a breath for one brutal moment as he reacted to her revelation. She knew. She knew and she was still here.

He told himself it was because she did not know the full, sordid truth. If Torrie's memories were not completely returned…hell, even if they were, it seemed unlikely he would tell his gently bred sister about the true evils lurking in the world.

Monty would have to tell her himself.

"One summer when I was down from Eton, my mother, father, and Catriona were in Scotland at Castle Clare," he began slowly. "I was given the choice of attending them there or remaining with Parkross in London. He is my mother's brother. It was to be a grand adventure in Town without my overbearing father, the duke."

"Oh, Ewan, my love," she said, stroking his cheeks, "you do not need to tell me. I understand."

He needed to tell her, he realized. To unburden himself. He wanted her to know the complete truth. "It started innocently enough. He took me to gaming hells, plied me with spirits. For the first time, I had escaped from my father's iron rule, for Eton was nothing more than an extension of that. But then, one night, he…he touched me. Asked me to touch him. He said it was part of becoming a man. I was so deep in my cups, I was seeing two of him. I…I did what he asked, and then I retched all over him. The next day, he apologized, said we must never speak of it. But that night, it happened again."

His cheeks were wet. Old tears, tears he had not shed in many years, emerged. Tears for the terrified lad he had been. Tears for all he had lost. For all he would lose still.

"One night, he attempted to force me. I was a skinny lad, but I fought him off, and I fled into the night…"

"Oh, my darling," she said softly. And then she was in his lap, her arms around him.

Somehow, she had not left. There was no disgust on her beautiful face. Only sorrow. He searched her gaze, looking for censure. For a sign she was repulsed. For pity.

"I should have told you before," he continued. "I had no right to keep it from you. To saddle you with me and all my demons. I have always told you that you deserve better than me. Now you can see for yourself, truer words have never been spoken."

"No, Ewan," she said, still holding his face captive. "Your past has no bearing upon the way I feel for you. How could you ever believe I would love you less because of what happened?"

"Because it is shameful, damn it."

His hands covered hers. He intended to push her away, but once his flesh touched hers, he could do nothing but hold her there. He loved her so much. Part of him was desperate to keep her, part of him knew he had to put her ahead of himself. He was at war, within.

"The only thing that is shameful is that a man you trusted—your own family member—would abuse you," she countered. "It was not your fault, Ewan. You were a boy. An innocent. Knowing what you have endured only makes me love you more."

"But you do not know everything," he persisted, because he had to. "What you saw today—him calling upon me—it was to threaten me. He is heavily in debt, and he is demanding ten thousand pounds from me. If I do not give him the funds, which I have sworn not to do, he threatened to tell you and to spread this putrid scandal all over Town."

"That spineless coward. How dare he?" Hattie frowned through the tears which had tracked down her cheeks. "You cannot let him win, Ewan. I will stand by your side with pride. Nothing he says or does will make me love you any less."

Just when he thought he could not love her more.

"Do you mean that, Hattie?"

"Can you doubt it?" She smiled then, through her tears. "I have loved you for so long, Ewan. Before you ever noticed me. Before we were married. And my love for you has only grown deeper and stronger with each day."

He slammed his lips on hers in a kiss. There was no sensual art in this kiss, no sweet seduction. It was not even gentle. It was brutal. A claiming and a declaration all at once.

He tore his mouth from hers, holding her gaze. "I love you, too, Hattie. Those women...I sent them away. I was desperate to make you leave me, and I knew you would never do so without good reason. I could not bear for you to stay, knowing what was going to happen. I thought your learning my sins would have been easier on the both of us if you already hated me. I still cannot bear the thought of the scandal and shame this may bring upon you, if Parkross carries out his threats."

"Do you mean it, Ewan?" she asked, awe in her voice. "You love me?"

"Desperately." He smiled back at her, joy bursting open inside him, like a bud transforming into a blossom. "You are the only woman for me. You always have been."

"I want a real marriage." She grew solemn. "I cannot bear for you to only be faithful to me until I bear you an heir."

"I *demand* a real marriage." He kissed her again, lingeringly. "I will not share you, and I want you to bear me at least half a dozen bairns."

"I would love nothing more," she told him.

"Even if Parkross attempts to ruin me?" he could not help but to ask. "There is every possibility it will be ugly, should he resort to such tactics. We could become social pariahs. I would never want that for you."

"Whatever happens, we will face it together." This time, she kissed him. "We will overcome it together. Ewan and Hattie."

"Hattie and Ewan," he agreed, so damn grateful for the woman in his lap. For this wife he still did not deserve. This magnificent angel who loved him in spite of all his flaws and sins. With her at his side, he knew he could face anything.

# EPILOGUE

## CASTLE CLARE, SCOTLAND, ONE YEAR LATER

The state dining hall at Castle Clare was truly a sight to behold. Its elaborate plasterwork had been painted by a supremely gifted German artist in the previous century. The table and chairs had been commissioned by Monty's grandfather during a visit to France and had cost an impressive fortune. The crystal chandelier was blazing, bathing the massive room in a warm glow. The portraits of generations of Hamilton ancestors watched over every gathering.

But for all the majesty of this impressive room, there was one sight that drew Monty's eyes more than all the rest—his glorious wife. His duchess. His heart.

*His Hattie.*

She was seated at his side, dressed to rival any queen. The diamond-and-gold filigree parure he had gifted her upon the birth of their son glistened from her throat, ears, and bodice. Her luxurious black hair had been captured in a soft style. Her green eyes caught his and held. The smile she gave him warmed him to his marrow. As always, she was the sun in his sky.

"This was a capital idea, Montrose," Crispin, the Duke of Whitley said, interrupting the maudlin bent of Monty's thoughts, "bringing all of us sinners and scoundrels together for a house party in the wilds of the north."

"Here now, Cris, speak for yourself," said Mr. Duncan Kirkwood, owner of the Duke's Bastard. "We are not all of us scoundrels any longer. I, for one, am quite reformed. Am I not, my dearest?"

Kirkwood directed his question to his wife, the famed novelist Lady Frederica Kirkwood, who had written *The Silent Duke* and *Lady Honoria's Revenge*. Lady Frederica gave her husband a secretive smile. "Entirely reformed, of course."

Kirkwood grinned back at her, and the two shared a silent exchange, which made Monty deuced uncomfortable. He flicked his gaze to Searle and his marchioness, also in attendance. "Well, Searle, what say you? Are you a reformed sinner and scoundrel as well?"

"You know I am." Searle flashed him a grin. "All it requires is the love of an excellent woman to bring a sinner to his knees and make him repent. If I did not have my Leonie, I shudder to think where I would be."

"Oh, my love," his marchioness returned softly, eyes filling with tears—undoubtedly because she was once more breeding. "I feel the same."

Monty had learned all too well that a delicate condition led to one's pragmatic, rational wife turning into a watering pot. And an insatiable bedmate. But he did not want to think about the last in relation to his cousin and his cousin's wife. *Beelzebub's earbobs*, the notion was enough to make him want to retch.

"For once, we are in accord, Searle," the Earl of Rayne chimed in wryly, his Spanish accent less pronounced now than it had once been since he had become domesticated and spent most of his time in either Wiltshire or London.

Although Searle and Rayne had once been bitter enemies, their feud had diminished over time, leaving them reluctant friends.

Monty was relieved the stubborn lords had worked through their differences, for he adored his sister Cat, and he considered Searle more a brother to him than a cousin. Searle and Rayne at odds was no damned good.

"I think the same can be said for the love of an excellent man," Cat said then, giving her husband a look that made Monty positively bilious.

Truly, what a group of milksops they all were. They had traveled here with their growing families, and they sat about at dinner drinking lemonade and talking about love and being reformed. There was a time when he would have sooner leapt from the turrets, without wings attached, than enjoy such a dinner.

Though his poor flying machine never *had* functioned. Perhaps one day. Lord knew he had not given up his love of adventure. Next year, he had every intention of taking Hattie and their son Titus on a tour of the Americas. Supposing Hattie was not increasing again by that time. And with as much time as they spent in each other's arms, such a happy occasion was certainly a possibility.

"We are so happy you could all join us here," Hattie announced, smiling to the gathering. "Each one of you is very dear to us, and we treasure your friendships, be you sinners, scoundrels, angels, or something in the middle."

He loved her so. Beneath the table, he surreptitiously ran his hand up her thigh. She clenched them through layers of silk and petticoats, casting him a sultry look from beneath her lowered lashes. Part of him had expected a subtle scold, for he ordinarily behaved himself in front of company. But his angel was being wicked tonight. He could already tell by the subtle curl to her full lips.

The party descended into happy chatter once more, and Monty was content to sit as he was and listen, slowly inching his caress farther up his wife's thigh. She had seen him through his darkest days, plucked him from the abyss, nursed him through his opium sickness, and then, when he had thought her lost to him forever, she had courageously stood at his side, ready to go to battle for him.

It had been Hattie who had informed his mother of the sins of her brother, and whilst Monty and his mother were not precisely on excellent terms, the old wounds between them had finally begun to heal. Aided, of course, by both her request for forgiveness and the demise of Arthur Parkross.

In the end, all Monty's fears had been for naught. After he had sent word to his uncle that the ten thousand pounds was not forthcoming, Parkross had not spoken a word of his sins, likely fearing he would implicate himself. Instead, he had drowned himself in the Thames the very next day. It had been assumed the devil had fallen into the waters in the darkness whilst in his cups, but Monty knew better. Parkross had either been pushed, or he had waded in himself, his desperation leading him to put an end to it all.

As far as Monty was concerned, the means by which his uncle had perished mattered not. What did matter was that he was gone, and he was no longer capable of hurting either Monty and his family or anyone else ever again.

"I love you," he could not resist murmuring to Hattie then.

He spoke the words often, but they never grew tired.

Beneath the table, her hand caught his, their fingers lacing. "I love you, too, my darling. So very much."

\* \* \*

Hattie had just returned to the duchess's chambers from the nursery, where she had wished both her beloved baby Titus and her beloved Sir Toby each a good night. Since Titus had been born, Sir Toby had taken an instant liking to him, which meant Hattie made certain a small, soft bed was laid out for him in the nursery at all times.

Her husband was already awaiting her, dressed in nothing but a dark silk banyan.

Her heart beat faster and her breath caught. He was so unfairly beautiful, and the way his molten-brown gaze slid over her body was like a caress. She closed the door behind her, feeling terribly overdressed in her evening gown and diamonds.

"You look divine in that gown, my love," he told her, giving her a slow smile that was pure seduction as he sauntered forward. "But I cannot stop thinking about taking it off you and fucking you while you wear nothing but those diamonds. What took you so long to get here?"

As usual, he was deliciously wicked in his words. They had their intended effect upon her, liquid heat pooling between her thighs. The delicious man knew she loved it when he said naughty things to her.

Two steps, and she reached him, belatedly recalling he had asked her a question. "I kissed our darling lad goodnight, of course."

"I did as well, and yet here I stand, ready for you." He held up his hands, palms toward her, grinning. "And do not lie to me, my darling, I know you kissed that arrogant little sack of fur, too."

He knew her so well.

She suppressed a smile. "Only the top of his sweet little head."

"I have not yet forgotten your suggestion I am his namesake," he told her with mock sternness. "That was a wretched thing to say. I am nothing like Shakespeare's character, you know."

It had taken the both of them attending the theater and watching *Twelfth Night* for her husband to finally comprehend her little joke. "You know I was only teasing you about that. And do forgive me the delay in preparing for slumber. I was detained a bit by chatting with your sister and the rest of the ladies."

She had not been exaggerating earlier at dinner when she had thanked their friends for joining them here in Scotland. She and Monty were so blessed in so many ways. She never could have imagined the joy they would find together, or the wonderful, true friends they would find. In the drawing room, the Duchess of Whitley had revealed she was expecting another babe, and Lady Frederica had made a happy announcement as well.

So much joy. So much love.

"Gossiping," her husband said, "when you could have already been on your back beneath me."

"Or perhaps you would have been on yours," she countered boldly. "You do like it when I ride your big, hard—"

"*God's fichu*," he muttered, interrupting before he silenced her with a deep kiss. "I love it when you say that word. But if you do, I cannot be held responsible for my actions. It turns me into a wild man every—"

"Cock," she said, cutting him off with her own wicked grin.

Then she took his hands in hers, turning them so his palms faced upward.

"Sweet minx."

He attempted to kiss her then, but she moved her head, not about to allow him to control this night. His lips grazed her cheek instead. Her husband gave her a frustrated glower, making a sound of protest.

"Have you ever heard of palmistry, my love?" she asked him, intentionally parodying the day he had asked her the same question when he had been courting her.

His sensual lips quirked. "Do not pretend you are an authority on it, pet. I was not born yesterday."

How he recalled her words from over a year ago, she could not say. But it was one of his quirks—he remembered *everything*. But she was not finished with him yet. She released his left hand, then used her right to stroke some of the ridges running through his broad palm.

"This line here." She stroked again. "It says you have married a woman you already know. Your friend's sister. She will give you everything you want, kiss you senseless as often as possible, and make you weak with desire by talking about your—"

"Not again," he interrupted on a groan. "Show a man some mercy, I beg you."

"—beautiful hands," she finished triumphantly.

"Hattie." His tone was steeped in warning.

"Ewan?" She blinked at him in feigned innocence.

"We both know you intended to say something else," he gritted.

Her smile deepened. "What else?"

That quickly, he flipped her hand around and he was the one in control, bringing her hand to his rigid cock. Even through the fine fabric of his banyan, his heat seared her. Between her legs, a new pulse pounded to life.

"This," he said.

"Oh." Her fingers shaped him, stroked him. The hunger within her intensified.

But she was not finished torturing him yet. She sank to her knees, making short work of the loose belt, which had been holding the twain ends of his banyan in place. The garment gaped, revealing a mouthwatering expanse of hard, male chest, muscled torso, and his staff, protruding thickly from a base of dark curls and the heavy weight of his ballocks.

"Cock," she said, and then she wasted no time in taking him in her mouth.

How she loved him, the musky, rich scent of him, the salty-sweet taste of him, the leashed power of his body, all at her command. She knew by now how to please him. Exhaling, she took him deep into her throat, worshiping him, this man she loved. He groaned above her, his hands sinking into her hair as his hips thrust. She cupped his sac, worked him, licked and sucked and pleasured him in every way she knew how.

But just when he was on the edge of release, he pulled away, bringing her to her feet. The ruddy flush in his cheeks pleased her. As did his breathlessness when he spoke.

"Enough, darling. I want to be inside you when I spend."

She could not argue with that. As one, they removed all her layers: gown, petticoats, chemise, stays, stockings. When she began to unfasten her earbobs, he stopped her.

"Leave the diamonds."

She did as he wanted, leaving them, and instead devoted herself to pushing his banyan off his broad shoulders. They fell into bed together, naked, with Hattie on her back and Ewan atop her. Her legs parted for the bold invasion of his body. She was ready for him, and he had scarcely even touched her.

"I wanted you on your back," she protested, pouting.

He kissed her, slow and deep, his tongue sinking inside to foray with hers. He tasted like lemonade, only more delicious, because he also tasted like himself. He dragged his mouth away for a breath. "In this, I win."

His fingers found her pearl, working over her.

"Your cunny is soaked, darling," he said.

More forbidden words. She undulated beneath him, seeking more. He sucked her nipple, then gently bit. She moaned, stiffening beneath him, already on the verge of spending when he sank two fingers inside her. His thumb played with the sensitive bundle of flesh while he fucked her swiftly, reaching that secret place inside her only he knew existed. She splintered, her release taking her by surprise in its sudden swiftness.

He kissed his way to her throat, to her ear. "I am going to fuck you now."

*Dear God.*

"Yes," she gasped. A desperate plea.

He withdrew his fingers, and she mourned the loss until he slammed back inside her with one deep thrust. He felt so good, filling her, stoking the passion inside her back into a roaring fire.

Their mouths met.

The rhythm he began was smooth, fast, hard. She lost herself far sooner than she had intended, tightening on him as splendor roared through her. Within moments, he was throwing back his head, releasing on a deep cry as his seed flooded her.

He collapsed atop her, his big, warm, beloved body pinning hers to the bed. Beloved weight. She wrapped herself around him, holding him tight. Their hearts thundered as one. United, just as they were.

*Forever.*

\* \* \*

THANK you for reading Monty and Hattie's happily ever after! I hope you loved their story! If you're looking for Torrie's story, you'll find it in Book 7, coming soon. Sign up for my newsletter here so you don't miss the release news!

Looking for more deliciously wicked Regency romance from me in the mean time? Check out some of my latest series, *The Sinful Suttons and The Wicked Winters*.

Please consider leaving an honest review. Reviews are greatly appreciated! If you'd like to keep up to date with my latest releases and series news, sign up for my newsletter here or follow me on Amazon or BookBub. Join my reader's group on Facebook for bonus content, early excerpts, giveaways, and more.

Read on for an excerpt from *Sutton's Spinster*, Book 1 in The Sinful Suttons.

\* \* \*

NOT BLOODY *AGAIN*.

Jasper Sutton's booted foot had connected with something soft as he seated himself at the desk in his office at The Sinner's Palace. The gaming hell he and his siblings owned together was teeming with drunken lords. The hour was despicably late by anyone's standards, even for a voluptuary such as himself. He wanted gin and he wanted quim, and not necessarily in that order.

What he did *not* want was one of his twin daughters hiding beneath his desk when she was supposed to be abed.

"Elizabeth," he guessed, for she was undeniably the naughtiest of the two children who had been unexpectedly delivered to his hell a fortnight ago.

*Abandoned* was a better fucking word for what their mother—whomever she was—had done. That was the trouble with possessing an insatiable appetite for rutting. Sooner or later, the rutting produced brats.

And sometimes, the mothers of the brats decided they did not want the burden of extra mouths to feed. And also sometimes, the mothers abandoned their daughters on the steps of a gaming hell at dawn and left them there for any despicable bastard to abuse, without a thought or a care. Until, *thank the Lord*, his men had arrived and taken the girls within before something had befallen them.

Jasper had always tried to take care to avoid siring a bastard. But he could admit the resemblance the children bore to him was apparent. Black hair, hazel Sutton eyes, the dent in his chin. There had been nights when he had been too deep in his cups to know where he'd spent his seed.

And now, he had daughters to look after. Twin devilish imps who were six years old and filled with mischief.

Still, no child emerged or responded. He tapped the girlish lump beneath his desk with the tip of his boot. "Anne?"

The rustle of fabric met his ears, followed by two sets of giggles.

*Christ.* The both of them were at it tonight. Sinner that he was, he sent a silent prayer for patience heavenward. And then with a scowl, he rose from his chair and hunkered down to peer beneath the massive piece of furniture which had only recently been repaired after a pistol had blown a portion of it apart. Two sets of grins and hazel eyes greeted him.

"Girls," he chastised sternly, "you are meant to be sleeping. What the devil are you doing hiding beneath my desk at this time of the evening?"

"We miss playing 'idey," Elizabeth announced, unrepentant.

*Hidey*, as he had come to learn, was a game his daughters had established to enliven their evenings when one of their mother's gentlemen callers paid a visit.

"Ma always told us it were fun to 'ide when the gentlemen arrived," Anne added brightly.

It was clear their mother had been a Covent Garden nun.

Could have been one of the doxies employed by The Sinner's Palace for the entertainments of his patrons. Could have been someone else. The girls said her name was Ma Bellington.

Bellington was a right fancy name for an East End whore. He suspected the woman had never told their daughters her true name, as Bellington did not mean a thing to him. Not that he expected it to. There had been occasions when he had not bothered to exchange names with his bedmates, it was true.

He wasn't proud of his past now that he was older and wiser. But he'd been a reckless, wild rakehell in his youth. No denying it. Just as there was no denying these hellions were his.

"Out from under the desk," he ordered the twins sternly. "We've talked about this before, no?"

"We wasn't tired," Elizabeth announced, crawling from beneath the desk in her nightdress and standing to eye him balefully. "It's right dull 'ere, it is."

Anne emerged from beneath the desk as well, frowning. "I told Lizbeth I didn't want to do it, but she made me."

He sighed. It had only taken him hours to discover that Elizabeth was the twin who delighted in galloping all over the hell, leaving mischief in her wake, and asking him so many questions he feared his head might explode like a melon tossed from a roof. Anne had a saucy disposition, was quick to turn into a watering pot, and liked to blame everything on her sister.

"What did I tell you yesterday when I caught you hiding beneath the hazard table?" he asked with as much calm as he could muster.

He'd been furious at the sight of his children wandering about the gaming hell, disrupting confused patrons. The discovery had made his need of a wife—someone to tame and look after his wayward offspring—all the more apparent.

"You said we couldn't go where the fancy coves be," Elizabeth said.

"You didn't say nothing about your desk," Anne added mulishly.

Before he could address either of them, a knock sounded on the door. Three raps in quick succession, which signified *more* trouble.

"Christ," he muttered.

"That's the Lord," Anne told him.

"I am aware," he said, silently praying for strength. And patience. And strength.

"You owe 'im an apolology," Elizabeth announced with a superior air.

*Sodding hell.* "*Apology*, Elizabeth," he corrected.

"What's sodding mean?" Anne asked.

*Damnation.* Had he said that bit aloud? To his utter shame, he discovered that he—Jasper Sutton, scourge of the East End—was bloody *flushing*.

He coughed to cover his embarrassment and called out to Hugh, who was on door duty this evening. "What is it now?"

"*She's* returned," Hugh called, his tone grim.

Jasper did not need to ask whom his man was speaking of. Over the last few months, one woman had continually appeared, ignoring his warnings, his threats—hell, even his kisses.

Lady Octavia Alexander.

And damn him if the mere name of the dark-haired beauty did not make his cock twitch to life. Until he recalled his children were still standing before him.

Children.

*His.*

He was yet growing accustomed to this abrupt change of circumstances.

"Tell her to go back to Mayfair where she damned well belongs," he ordered Hugh, for he had far more important matters awaiting him this evening.

Namely, the twins who had once more escaped from their shared room to wander about unattended.

The door burst open, and Lady Octavia crossed the threshold, elegant, beautiful, and maddening as hell. Her vivid brown eyes settled upon him first, and how he despised the bolt of lust that hit him. So, too, the memories of the frantic kisses they had shared, her tongue in his mouth.

The minx.

*Christ*, she was delicious.

And infuriating.

And delicious.

*Damnation.*

"You are not welcome here, Lady Octavia," he told her, just as he had on numerous occasions in the past. "I will have one of my men escort you back to the safety of your sister's home."

"Children, Sutton?" she asked, her gaze flitting from his daughters, to him, then back again.

"Aye," he ground out. "Children. *Mine.*"

She had not trespassed at The Sinner's Palace in three weeks. Not that he had been counting. And not that he had missed her irritating intrusions. Because he most certainly had not.

Her mouth dropped open. Pretty, lush mouth. Not a spinster's mouth at all, and that bothered him for reasons he didn't care to examine. Lady Octavia Alexander had no desire to marry. All she wanted was to be at the helm of a gossip journal. Hers, of course. When she had initially approached him with the idea, he had laughed. And then he had kissed her senseless. And then *she* had been the one laughing.

The bloody nuisance.

"*Your* children," she repeated at last.

"Mine," he said again, willing her to go away.

To go far, far away.

To the Continent, in fact.

Or mayhap the Americas.

Out of his reach, wherever that took her.

Was the moon a possibility?

"*You* are a father."

He did not miss the manner in which she emphasized the *you*, as if the very notion of his paternal state were blasphemy.

"Aye," he gritted, frowning at her. "Are you daft, woman? I've just said so."

He was being rude, and he knew it. Also, he did not care.

"Don't say *daft*," he added as an afterthought, addressing his wide-eyed daughters.

"I would never," Anne breathed. "It would be unkind, Papa."

*Papa.* His cold, dead heart never failed to warm at the title, and curse him if he knew why. He'd certainly not wanted spawn. Still didn't want them. Not particularly. They were trouble, these two.

Hence his need for a wife.

*Yesterday.*

A plain, appreciative woman without expectations who was willing to guide his children and turn a blind eye to whatever the hell he wished to do that did not involve her.

Lady Octavia was grinning at him like the cat who'd got into the cream. "Yes, Papa. It is most *unkind* to call a lady who has only ever been polite to you *daft*."

"Do not call me Papa," he growled at her, stalking forward.

Toward her.

*Pulled.*

Always, always pulled. This woman was vexing and she was intoxicating, and he wanted more of her, and he wanted her to go away and never to return.

But mostly, he wanted more of her.

"Papa?" asked one of his daughters, and he was ashamed to admit that with them at his back, he could not distinguish one voice from the next.

He paused, stopping just short of Lady Octavia. "What is it now, daughter?" he asked, casting a glance over his shoulder.

"I want a cat," Anne said.

"I want a dog," Elizabeth announced.

"Then you shall have both," Lady Octavia proclaimed, her voice cheerful, benevolent.

*Annoying.*

He turned back to her, pinning her with a glare. "Hold your tongue, Lady Octavia."

She winked, the outrageous baggage. "Force me to if you dare."

*Challenge accepted, milady.*

He would have great fun with her tongue. Later. Not with his children as an audience. Kisses could wait. Anne and Elizabeth needed to get to bed.

Want more? Get *Sutton's Spinster* now.

DON'T MISS SCARLETT'S OTHER ROMANCES!

Complete Book List
**HISTORICAL ROMANCE**

Heart's Temptation
A Mad Passion (Book One)
Rebel Love (Book Two)
Reckless Need (Book Three)
Sweet Scandal (Book Four)
Restless Rake (Book Five)
Darling Duke (Book Six)
The Night Before Scandal (Book Seven)

Wicked Husbands
Her Errant Earl (Book One)
Her Lovestruck Lord (Book Two)
Her Reformed Rake (Book Three)
Her Deceptive Duke (Book Four)
Her Missing Marquess (Book Five)
Her Virtuous Viscount (Book Six)

DON'T MISS SCARLETT'S OTHER ROMANCES!

League of Dukes
Nobody's Duke (Book One)
Heartless Duke (Book Two)
Dangerous Duke (Book Three)
Shameless Duke (Book Four)
Scandalous Duke (Book Five)
Fearless Duke (Book Six)

Notorious Ladies of London
Lady Ruthless (Book One)
Lady Wallflower (Book Two)
Lady Reckless (Book Three)
Lady Wicked (Book Four)
Lady Lawless (Book Five)
Lady Brazen (Book 6)

Unexpected Lords
The Detective Duke (Book One)
The Playboy Peer (Book Two)

The Wicked Winters
Wicked in Winter (Book One)
Wedded in Winter (Book Two)
Wanton in Winter (Book Three)
Wishes in Winter (Book 3.5)
Willful in Winter (Book Four)
Wagered in Winter (Book Five)
Wild in Winter (Book Six)
Wooed in Winter (Book Seven)
Winter's Wallflower (Book Eight)
Winter's Woman (Book Nine)
Winter's Whispers (Book Ten)
Winter's Waltz (Book Eleven)
Winter's Widow (Book Twelve)

DON'T MISS SCARLETT'S OTHER ROMANCES!

Winter's Warrior (Book Thirteen)

The Sinful Suttons
Sutton's Spinster (Book One)
Sutton's Sins (Book Two)
Sutton's Surrender (Book Three)

Sins and Scoundrels
Duke of Depravity
Prince of Persuasion
Marquess of Mayhem
Sarah
Earl of Every Sin
Duke of Debauchery

Second Chance Manor
The Matchmaker and the Marquess by Scarlett Scott
The Angel and the Aristocrat *by Merry Farmer*
The Scholar and the Scot *by Caroline Lee*
The Venus and the Viscount by Scarlett Scott
The Buccaneer and the Bastard *by Merry Farmer*
The Doxy and the Duke *by Caroline Lee*

Stand-alone Novella
Lord of Pirates

**CONTEMPORARY ROMANCE**
Love's Second Chance
Reprieve (Book One)
Perfect Persuasion (Book Two)
Win My Love (Book Three)

Coastal Heat
Loved Up (Book One)

ABOUT THE AUTHOR

*USA Today* and Amazon bestselling author Scarlett Scott writes steamy Victorian and Regency romance with strong, intelligent heroines and sexy alpha heroes. She lives in Pennsylvania and Maryland with her Canadian husband, adorable identical twins, and two dogs.

A self-professed literary junkie and nerd, she loves reading anything, but especially romance novels, poetry, and Middle English verse. Catch up with her on her website http://www.scarlettscottauthor.com/. Hearing from readers never fails to make her day.

Scarlett's complete book list and information about upcoming releases can be found at http://www.scarlettscottauthor.com/.

Connect with Scarlett! You can find her here:
  Join Scarlett Scott's reader group on Facebook for early excerpts, giveaways, and a whole lot of fun!
  Sign up for her newsletter here
  https://www.tiktok.com/@authorscarlettscott

- facebook.com/AuthorScarlettScott
- twitter.com/scarscoromance
- instagram.com/scarlettscottauthor
- bookbub.com/authors/scarlett-scott
- amazon.com/Scarlett-Scott/e/B004NW8N2I
- pinterest.com/scarlettscott

Printed in Great Britain
by Amazon